MURDER IN THE
ARTS DISTRICT

Reviewers Love Greg Herren's Mysteries

"Herren, a loyal New Orleans resident, paints a brilliant portrait of the recovering city, including insights into its tight-knit gay community. This latest installment in a powerful series is sure to delight old fans and attract new ones."—*Publishers Weekly*

"Fast-moving and entertaining, evoking the Quarter and its gay scene in a sweet, funny, action-packed way."—*New Orleans Times-Picayune*

"Herren does a fine job of moving the story along, deftly juggling the murder investigation and the intricate relationships while maintaining several running subjects."—*Echo* Magazine

"An entertaining read."—*OutSmart* Magazine

"A pleasant addition to your beach bag."—*Bay Windows*

"Greg Herren gives readers a tantalizing glimpse of New Orleans." —*Midwest Book Review*

"Herren's characters, dialogue and setting make the book seem absolutely real."—*The Houston Voice*

"So much fun it should be thrown from Mardi Gras floats!"—*New Orleans Times-Picayune*

By The Author

The Scotty Bradley Adventures

Bourbon Street Blues

Jackson Square Jazz

Mardi Gras Mambo

Vieux Carré Voodoo

Who Dat Whodunnit

Baton Rouge Bingo

The Chanse MacLeod Mysteries

Murder in the Rue Dauphine

Murder in the Rue St. Ann

Murder in the Rue Chartres

Murder in the Rue Ursulines

Murder in the Garden District

Murder in the Irish Channel

Murder in the Arts District

Sleeping Angel

Sara

Timothy

Lake Thirteen

Dark Tide

Women of the Mean Streets: Lesbian Noir

Men of the Mean Streets: Gay Noir

Night Shadows: Queer Horror
(edited with J. M. Redmann)

Love, Bourbon Street: Reflections on New Orleans
(edited with Paul J. Willis)

Visit us at www.boldstrokesbooks.com

Murder in the Arts District

by

Greg Herren

A Division of Bold Strokes Books

2014

THIS TRADE PAPERBACK ORIGINAL IS PUBLISHED BY
BOLD STROKES BOOKS, INC.
P.O. BOX 249
VALLEY FALLS, NY 12185

FIRST EDITION: OCTOBER 2014

CREDITS
EDITOR: STACIA SEAMAN
PRODUCTION DESIGN: STACIA SEAMAN
COVER DESIGN BY SHERI (GRAPHICARTIST2020@HOTMAIL.COM)

Acknowledgments

Chanse MacLeod and I have been together for a very long time. I first dreamed him up back in 1990, when I was living in Houston. I was trapped in traffic one night on my way home from work on I-45 South, and while I sat there waiting for traffic to start moving again, I started thinking about the private eye novel I wanted to write—and his name just came to me: Chanse MacLeod. I started scribbling notes in a notebook, and when I got home I started writing. I worked on Chanse in bits and pieces, here and there, until 1997, when I opened a Word document and started writing the manuscript that eventually became *Murder in the Rue Dauphine*. That was my first novel to get published (in January 2002), and now, the last Chanse book is going into print.

The road Chanse and I have traveled together for the last twenty-four years or so has been bumpy sometimes, rocky at others, and smooth for long stretches. Saying good-bye to him wasn't an easy decision to make, and it may not be permanent—but after seven novels with him, and a total of thirteen novels about private eyes overall, I want to do some different things. Maybe Chanse will come back someday; who knows? But for now, we're going our separate ways, at least for a while.

If I listed everyone who has had a hand in the Chanse books and my career since that hot August day I was stuck in traffic, this book would be about as thick as a James Michener novel. I've been incredibly blessed in my life to have any number of wonderful people pass through it, and each and every one of them has made my life richer for being a part of it.

There are some people who simply have to be named, because to not acknowledge their importance would be criminal.

Everyone at Bold Strokes Books, from Radclyffe to Sandy Lowe to Cindy Cresap to Stacia Seaman to Ruth Sternglantz, has been absolutely amazing to me ever since they gave me a publishing home. Being a part of the company and getting to know the rest of the Bold Strokes family has been one of the most pleasant experiences of my life. Thank you all for that, with a special nod to Lady Hermione, Nell, Trin, Lynda, Niner, Lisa, Rachel, Annie and Linda, Ashley, Rebekah, Kim, Xenia, and anyone I may have overlooked—y'all are a lot of fun to spend time with, whether it's watching *Rosemary's Baby* at Garnet Hill Lodge, exploring a cemetery or a nearly abandoned town or the Joshua Tree park, or just hanging around eating candy and talking smack—thank you for the amazing memories and being just great people.

The people I always think of as my blog friends ('Nathan, Jeffrey, FARB, Timothy, Becky, Lisa, David, Tim, Rhonda, Lindsay, Jim, and whomever else I am forgetting) have brought me lots of joy and laughter over the years. (I haven't forgotten the dog-gnawed roll, Jim—just you wait.)

Some of the great bookstores who have been supportive of me and my books over the years are no longer around, but I shall never forget Outwrite in Atlanta, Giovanni's Room in Philadelphia, A Different Light in both West Hollywood and San Francisco. Murder by the Book and everyone there in Houston are amazing. Thank you all.

My New Orleans friends are like family to me, and I thank God for all of you every day: Jean Redmann, Gillian Roger, Konstantine Smorodnikov, Pat Brady, Michael Ledet, Bev and Butch Marshall, Jesse and Laura Ledet, Billy Martin, Josh Fegley, the evil Mark Drake, Allison Vertovec, Brandon Benson, Augustin Correro, Tiffany Medlock, Nick Parr, Drew Davenport, Jeremy Bickford, Mark Smith, everyone at the NO/AIDS Task Force, Jacob Rickoll, Joey Olsen, Stan and Janet Duval Daley, Harriet Campbell Young, Michael Carruth, John Angelico, Karissa Kary, Chris Wiltz, and Susan Larson. My other longtime friends from all over the country are also like family: Stephen Driscoll, Stuart Wamsley, Carol Rosenfeld, Michael Thomas Ford, Michele Karlsberg, Mike Smid, Karen Bengtsen, Kara Keegan Warnke, Dawn LoBaugh, Darren Brewer, Heidi Haltiner, Ryan McNeeley, Vince Liaguno, Lisa Morton, Ricky Grove, and so many others I can't even begin to name them all.

Martin Strickland, Robin Pearce and Meghan Davidson—not a day goes by when I don't miss you. When are you coming home for good?

And then there's the Vicious Circle. How would I get through a day without your help rappelling down mountains, installing air conditioners, drinking vodka that tastes like bad cake batter, or running for mayor of Puerto Vallarta? Woo-hoo! I hope I never have to find out—or get hit in the face with a flying wineholder made from plastic.

And of course, Paul J. Willis, who believed in me when no one else did including myself—you've made my life so much better and helped make all my dreams come true. Thank you.

This is for Diana Pinckley,
gone too soon but never to be forgotten.

"My luck had run out, you know luck does that sometimes, it peters out on you no matter how hard you try."

Tennessee Williams, *Kingdom of Earth*

CHAPTER ONE

The electronic gate began rolling to the left with a loud clamor.

I closed the driver's side window of my "billet silver" Jeep Cherokee, shivering. I turned the heater back up to high. I was cold even though I was wearing my black trench coat and a black knit Saints cap. It was in the low thirties. The sky was gray and covered with clouds, the air the kind of chilly damp that goes right to your joints. Last night there had been a freeze warning for all of southeastern Louisiana, so I'd had to turn all my faucets on to a trickle all night to keep the exposed pipes under my house from freezing. The grass on either side of the paved driveway had turned brown, and in the rearview mirror I could see the grass on the levee on the other side of the road behind me had as well.

This cold snap had every New Orleans weathercaster worked up into the kind of energetic, wide-eyed frenzy they usually reserved for hurricane season. The possibility of snow either tonight or sometime tomorrow had them practically drooling. The one currently breathlessly going on and on about how we all needed to make sure to bring all plants and pets inside before sunset was getting on my nerves, so I turned the radio off. It had snowed maybe three times in all my years of living in New Orleans. Those rare, occasional snowstorms always brought the city to its knees. Businesses closed, people holed up in their homes afraid to drive anywhere, and nothing got done.

I drummed my fingers on the steering wheel as the gate lumbered open slowly. My lower back was starting to ache, which wasn't a good sign. I pressed the button on the steering wheel that controlled the heater in the driver's seat. Heat always seemed to help with the pain, but taking a pain pill wasn't an option. Not if I wanted my brain to be functional when meeting a pair of prospective new clients, anyway.

Finally, the gate was open wide enough for me to drive through, and I pushed the gas pedal down.

With the big metal gate open, I could see the house. In spite of myself, I gasped. I'd seen Belle Riviere depicted many times on postcards, but the reality took my breath away.

Belle Riviere was one of the more famous old plantation homes in Louisiana. Painted a pale shade of coral, six enormous round columns rose two stories high from their bases to support the roof on every side of the house. There was a gallery running around the house on both the first and second floors. The incredible view of the front was framed by the Spanish moss–festooned branches from the enormous matching rows of ancient live oaks on either side of the paved driveway. The branches made a natural arch overhead. Legend held that the original builder had the trees dug up from the nearby Atchafalaya swamp basin and transported to create an impressive pathway to his front door so his guests would always approach the house shaded from the sun—and frosted glasses of mint juleps would be waiting for them on the gallery.

Southern hospitality at its finest, if you could overlook the fact that slaves did all the work.

Pictures of the mansion were in every book about

Louisiana history and every coffee table book about the state's famous old homes. Numerous films and televisions programs had been filmed on the grounds. It had served as the backdrop for a romantic story line for one of daytime drama's most famous divas. But it was probably best known as the setting for a dark noir film from the mid-1960s starring two fading female superstars from Hollywood's Golden Age who'd despised each other. Several books and documentaries detailed every bit of gossip from the filming and their infamous feud. The film had become a camp classic, de rigeur viewing for every gay man. Any number of gay men dressed up as the characters from the film at Halloween and on Fat Tuesday, and the characters were also very popular with drag queens.

As I drove down the long drive through the live oaks, I could see the perfectly manicured landscaping through the gnarled trunks. Enormous fountains spewed water from bronze sculptures. Above me, the Spanish moss swayed and moved in the wind from the river. The driveway ended in an enormous paved oval, with clearly marked parking spaces. I could see that the drive continued around the right side of the big house. There were several buildings scattered about at varying distances from Belle Riviere, and there was also a huge gazebo in the shade of another enormous live oak on the left side of the house. Several cars were parked at the left side of the big oval: a silver Mercedes, a gray Jaguar sports coupe, and a black Rolls-Royce Silver Cloud. I whistled at the sight of the expensive cars, then laughed at myself.

Anyone who could afford to own Belle Riviere wouldn't drive a Kia.

I parked in the open spot next to the Mercedes. I got out of the car just as the icy wind picked up again. I winced. My back had tightened much worse than I'd thought. When I stood up, dull pain throbbed. It felt like a bowling ball was sitting on the base of my spine. I tried to crack my back, twisting from one side to the other, bending forward at the waist and then leaning backward. It didn't work, and as tempting as it was to take one of the pain pills I kept in the armrest, the Vicodin always made my brain a little fuzzy.

Not that I really need to be alert, I thought, wincing as I slowly climbed the steps to the first level gallery. *This is just a courtesy call. I doubt they need a private eye.*

Most people who consulted with me didn't. I'd listen to what they had to say, and if by some weird chance they actually did need one, I'd pass it along to my business partner, Abby Grosjean.

To be honest, I wasn't really sure what I was doing here. My old buddy Blaine Tujague's longtime partner Todd Laborde had asked me to come out here as a personal favor. All I'd been told was Todd's old friend Bill Marren, who owned Belle Riviere, needed to hire a private eye. I wasn't looking for new work, and driving all the way out to Redemption Parish to do a favor was pushing the boundaries of friendship. I had briefly considered sending Abby in my place. Besides, Todd and I weren't exactly friends. I'd never felt comfortable around him and always got the sense he didn't like me. But I hadn't yet taken my new Jeep SUV for a drive out of the city and I had nothing else to do except sit around the house and mope, so here I was.

And having Todd owe me wasn't exactly a negative.

I shivered as another blast of cold wind whipped around the corners of the gallery. It was definitely much colder out here than it was back in New Orleans, and the cold in New Orleans was bad enough. We might not get the winter extremes the way they do up north, but winter in southeastern Louisiana is bitter, a cold damp that gets into your bones and joints and makes them ache. The houses are built for heat to escape in the summer, so all the heat rises to the high ceilings. The old houses aren't insulated, the pipes are exposed underneath, and the cold wet wind always manages to find every crack and crevice in the walls.

Fortunately, our winters never last longer than a couple of months. Some winters are just a couple of weeks.

The front door started opening as I climbed the steps and made my way across the wide gallery. A black woman stood there, wearing the traditional maid's uniform with the white apron and white cap. Watching me intently with no expression on her face, she looked young—mid to late twenties at most. Her hands were in the pockets of her apron.

She bent her head forward in a slight nod. "Mr. Marren and Mr. Ziebell are in the drawing room. If you'll follow me?" Her voice was soft and unaccented. She opened the door wider and stepped aside.

"Thank you." I stepped past her into the main hallway of the enormous house and she shut the door behind me. The change in climate was a shock. It was incredibly warm, almost hot, inside Belle Riviere. She took my coat when I slipped it off, folding it over her arm. The hallway ran the length of the house. A hanging stair was in the direct center of the house, leading upstairs. At the end of the hall I could see a set of enormous double doors with enormous panes of frosted glass set into them, through which I saw a fountain bubbling and a vast expanse of green lawn and more outbuildings. The walls of the hallway were painted a dark forest green, with gold fleur-de-lis stenciled at even intervals. Several doors were open on each side of the hallway. Antique tables were placed against the walls, with vases filled with red and yellow roses and baby's breath centered. There was no dust to be seen, and the surfaces of the tables had been polished to an almost startling shine. Above each table was an enormous oil portrait of someone from a previous century in a gilt frame. An enormous chandelier hung from the ceiling, every crystal sparkling and shooting red and blue flame each time it caught the light.

"This way, sir," she said with a slight tilt of her head. I followed her down the hallway. She indicated an open door on the right, and I walked into an enormous room that was even hotter than the hallway. She'd called it the drawing room, but I would have called it the library. Every wall had bookshelves running from the floor up to the ceiling, eighteen feet above. Every shelf was filled with neatly organized hardcover books. There was another glittering chandelier hanging from the center of the ceiling. To my right, enormous ten-foot windows rose from the floor. The shutters were closed, but the window treatments were green velvet, tied back with gold cord that ended with enormous tassels. The floor was hardwood, also polished and buffed so I could almost see my reflection in it. An antique wooden desk was placed between the two windows, facing out into the room. An enormous green and gold Oriental rug covered the floor between the enormous antique desk and several wingback chairs. I heard the door behind me being shut softly.

The source of the heat was an inferno in the fireplace. Over the mantel an enormous oil painting of some nineteenth-century grandee glared out over the room. A man in jeans and a navy blue polo shirt was kneeling in front of the fire, poking at the logs with an enormous cast iron poker. Another man stood facing the door with his hands folded in front of him as I entered.

He looked to be about sixty years old or so, with a shock of thick white hair. His bright blue eyes were alert and alive. He was tan, the wrinkles around his eyes and the corners of his mouth adding strength and character to his handsome face. His nose was long and patrician, his mouth wide with thin lips over a strong chin. A pair of gold-framed spectacles was tucked into his shirt pocket. He was wearing a pair of navy blue slacks, a white button-down shirt, and a very bright red tie. He was slender, but his grip was strong as he shook my hand. "Thank you for coming, Mr. MacLeod. I'm Bill Marren, and this is my partner, Tom Ziebell."

The man at the fireplace stood up and stretched in one fluid motion. The muscles in his back flexed beneath his tight shirt. I gave an involuntary start when he turned around. *I know him from somewhere*, I thought as he crossed the room. I racked my brain to remember where I could have met him as he crossed the Oriental rug to shake my hand. I had a brief flash of him standing in a poorly lit room, wearing only a pair of white boxer briefs that clung tightly to him, and then it was gone.

He was in his late twenties, possibly his early thirties, with curly light brown hair and round green eyes. His jaw was square and strong, and there were dimples in his cheeks and another in his chin. His lips were thick and sensual. When he smiled, his teeth were straight and white. The navy blue shirt fit snugly across his deep chest, and the loose jeans accentuated his strong, athletic body. He was stocky, thickly muscled like a football player rather than lean. He was maybe five-nine. His hand was big and strong, the handshake firm. "Yes, thanks for coming. Can I get you anything to drink? Anything to eat or snack on?" His voice was a soft yet deep baritone. "Thank you so much for driving all the way out here."

"No, I'm fine, thank you." I smiled back at him. "I'm sorry, but you look really familiar to me. Have we met before?"

He laughed. "No, I'm pretty sure I'd remember you."

"Are you sure? In New Orleans somewhere?" I couldn't get the image of him in the boxer briefs out of my head.

"I don't get into the city very often, if at all." He gestured to another wingback chair. "Please, have a seat." As I sat down, Tom added, "Todd recommended you very highly. Did he tell you anything about what we need you to do for us?" Tom sat down in a chair next to mine, while Bill sat down behind the desk.

The chair was extremely comfortable, but my back was still throbbing. "No, I actually didn't talk to Todd. He asked Blaine to ask me." There was no need to explain the complex dynamics of my relationship with Blaine and his partner to them. Blaine and I used to have a friends-with-benefits arrangement, and even though he always swore to me he and Todd had an open relationship, I wasn't quite as sure as Blaine that Todd was completely on board with that. Todd had always seemed distant, cold, and unfriendly to me. I didn't blame him. I couldn't imagine being in a relationship and allowing my boyfriend to sleep around with other guys. But if it worked for them, who was I to judge? Todd was a little younger than Bill, and owned an art gallery on Magazine Street near the corner at Julia. Blaine always said that Todd was a big deal in the art world, nationally known, but I'd never set foot in the Todd Laborde Gallery. I never felt comfortable around Todd, even if Blaine laughed at me whenever I told him Todd didn't seem to like me.

The two exchanged glances, and Bill lifted a teacup to his lips with trembling hands. "We were robbed a few weeks ago," Bill looked over at Tom again. "And the police—well, the police have been no help at all." He closed his eyes and shook his head softly.

"The police of Redemption Parish," Tom said, his voice shaking with barely contained anger and his face reddening, "are corrupt homophobic assholes who think we staged the robbery ourselves."

"What?" I shook my head. I looked from one serious face to the other. "They actually said that to you? They think you were trying to commit insurance fraud?"

"Please excuse Tom, he tends to get a little worked up," Bill replied in a slightly patronizing tone and a slight shake of his head. "He has his own history with the Redemption Parish police."

Tom flushed. "Bill doesn't think it has anything to do with how they're treating the robbery. I ask you, Mr. MacLeod, is it beyond the realm of possibility that we're being singled out because the law firm I work for is suing the sheriff's department?"

"Perhaps we should start at the beginning?" Bill said before I had a chance to respond.

"That's always a good idea." I glanced at Tom out of the corner of my eyes. I couldn't shake the feeling I'd seen him before somewhere.

"There's no insurance money to be had anyway, which makes their accusation so incredibly strange." Bill took a deep breath. "As you are no doubt aware, Mr. MacLeod, I am a very successful man." He gestured about the room in an expansive way. "I've done very well for myself. I am not entirely a self-made man, but I took my modest inheritance and invested wisely and well. I am now able to live very comfortably in my old age." Tom started to say something but a hand gesture stopped him. "I love art and have managed to collect some really wonderful pieces over the course of my years. I was approached several months ago by a dealer with whom I've worked before who said that some paintings, missing for quite some time, had resurfaced and their owner was looking to sell them discreetly, and would I be interested?" He smiled faintly.

"The dealer knew, of course, that I was interested in the artist. I already have several of his works, which she acquired for me. I—and many others—had long believed the paintings to have been destroyed." He closed his eyes. "A lot of art disappeared during the Second World War, Mr. MacLeod. Some of it was stolen, of course, but a lot of it was destroyed."

I nodded. "So, just how valuable were these paintings?"

"Have you heard of Benjamin Anschler, Mr. MacLeod?"

I shook my head. "I'm sorry, I don't know a lot about art, I'm afraid. I took an art history class in college, but other than that…" I shrugged.

He cleared his throat. "Anschler was a Dutch Jew, Mr. MacLeod. He was an Impressionist and studied in Paris with some of the great masters. He was crippled with arthritis and had to give up his art far too soon. He was an old man when the war broke out…but he was a Jew, so of course his age didn't matter to the Nazis. He and his family were sent to the camps, where they died. But in his home in Rotterdam he had kept his three best works. Those paintings disappeared." He paused again. "There have been rumors over the years, of course. Anschler had sold them to private collectors to raise the money to smuggle his family out of Europe, a Nazi officer stole them, they were in a bank in Switzerland." He cleared his throat. "The seller wanted two million dollars for the three paintings. It was quite a bargain."

I whistled. *Two million for three paintings is a bargain?*

We clearly came from different income brackets.

Bill smiled. "Believe me, Mr. MacLeod, just one of those paintings could bring in more than that at an auction."

"So why weren't they insured? That doesn't make any sense. Surely that's not common practice?"

The two exchanged another glance. Bill looked uncomfortable and turned his head away from me. Tom spoke up. "We have to tell him, Bill. We talked about this. He can't help us if we don't tell him the truth. That's what got us into trouble with the cops in the first place."

"Tell me what?" I looked from one to the other.

Bill tented his fingers in front of his face and looked down at this desk. Tom shook his head. "We hadn't insured the paintings yet because we hadn't been able to establish their provenance. You can't get insurance without the provenance."

"Provenance?"

"Provenance means their ownership history, Mr. MacLeod." Bill's voice was clipped. "You have to be able to prove to the insurer that the paintings belong to you properly, that at some point in their history they weren't stolen or obtained by other nefarious means." He waved his hand. "Usually, the provenance is provided at the time of purchase, but that wasn't the case this time." He sighed. "And especially in a case like this, the provenance is crucial. No one is really sure what happened to the paintings—if Anschler or his family were able to sell them or if they were part of Nazi loot. Obviously, if the paintings were stolen by the Nazis, the Anschler heirs would have a claim to ownership. I wasn't going to finish paying for the paintings until I had the provenance in my hands proving I wasn't buying war loot." He paused. "The dealer who was making the arrangements—I trust her implicitly, Mr. MacLeod, but now…now I'm beginning to have my doubts." He glanced over at Tom again and then back to me. "Please bear in mind this must be kept confidential."

"Anything said in this meeting will be kept confidential, of course." I looked from him to his partner and shrugged. "Obviously, I can be compelled to testify in court, but I'm not a gossip, Mr. Marren, and I don't make a habit of talking about my clients' business."

"The paintings disappeared sometime before, or during,

the Second World War, Mr. MacLeod, no one is really sure when. All that's known for sure is they were missing after the German surrender." Tom took the tale up now. "The dealer— well, since the paintings were stolen from us, we're not quite as sure as we were before that the paintings weren't actually Nazi plunder."

"And why exactly is that? Why did the theft make you think differently?"

Bill said, "According to the dealer, Anschler's daughter Rachel took the paintings to sell to a friend who had already escaped to England, a Jewish Dutch investment banker by the name of Jacob Lippmann. Lippmann already owned some of Anschler's paintings, was an old family friend, had loaned the Anschler family money from time to time." Bill hesitated. "But the entire Lippmann family was killed during the war, during the Blitz. Rachel herself died in the 1960s. She left everything she owned to charity, and all of her art to the New Orleans Museum of Art."

"NOMA? Why?"

Tom nodded. "She had roots in New Orleans and emigrated there after the war. The story we were told is that she took the paintings to London to try to raise the money to get the family out. The Germans swept through the Netherlands while she was there, and she couldn't get back home. She spent the entire war trying to locate her family. Her mother's family was from New Orleans. But these three paintings were not part of the collection left to NOMA. Our dealer told us Rachel had sold the paintings before she died because she needed money. But…"

"If that was true, then why did your dealer have so much trouble coming up with the—what did you call it—the provenance?" I bit my lower lip. Something here wasn't adding up. "That's an awful lot of money to spend on paintings you can't insure. And if it was proved they were Nazi loot, wouldn't you lose the money?"

"The money was put in an escrow account," Tom interrupted. "There was a security deposit of several hundred thousand dollars, but the rest was put in escrow pending the provenance. If the provenance wasn't forthcoming—"

"The dealer assured me that it was," Bill finished for him. "And I've known this dealer for a number of years, and I know she is trustworthy."

I pulled out my phone and typed some notes. "And what is her name?"

They exchanged another glance. "Myrna Lovejoy," the older man said after a moment of silence almost long enough to become awkward. "I've known Myrna for years—I also knew her father back in New York. She's recently relocated to New Orleans and opened a gallery on Camp Street, near Julia, in the Arts District."

I inhaled sharply. I knew the name, of course—most people in New Orleans did.

Just three weeks ago, no one outside of her immediate circle of friends or the New Orleans art community had the slightest idea who Myrna Lovejoy was, nor would they have cared. That all changed when a travel writer from the *New York Times* decided to write a piece on the "new" New Orleans and use his old friend Myrna as the focus.

I've lived in New Orleans ever since I got out of college, about fourteen or fifteen years, give or take a few months. It took years for me to get to the point where I was considered a local rather than a *parvenu*—and even then, it was a kind of second-class local status. To be a true New Orleanian one has to be born there—and the locals hate nothing more than a *parvenu* who comes to New Orleans and tries to throw their weight around. Over the years since I settled there after college, every once in a while a journalist from some major city newspaper would come to New Orleans, decide to write an article so they could write off the trip on their taxes or charge it to their employer. Inevitably, they wouldn't do even the most rudimentary research to get things right. The arrogance of these journalists—and the enormous mistakes they made in these articles—never ceased to infuriate New Orleanians. New Orleanians take a fierce pride in our city and hold on to it with the possessiveness of a spoiled only child—and that pride only grew more defiant and defensive in the wake of Hurricane Katrina and the flood caused by the failure of the federally built and maintained levees.

Unfortunately, since the flood those types of pieces seemed to be becoming more frequent, and even more condescending and insulting than we could have ever imagined. My best friend, Paige, who's editor-in-chief at *Crescent City* magazine, hates those articles with a passion she reserves for very few things in life. I wouldn't have even known about the Myrna Lovejoy article had Paige not sent me an email with a link to it.

I'd read it and was more amused than offended. Like all these types of pieces, this one had an air of the "white man exploring darkest Africa on safari" to it, a rather breathless tone that reminded me of old *Mutual of Omaha Wild Kingdom* reruns I'd seen on some cable channel one afternoon when I was too stoned to get off the couch or reach for the remote control. I didn't see any point in getting angry—it wasn't the first such article, and it definitely wouldn't be the last. The nonsensical premise that Myrna had bravely left "civilization" for the uncharted territory of New Orleans, "where it's hard to find kale in the grocery store," struck me as more laughable than anything else. She even referred to the house she and her husband had bought as "crumbling and decayed," when it was actually in the Garden District on Coliseum Street just a block or so from Commander's Palace. I knew the house. It was near my landlady and main client Barbara Castlemaine's mansion. There were any number of adjectives that could be used to describe the place, but "crumbling" and "decayed" weren't two of them.

To me, Myrna came across as nothing more offensive than a clueless transport, a privileged and spoiled woman playing at being Bohemian in New Orleans, like the other hipsters who were descending on the city like flies on shit.

She couldn't be held responsible for the tone of the piece, of course, since she hadn't written it. And maybe her quotes were taken out of context—but it was also stupid for someone trying to make a life and start a business in an insular city like New Orleans to say some of the things she said. How could she have thought it would do her gallery any good? I knew instantly the reaction most locals would have, and I wasn't wrong.

Blogs and websites ripped Myrna to pieces. Paige herself wrote a lengthy editorial for her old employer the *Times-Picayune*, ripping the piece to shreds. In her own magazine, she used the article as the basis for a longer piece about the gentrification of New Orleans after the storm—and what the city was losing in terms of art and culture as a result of this flood of porkpie- and skinny-jeans-wearing "feauxhemians," a term everyone now used.

Apparently, my poker face had slipped because Tom said quickly, "Myrna is nothing like the piece in the *Times* made her out to be." He shook his head sadly. "We've known her for years. She loves New Orleans and was absolutely mortified when that piece came out. That wasn't Myrna at all."

"It doesn't matter to me one way or the other," I replied.

"Myrna's father and I went to college together," Bill went

on. "He was very big in the gallery scene in Manhattan for years, and of course he was my go-to when I started collecting art. Alas, he was killed in a robbery at his gallery about ten years or so, but Myrna was fresh out of college and ready to take over the gallery. I've always been fond of the girl—she's like a daughter to me—and I was, of course, delighted when she and her husband decided to relocate to New Orleans, which meant she would be close by. So of course, when she told me about the paintings, and showed me photographs…I was interested."

"Who else knew the paintings were here?" I frowned. "And is it standard to take possession of paintings before getting the provenance and finalizing the sale?"

"It was a bit odd," Bill admitted, "but Myrna was nervous about keeping them in her gallery, obviously, and so once the money was put in the escrow account and the deposit paid, she brought the paintings out here. She hired security, of course, to escort her."

"Did anyone else beside Myrna and the security guards know the paintings were here?" I kept typing madly away at the touch screen keyboard on my phone.

"We didn't tell anyone," Tom said.

"You don't think Myrna had something to do with the robbery?"

Bill shook his head. "She would never do such a thing— especially since her father was killed during a robbery."

"What kind of security do you have?"

"Alarms and motion detectors, of course. But we weren't keeping the paintings in the house," Tom replied.

I raised my eyebrows.

"We are planning on opening Belle Riviere to the public," Tom went on hurriedly. "And we're planning on using what used to be the slave quarters—well, we've renovated them and turned them into a gallery to display our art collection. It's climate controlled, of course, and there's a generator in case of power failures, to protect the work. The paintings were out there."

"And the thieves didn't trigger the alarm?"

"The alarm wasn't on." Tom made a face. "I'd swear I turned it on, Mr. MacLeod, that night. I am curating the collection until we can hire a professional—Myrna was looking into hiring someone for us. I finished working down there that night and set the alarms, and came back up to the house. The following morning when I went down there, the door had been kicked open and the three crates were gone. I immediately called the police, of course. They came out, looked around, and did absolutely nothing…and now claim that we never had the paintings in the first place and are trying to pull some sort of scam." He rolled his eyes. "But like I said, the parish sheriff has it in for me because the law firm I'm clerking at while I study for the bar is suing the sheriff's office." Bill started to say something but Tom held up his hand to cut him off. "I think he's trying to discredit me and Bill by making us look like criminals, and since I work at the firm," he shrugged his muscular shoulders, "by extension he'll discredit the firm. Can you help us?"

"Did anyone else know how to turn off the alarm? Who all knew the code?"

"Just me and the alarm company." Tom licked his lower lip. "Bill didn't even know it. I must not have turned it on that night…"

Strange coincidence that you didn't turn on the alarm the night someone broke in, I thought.

"We're responsible for the paintings." Bill's expression

was serious. "The owner has them insured, of course, but without a police report proving they were stolen…I'm financially responsible for them. I'll have to pay for them."

"Which Sheriff Parlange is well aware of," Tom went on grimly. "So, what do you say, Mr. MacLeod? Do you think you can help us?"

I thought about it for a few moments. *Ah, what the hell, Todd will seriously owe me one.*

"I can't guarantee I'll find the paintings, or who stole them," I replied. "But I can certainly look into it."

"Well, we can't ask for more than that," Bill replied, removing a checkbook from his inner jacket pocket. "It's certainly more than we're getting from the police."

I briefly explained how I worked and how much I charged. I found a blank contract on the Dropbox app on my phone and sent it to the email address Bill provided. Bill wrote out a check, which he handed to me with a flourish. "I'll print out your contract and sign it. I can fax it, or have it scanned and emailed to you?"

"Scanned and emailed would be great," I replied, standing up and shaking his hand. "Either I or my partner will email you progress reports every few days or so, and you can decide to terminate our services at any time, of course."

"Did you want to take a look at the gallery?" Bill's voice sounded tired.

"Actually, I have another appointment in the city," I lied. The truth was my back was beginning to throb more, which wasn't a good sign. It was also information I didn't want to share with a client. "Either I or my partner will be back out tomorrow or the day after."

"Tom, would you mind showing Mr. MacLeod out?" Bill asked. He closed his eyes and slid down a bit in his chair.

"He's having some heart trouble," Tom said in a low voice as we walked out the door, which he closed behind us.

"I'm sorry to hear that." I replied.

He brushed against me slightly as we started walking down the enormous hallway to the front door. "This whole mess isn't helping matters any."

The maid materialized with my cap and trench coat, which she handed to me before disappearing through another doorway. "I would imagine not."

"I'm sure you'll get to the bottom of it in no time." His smile grew broader, and he winked at me.

Is he flirting with me? With his sugar daddy just down the hall? "Like I said, I can't promise results."

"Well, thank you so much for taking our case." He opened the front door, holding out his hand.

I finished buttoning my trench coat and shook his hand. He held on to mine for just a couple of beats too long. "You're sure we've never met before?"

He laughed. "Trust me, I would remember you." He gave me yet another wink as he shut the front door.

CHAPTER TWO

B y the time I was heading up the on-ramp onto I-10 East, my back was hurting so badly I wasn't completely sure I'd be able to drive back to New Orleans.

I'd been afraid this was going to happen. Todd and Blaine were going to owe me *big* time. I took a deep breath and gritted my teeth. I was about forty minutes from home, give or take, depending on how heavy traffic was. If this was just a minor twinge, I'd make it with a minimum of discomfort. If it was one of the bad ones—well, hopefully I could make it at least to Kenner before it got so bad I'd have to pull over. If I could make it at least to the dry ground on the other side of the bridge, I could pop a painkiller then and make it home before my mind swam out of focus.

I floored the gas pedal as I merged onto the highway. There was an eighteen-wheeler coming up fast in my lane. I watched as the numbers on the digital speedometer shot up until it read eighty miles per hour—ten miles over the speed limit. Most highway patrol officers would turn a blind eye to that—it was the parish police trying to make quotas I had to worry about. I'd never heard of any speed traps between Redemption Parish and New Orleans, so I set the cruise control and tried to relax. I twisted a bit in my seat, trying to ease the pressure on my lower back, and turned the seat warmer back on, hoping the heat might loosen the muscles a bit and relieve some of the throbbing going on back there.

It's funny how your entire life can change in the blink of an eye.

Just four months earlier I hit the big milestone of my fortieth birthday. Everyone I knew had been giving me hell about what this birthday meant—the usual "one foot in the grave and the other on a banana peel" kind of thing. I laughed along with them. Getting older wasn't something I'd ever been overly concerned about. I'd spent most of my teens waiting for eighteen—which was when I started counting down the days till I turned twenty-one. The other milestones had come and gone without anything changing—twenty-five, thirty, thirty-five. I certainly had no reason to believe forty was going to be any different. Sure, I was now shaving my head—but my hairline had started receding in my early twenties. Some of the stubble was now grayish or silver, but so what? I was in good health, I was in probably the best physical condition of my life, and even my emotional state was probably the best it had ever been. Sure, I didn't have the same energy I used to have, and sometimes when I really pushed myself at the gym the soreness didn't seem to go away as quickly as it used to—and sometimes there were aches and pains in my joints and muscles that didn't used to be there. But I had nothing to complain about, really.

It was about three weeks later when it happened, when everything changed. I was heading uptown on Prytania Street on a beautiful early September afternoon, one of those gorgeous days after the humidity has broken and the heat has dropped down to the high seventies/low eighties, when everything is green and the sky is cerulean blue without a wisp of cloud and the perfume of the sweet olive still hangs in the air. I had turned off the air-conditioning in my car and had the driver's side window down, my arm resting on the door frame as I cheerfully hummed along with an old ABBA tune playing on the car stereo. The light at Washington turned green and I floored the accelerator. As I went past the cemetery I was aware I was speeding—maybe about forty in a thirty zone. I was coming up to the intersection at Seventh Street when I noticed a police car stopped at the corner. I took my foot off the gas pedal, worried about possibly getting a ticket, when I noticed the police car was a little farther into the intersection than it should be. As I got closer, I saw that it was starting to creep forward slowly, and the female officer behind the wheel was looking the other way.

Oh my God she is going to pull out in front of me and doesn't know I'm coming LOOK OUT YOU STUPID—

In a split second I checked to make sure the other lane was free and started to turn my wheel while honking the horn at the same time and shifting my foot to the brake pedal—and then there was the loud crash and my car stopped dead.

My ears were ringing as the airbag deflated. I could taste chemicals in the back of my throat and I started coughing. Everything seemed surreal—the daylight streaming through my windshield now spider-webbed with cracks, the green leaves on the branches of the live oaks hanging over the street, and my inability to hear anything over the ringing of my ears. I began to tremble as the adrenaline drained out of my system, and I knew the weirdness was shock. My heart was pounding in my ears and I tried to control my breathing because I knew I was close to hyperventilating. I could see the female officer was slumped over the steering wheel. In the haze I somehow noticed in the rearview mirror that a fire truck had already blocked the street behind me and there were police cars everywhere, their lights flashing. *Man they got here fast*, I thought as I reached to open my door, get out and make sure she was okay, make sure I was okay. My hood was crumpled and smashed, and so was the fender on the right side of the car. I could see steam coming out from under the police car's hood but none from mine. But when I tried to move, bolts of agonizing pain shot from both my neck and my lower back. *Oh my fucking God I'm injured* went through my head over and over again as I collapsed, wincing, back against my car seat.

I'd never felt anything like this pain, and I'd played football for eight years—four at the collegiate level at LSU. It felt like my back was broken. My neck was so stiff and painful I couldn't turn it.

And no matter how much I coughed, I couldn't get that goddamned chemical taste out of my throat.

All I could do was close my eyes, bite my lower lip, and grip the steering wheel while I tried not to scream.

An eternity later—but it was really only a couple of minutes—I was trying to listen to the accident investigator over the roaring in my ears. I kept apologizing and pointing out that I was in excruciating pain. I could see the sympathy in his face as he knelt next to my open car door, taking notes as EMTs dealt with the other driver. Messed up and in pain as I was, I had enough presence of mind to not admit to speeding. Finally he was finished and an EMT was asking me questions, shining a penlight into my eyes, probing at my neck with her fingers. Carefully, they moved me from the car to a stretcher and loaded me into the back of an ambulance. I also had the presence of mind to tell them to take me to Touro Infirmary rather than LSU Medical Center. I wound up staying in the hospital overnight. I had a ridiculous battery of tests and

X-rays and consultations with experts and nurses and physical therapists and surgeons—all of whom I had difficulty hearing, and that damned chemical taste would not go away.

Finally, I was released the next day with prescriptions for pain pills ("the Vicodin is for moderate pain and the Oxycontin for overwhelming pain") and a referral to a physical therapist. I also had follow-up appointments. The X-rays showed damage to some of my lumbar vertebrae—compressed disks that caused bulging cartilage, and incredible pain. My options were to have surgery or to try to rehabilitate it by making my back stronger through stretching and exercise. I chose to try rehabilitation. Both options involved painkillers. I wasn't too thrilled about that. After Katrina I'd had a problem with prescriptions for anxiety and panic attacks. I wasn't too keen on risking another addiction, so at first I decided to only take a pill when the pain became too unbearable.

I got over that pretty damned fast.

My car was totaled, a complete loss—which only made sense, since I'd just finished paying it off the month before.

I was also forbidden from working out at my gym— anything other than yoga or the exercises my physical therapist took me through twice a week. I gained about five pounds the first week of not going to the gym. I was used to going a minimum of three times per week, with an hour devoted to weight lifting and another hour on one of the cardio machines. Reluctantly I cut everything fattening out of my diet and started trying to eat smaller portions.

It was a miserable existence.

And now, driving back home, the pain was starting up again. I had some of my pain pills in the armrest between the front seats, but rather than taking one I slipped a lumbar pillow behind my lower back for extra support. I drove up onto the bridge over the lake marshes and the Bonnet Carré Spillway.

The traffic was light, and by controlling my breathing I was able to focus on something besides the dull ache in my back. *Just get home and take a pill*, I reminded myself. It was only about another twenty minutes. I would have taken one in the car but I hadn't had lunch so there was nothing to delay the pill taking effect, and I worried I might start get loopy and woozy around the time I passed the parish line from Jefferson into Orleans. I'd made the mistake of driving on Vicodin once. The second time I went through a red light because my mind was wandering and I couldn't focus was when I realized I was a danger to everyone, so I turned the car around and headed home as quickly as I could.

To take my mind off my back, I started thinking about the case.

And the more I thought about this case, the less I liked it.

I seriously doubted they'd given me the whole story. It wouldn't be the first time a client had lied to me, nor would it be the last. In my line of work, you kind of get used to being lied to by clients. Maybe they just weren't telling me everything. That was possible. Their story just didn't add up for me. Tom was handsome and had a great body, but he'd been to law school and was clerking at a law firm. Sure, even the smartest people fuck up from time to time, but not setting the alarm for a building with several million dollars' worth of art stored inside had to take the prize for stupidity. And of course that just happened to be the night the thieves showed up. I kind of saw the Redemption Parish sheriff's point—it did look bad for Tom, especially if he was the only one who knew the alarm code.

I'll be the first to admit I don't know anything about art. The only art in my apartment was black-and-white photography, mostly landscapes and male nudes. Most of those had been gifts; I'd bought the others at gallery shows Paige had dragged me to when she didn't have a significant other. I'd never paid more than five hundred bucks for art, so the concept of putting a couple of hundred thousand dollars into escrow for the right to buy some paintings wasn't something I could wrap my head around. Taking possession of extremely valuable paintings I might not wind up owning also seemed a little odd to me.

Then again, maybe that was the way the art world worked when it came to big-ticket items. I was neither an art collector nor rich beyond belief. However, I did know several people who were one or the other or both. My landlady and primary employer, Barbara Castlemaine, lived in a mansion in the Garden District filled with art she'd collected. She wasn't in town at the moment—she was actually in Europe, buying art—but she was due back on the weekend.

And since he'd gotten me into this, I was definitely going to talk to Todd Laborde about his friends.

Bill had seemed a little evasive about how he made his money, so that was also something I'd have to look into—if he wasn't above cutting a corner here or there to make money, it was logical to assume he wouldn't be above questionable legal tactics when it came to collecting art. And restoring Belle Riviere must have cost a small fortune. The *New Orleans Advocate* had run a story when Bill bought the place. The previous owners had gone bankrupt trying to maintain the property and had let it go a bit to seed over the years. The monthly power bill alone had to run to the thousands. The cost of the renovations had to have been astronomical—so Bill was clearly sitting on top of quite a fortune.

It was enough of a fortune to acquire a hunky boy toy. *You're being a dick*, I told myself. *Tom has a law degree. He's clearly not some dumb hunk—but he is pretty.*

And I knew I shouldn't be judgmental about their age difference, and so quick to assume it had everything to do with

Bill's fortune. It was *possible* they were in love. Just because it would be hard for me to fall in love with someone that much older than me didn't mean it couldn't happen for other people. I'd been pretty judgmental when I was younger but had mellowed out about a lot of things as I got older. Really, who was I to judge? I was dating a guy almost ten years younger than me.

Todd was about twenty years or so older than Blaine. I'd never understood how their relationship worked when I was younger. Blaine was free pretty much to sleep with whomever he wanted whenever he wanted—and Blaine did go through periods of time when he was doing a lot of trolling around for sex. Yet Todd never seemed to have any problems with Blaine's extracurricular activity, some of which had been with me. I could never be comfortable having anyone I was seeing whore around the way Blaine occasionally did. I also couldn't understand why Blaine would stay with someone who didn't care if he was faithful or not. Blaine and I had slept together a few times when I was younger and a lot more foolish. As a result, I always felt like Todd disliked me intensely and only tolerated me to be polite. Paige always said I was projecting my own hang-ups onto him whenever I brought it up. It was possible, but I was also pretty sure Todd barely tried to hide his disdain for me beneath a veneer of New Orleans society social politeness.

But I'd learned there was more than one way to love someone, and there was more than one kind of relationship—

I almost screamed as a jolt of pain shot out from my lower back.

Fuck it, I thought, gritting my teeth and blinking back involuntary tears. I flipped open the console between the front seats, felt for the pill bottle while keeping my eyes on the road, and shook a pill out into my hand. I swallowed it dry, making sure to cap the bottle before putting it back inside the console. The pain was already so intense I could barely focus on the road. *Another ten minutes*, I thought as I grimly tried to push the pain out of my head, hoping it wouldn't make it impossible for me to keep driving. *Maybe I should just pull over and call someone to come get me* flashed through my mind. I dismissed that option. The only person I knew who wouldn't be at work was out of town, so the only option would be a cab.

I can make it home. I just need to focus.

My car came down from the bridge to dry land and the traffic began to get thicker, the way it always did out by the airport. I still had hope it was early enough that traffic wouldn't be backed up anywhere. If I got stuck in bumper-to-bumper stop-and-go traffic—*no, don't think that way, stay positive*, I reminded myself as I checked my side mirrors. I gritted my teeth as I swerved around cars so I wouldn't have to slow down, mumbling swear words out the side of my mouth. The dull ache was getting more pronounced with each turn of the wheels on the road, with each tick of the second hand—but at least the sharper, knifelike agony hadn't come back. I flew past exits with the speedometer holding steady at eighty, thanking God for light traffic.

Half an hour later and I would have been stuck between the Clearview Parkway and Causeway Boulevard exits for sure.

The car handled beautifully as I flew around the curve after the 610 split, passed another couple of slow-moving cars as I went past the cemeteries and the Superdome came into sight as the highway turned back again toward the river.

And as I finally passed the Superdome/Claiborne Avenue exits, the pain suddenly went away.

I sat up straight, happy the pain pill had finally kicked in. I had another five or ten minutes of lucidity before the world started melting around the edges of my vision, and that had to be enough time for me to make it home.

And it was.

I pulled into my parking space, turning off the engine with a sigh of relief just as my mind started taking on that weird numb feeling I now associated with Oxycontin.

My hand was trembling a bit as I slipped my key into the dead bolt of the back entrance to the house. I had to put my hand against the back door to my apartment as I tried to figure out which of my keys would unlock it.

I could feel my head getting heavier as I tossed the keys onto the nightstand next to my bed.

My cell phone started ringing as I collapsed facedown onto my bed, stretching out my body. I looked at the screen—it was my business partner, Abby Grosjean. "Hello?" I said into the phone, wincing a bit at how slurred my voice sounded.

"Dude—you hurting?"

"I was," I replied, rolling over onto my back. I reached for the heating pad sitting on the nightstand, turned it on, and slipped it into the slight arch above my butt, which was where the pain always came from. "I took a pill, fine now. Just a little on the loopy side."

She clicked her tongue. "Sorry, man. I told you I'd take the meeting if you wanted me to." Her disapproving tone clearly was saying *You need to take it easy and stop pushing your luck—you wanna be crippled for life?*

"It's not that I didn't want you to—believe me, I would have been more than happy to let you go out there, but they were kind of insistent on talking to *me.*" I could feel the heating pad warming up and shifted a bit so I could pull my shirt down to protect my skin. "It's a weird fucking case. I don't know what to make of it. What do you think of this?" I filled her in as best I could. My voice sounded hollow to my ears, echoing inside my head like it was an empty chamber with air blowing through it.

That was one of the many reasons I hated having to take Oxycontin. Percocet and Vicodin didn't have the same effect, but they didn't take the pain away completely when it got really bad. They also didn't last as long. And when the pain got that bad, I didn't care what I had to suffer through to make it go away. If it meant being empty-headed and being unable to focus, so be it.

I was very worried about addiction. I'd flirted with addiction to Xanax after Katrina, and that breakup had been bitter and difficult. I'd also managed to quit smoking, and when I'd gotten that monkey off my back I'd vowed to never let anything like that happen again. But much as I hated the thought of being addicted to something else, sometimes the pain was too much for me to handle with non-prescription medication. I tried to deal with the pain the best I could. Learning to live with the dull, constant, steady ache hadn't been easy but I could manage it. It was when the pain got worse that I couldn't deal. In the early days of the injury I tried to see how long I could go without taking something stronger than Aleve—and had learned my lesson the hard way.

I'd also learned to recognize the signs of when the pain was going to become soul destroying, and to pop a pill before it got so bad.

The physical therapy *was* helping. I didn't want to have surgery—that was going to be the last resort—and there was a possibility that I could strengthen the back without having to go under the knife.

The thought of having an operation of any kind on my spine wasn't exactly appealing.

She whistled when I finished. "You're right, Chanse, it

does sound funky to me. You say the cops in Redemption Parish think the whole thing is fraud?"

"Yeah. Tom, the younger one, claimed it had to do with him clerking at some law firm suing the sheriff's department on an unrelated matter, trying to make the firm look bad, as well as homophobia"—I winced as I shifted on the bed to get more comfortable—"but not everything is homophobia, you know what I mean?"

"You want me to head out there tomorrow, nose around the sheriff's office?"

It was uncanny how she always seemed to know what I wanted her to do before I could tell her. It was one of the many reasons I'd made her a full partner. "Yeah, see what you can find out. And look into this lawsuit. I'm going to go check out the dealer who made the sale and also appraised the paintings for the insurance company tomorrow." I'd wanted to stop by her gallery on my way home, get a feel for her and her business—but that was before my back pain started spiraling out of control. "You don't know anything about Myrna Lovejoy, do you? Have Jephtha do a web search on her, find out what he can, and email a report to me later." Jephtha was her boyfriend, a computer whiz who was able to do things online that I preferred to know nothing about. He'd been busted for credit card fraud in high school and done some time in a juvenile detention center in Jefferson Parish. That conviction kept him from getting work in his area of expertise—well, that and his lack of a college degree. He'd gotten his GED and taken some classes at Delgado Junior College, but he found it boring and quit. "I know more about computers than my teachers," he said with a shrug, "and they don't like it when I tell them they're wrong about something." He did some freelance web design work, but his real passion was designing computer games. He'd done a few already that hadn't been licensed—the market for them was too narrow—but there was no doubt in my mind Jephtha was going to strike it rich someday. It was just a matter of time and finding the right game idea. I kept him on retainer to do work for me. He was a whiz at computers and the Internet, and his help had upped my game in the security market.

I preferred not to know how or where he found his information. I suspected Jephtha wasn't above hacking, so I liked to keep a firewall up between us.

"Myrna Lovejoy?" Abby snorted. "That pretentious bitch from New York? She was the one who set this ball rolling?"

"You know who she is?" It shouldn't have surprised me. Abby seemed to know everyone in New Orleans.

"I know her and her husband." Her tone made it very clear her opinion of the Lovejoys was not a high one. "They're both pieces of work. Idiots. Jephtha did her website for her. What a pain in the ass."

"What does the husband do?"

"Lives off his wife, apparently." She laughed snidely. "He's here trying to get work in film and television but hasn't found anything yet. He's a big talker—you know the type. Refers to stars by their first names, like they're close, personal friends. He somehow manages to drop in a 'George' or 'Julia' or 'Matt' or 'Jennifer' in every conversation." She snorted again. "Like any major star would have anything to do with him. He used to be an agent in New York, worked for the Johnson Harris Agency. Mostly represented soap stars and Broadway wannabes, best as I can tell."

"So why isn't he working as an agent anymore? I can't imagine moving to New Orleans from New York is a strategic career move."

She laughed again. "Trust me, I found out everything I could about him and his wife once I'd met them. There was a *scandal*."

"Oh?"

"Yeah, he had to resign from Johnson Harris and no one would hire him. Apparently, Myrna was having an affair with one of the agency's senior partners and was using pillow talk to try to advance her hubby's career. The senior partner got quietly bought out, and dear Collier was also let go. That's the real reason they moved down here, you know. They figured no one here would know—or care—about their scandalous past." I could see her rolling her eyes as she said the last.

"Well, New Orleans does tend to draw people needing to reinvent themselves," I observed. It was true. People came to New Orleans all the time to start over and leave their pasts in the dust. For an extremely insular city, New Orleans was very welcoming and no one ever bothered to check out new people's pasts. This did result in temporary success for the occasional con artist, who eventually ended up sneaking out of town under the cover of darkness before his or her scam blew up completely in his or her face. "So what exactly did they do to get your hackles up?"

She hesitated for a moment. "I told you—Jephtha did her website, and then the bitch tried to get out of paying him, so I dug up some dirt on Myrna to get her to pay, is all. She paid, all right. She doesn't want anyone in New Orleans to know she and her precious Collier basically got run out of New York."

I whistled. "Damn."

"She's still got some connections up there," Abby went on, "which is how that piece in the *Times* got published. You're going to have to go talk to her yourself, though. You can bet she won't want anything to do with me."

"Hopefully tomorrow I'll be able to stop by her gallery." The heating pad was getting a bit too hot, so I turned it down a bit.

"I'll see what I can find out in Redemption Parish," she replied. "You rest and make sure you take care of yourself, hear? And I'll have Jephtha send you some reports on these people, okay?" She hung up.

I glanced over at the clock. It was getting close to three. I was supposed to have dinner with Rory and another couple we knew at seven thirty.

I took a deep breath and typed a text out to him. *Baby I don't know about tonight my back's flared up again and I took a pill.*

I hesitated before hitting send.

It wasn't the first time I'd backed out of something recently because of my back.

It was starting to get on Rory's nerves.

We'd been dating off and on now for going on five years, hard as that was to believe. I'd actually met Rory while working on a case, and our attraction to each other had been immediate. We started seeing each other after I closed that case. He was sexy and smart, and we liked the same kinds of movies and television shows. He also was able to make me laugh harder than anyone I'd ever known before. When we met, he'd been finishing his master's in public health at Tulane and was working at the NO/AIDS Task Force, running their young men's social group and doing testing work. Rory wasn't looking for anything committed—he didn't like the idea of whoring around and playing the field, but he wasn't, he told me, looking for anything lifetime commitment-like. Even though he came from an old New Orleans political family— his father had been mayor—and money, he was determined to work on his career and getting his life together before making any kind of commitment.

That was more than fine with me—I've always been a bit of a commitment phobe. The one time I ever had a serious relationship with another guy, I'd ruined it with my selfish and jealous nature—and before I could fix things he'd been killed.

So, yeah, I wasn't ready for anything serious. I'd pretty much decided to live the rest of my life alone.

But now Rory and I were falling into a kind of rhythm, a comfort zone where we didn't talk about the future and all we cared about was the present. The sex was amazing, Rory was incredibly creative and adventurous, and it was hard to believe that so much time had passed.

Rory had recently gotten a major promotion into management with NO/AIDS…and at the same time he'd come into an inheritance from a relative—I think an aunt.

Now he was ready for a lifetime commitment.

And I wasn't so sure I was.

He was a great guy, but I didn't love him the way I'd loved—

A few moments later my phone vibrated.

ok was all he sent back.

That wasn't good.

I took a deep breath and closed my eyes.

I'll worry about this later.

CHAPTER THREE

The sound of a garbage truck woke me from a deep, restful sleep.

I opened my eyes and stared up at the ceiling. My room was filled with the grayish light of the pre-dawn. The glowing digital numbers on my alarm read 6:04. I was warm beneath my blankets, but my face was exposed and cold. I resisted the urge to pull the blankets over my head and go back to sleep. I knew from bitter experience just how cold it would be out of my warm cocoon. I sighed and rolled over to my side. The good news was that my back wasn't hurting, just the low dull throb I'd gotten so used to and rarely noticed anymore. It was just something to be endured every day. It had only been a few months but I couldn't remember what my life had been like without back pain. But I usually took waking up with just the throb as a sign it would be a good day. At least I'd slept through the night. I hated those nights when the pain woke me up writhing in agony. I'd learned to keep the pill bottles on the nightstand the first time that happened and I could barely make it to the bathroom, each step a fresh hell of suffering.

I closed my eyes again in a vain attempt to see if my mind would shut down and let me go back to sleep. But it was no use, I was wide-awake. No matter how long I stayed burrowed under the covers with my eyes closed, I wasn't going to fall back asleep.

I had no memory of going to bed, nor did I remember getting undressed. That was another strike against taking Oxycontin: memory loss. The last thing I could remember about the previous day was talking to Abby on the phone.

There was undoubtedly a report waiting for me in my email inbox. Both Abby and Jephtha were nothing if not efficient, which was why she was my partner and I kept him on a healthy retainer.

I grabbed my cell phone from the nightstand and pressed the button to bring it back to life. Nothing—the battery was dead. In my drugged-out stupor I'd forgotten to charge the damned thing. *Stupid fucking Oxycontin.* I sat up, keeping the blankets covering as much of my body as I could. I inhaled sharply. I had no choice now but to get out of bed.

I pushed the covers off and immediately began shivering. The cold washed over my body, goose bumps rising on my skin, and my teeth started chattering. I hate being cold more than almost anything. My house was raised at least four feet off the ground—and the floor wasn't insulated. Before electricity, the fireplaces worked—which was also why the city burned to the ground any number of times. My first winter living in my apartment I'd done my best to make the place livable. I ran the heater nonstop and bought some space heaters, and my reward was an apartment filled with stuffy dry air, cold floors, and an astronomical Entergy bill. After that, I learned to just dress in layers, run the heat for brief spurts to take the edge off, and pray for winter to end.

My purple LSU sweats were folded neatly on the nightstand where I'd put them yesterday morning after getting ready for the trip to Belle Riviere. I slid the pants on and slipped my bare feet into my faux-fur-lined house shoes. I pulled the hoodie on over my head, walked into the bathroom, and turned on the water spigot. While I waited for the water to get hot, I went into the kitchen and started a pot of coffee. Another strike against Oxycontin: I'd forgotten to get the coffee ready last night and set the timer. While the coffee brewed I went back into the bathroom. I brushed my teeth and thoroughly washed my face with the hot water. The room was so cold tendrils of steam drifted up from the stream of water, misting up the mirror. By the time I got back into the kitchen there was enough coffee in the pot for a cup.

After I stirred a Sweet'N Low packet and a healthy dollop of French vanilla creamer into my big mug, I realized Rory hadn't come over to spend the night.

Of course, that didn't mean anything. It was possible he may have come by and found me dead to the world thanks to the Oxycontin (strike three). If he had, I couldn't blame him for not staying.

No, he didn't come by, because if he had, he wouldn't have left without checking to make sure the coffeemaker was set. It was the kind of thoughtful thing he always did. Before his promotion he used to have to work late nights doing HIV testing in the French Quarter's gay bars. I'd try to wait up for him but would fall asleep on the couch. He'd always wake me up and make me get into bed, and before he joined me he'd always make sure the coffee was set so it would be ready for me in the morning.

He was a great guy, thoughtful and considerate and ruthlessly efficient.

It was, I had to admit, a weird relationship. We were comfortable with each other, which was probably a terrible way to describe a relationship. We made each other laugh, and I enjoyed talking to him. But was it a relationship, really? I went with him to NO/AIDS events or parties where he needed a date. We didn't go out much together other than that. I had a key to his place in the Bywater and he had a key to mine. Every once in a while he'd decide he needed to be single and I wouldn't see him for a few months—but then he'd call and we'd start up all over again. I was never upset or hurt when he'd have one of his "I need more than this" moods, and I always took him back.

And now that he'd gotten the promotion he'd wanted, he was talking about settling down. I wasn't sure what that meant and never asked. He never offered an explanation, either.

He must be really pissed at me for bailing on him last night if he didn't come by.

My best friend Paige said it was past time for us to either "shit or get off the pot." It was hard to believe that we'd been seeing each other off and on for almost five years. *Five years.* Much as I hated to admit it, she had a point. Were we ever going to commit, move in together and set up a joint household? I wondered myself sometimes. But whenever it had come up in the past, it seemed like there was always a good reason to table it, put it off, push it aside and pretend it had never come up. Things worked between us the way they were.

Was the reason I never asked what he meant by settling down because I wasn't ready? Or did I not want to settle down with Rory?

I'll figure out a way to make it up to him, I decided as I sat down on the sofa in my living room, putting my feet up on the table. I wasn't good at romantic gestures, but unlike other guys in my checkered past, Rory never seemed to mind. That was another reason we clicked. I liked that he didn't make me feel guilty for forgetting made-up anniversaries like "our first date" or "the day we met" or other ridiculous sentimental occasions. He didn't want me sending him flowers or buying him little gifts. He didn't get his feelings hurt when I wanted alone time or when I was feeling moody.

I plugged my phone into the charger and set my mug down on the coffee table. I leaned back on the couch. My back was still not hurting, but the muscles felt tight.

I picked up the remote for the DVD player, pressed the play button, and took a sip of my coffee as the yoga DVD started up.

Yoga was part of my regimen for my back. I'd been resistant when my physical therapist recommended daily yoga as part of my regimen. He'd given me phone numbers for several yoga studios in the city, but I just couldn't see myself going to a group class. Yoga was for women, not former college football players who stood six foot four and weighed in at more than 240 pounds. Sensing my reluctance, my therapist rolled his eyes and gave me a DVD. "Try this," he said with a slight shake of his head, "there're routines for beginners, intermediates, and advanced. You might actually like it." He looked me up and down. "It wouldn't hurt you to work on your flexibility anyway."

I put my yoga mat out on the floor and sat down. The DVD featured an incredibly ripped and hot man with dark olive skin and long bluish black hair pulled back into a ponytail, wearing nothing more than black tights over his legs. His voice was calm and soothing. I'd felt pretty silly the first time I'd done it—if anyone had told me back in the days when I was playing football at LSU that one day I'd be doing yoga I would have laughed in their face—but now I actually looked forward to doing my yoga routine every morning. I'd never really been much of a stretcher before—I always just went through the motions of stretching before practice and games—but I found myself enjoying it. The stretching felt good, and the breathing method *was* calming.

As I closed my eyes and listened to Yogi Rafael's soothing voice, the music playing gently in the background, and focused on controlling my breathing the way he softly prodded me to, I found my mind wandering back to the meeting at Belle Riviere.

Where do I know Tom from? I asked myself as I moved from Mountain Pose to Warrior, and then into Child's Pose, feeling the gentle pull of the tight muscles in my back. *I know I've seen him before, shirtless. Maybe it was at Decadence, or the dance floor of one of the bars, or Mardi Gras? But I haven't been to bars in years...*

The weird thing was the memory was pretty clear. He was shirtless, his pale skin covered with a light sheen of sweat, and he was wearing clinging white boxer briefs as he leaned against a black wall with his eyes closed. It was like he was right there in front of me, his light brown curls dusted with drops of sweat.

Where? Where do I know him from?

New Orleans is a very small town. Many times I would see someone who looked familiar to me but I couldn't place the face. I saw so many people in my day-to-day existence—the cashiers at the grocery store or the Walgreens on St. Charles, the trainers and front desk clerks at my gym, the people who worked at the rehab facility at Touro—and when I saw them out of context I couldn't place them. Maybe that's all it was with Tom. Maybe he'd put himself through law school dancing for dollars in the gay bars. Maybe I'd seen him in the locker room at the gym sometime. I'd eventually remember. I always did.

Finally, I pushed the thoughts out of my head and focused on the yoga.

Before I knew it the workout was over, with Yogi Raphael placing his hands together and saying *namaste*. I got to my feet slowly, rolled up the mat, and stored it back under the sofa. I got another cup of coffee and took a shower.

I wanted to catch Todd before he left for the gallery. I figured it would be easier to talk to him at home. The Todd Laborde Gallery was always filled with potential buyers, and I knew he had five or six salespeople working all day. I'd been to openings there, and the guest list was the highest echelons of New Orleans society. Blaine had been born into that world—his family went back to even before the Spanish took over New Orleans in 1763, and his mother was the grandest of New Orleans's grande dames—but I always felt uncomfortable in those situations. I'd grown up in a trailer park in a Podunk town in East Texas, and going to openings at Todd's gallery made me very aware of that past. As I got dressed, it hit me that Rory's family was kind of the same as Blaine's—maybe that was the reason I was so on the fence about everything with him?

I pushed that thought to the back of my mind. I didn't have time to think about that now.

I locked my front door and crossed Camp Street, cutting through Coliseum Square. Blaine and Todd lived on Coliseum Street on the other side of the park, between Polymnia and Race Streets. I turned up my leather jacket's collar as the cold, damp wind blasted at me. Some dog owners were huddled together over by the fountain, clutching Styrofoam cups of coffee in their hands as their dogs went about their business. Blaine and Todd's beautiful old house was almost directly kitty-corner from mine. It had taken them several years to renovate it. I'd just moved into my place when they bought it. The place looked like a derelict wreck at the time, like one good shove and the whole place would collapse into a pile of rotting wood and decayed plaster. Todd bought it for practically a song. They'd been living pretty far uptown, in Riverbend, and this was a lot closer not only to Todd's gallery but the 8th District police station where Blaine was based.

At that time, the whole neighborhood was in pretty bad shape. The park wasn't lit up at night—all the streetlights had been shot out and never replaced. Peering through my blinds I could see the drug dealers and their clients out there, dim shapes in the dark, the occasional flare of a cigarette lighter and the glowing red end as someone inhaled. The houses around the park, with a few exceptions, all looked abandoned and blighted. But once Todd and Blaine got their house and got the renovation started, the other wrecked houses started getting bought up by other gay couples and the gentrification began. Within a year or two, *Utne Reader* declared the Lower Garden District to be "the coolest neighborhood to live in the United States." The Coliseum Square Association was formed by the new homeowners around the park and the other streets in the neighborhood. They'd spent a lot of money renovating their homes and turning them into show places. Eager to protect their investments and increase their property values, they pressured the city into fixing the streetlights in the park, then pressured the police department into chasing the drug dealers and users out of the park. Now Coliseum Square was well lit all night long. The fountain had been repaired and was also lit at night. It was now safe for the young urban professionals who'd moved in to walk their dogs alone after dark.

It was my first experience with gentrification, and I really couldn't complain about it. I didn't mind coming home at night and not having to worry about being harassed—or shot—by drug dealers and their clientele. The park was beautiful now.

Gentrification, though, was now becoming a dirty word in New Orleans.

The whole city had changed a great deal since Katrina. The first few years after had been difficult as we struggled to rebuild the city with a corrupt and ineffective mayor who didn't give a damn. But things began to pick up once a new mayor was voted in. It had actually taken years, but now it seemed like the city had changed overnight.

Rory's neighborhood—the Bywater—had changed so dramatically it was almost unrecognizable. His own rent had been raised several times, and he was tired of it. He was looking for a new place to live, maybe even a condo to buy. Rory called the people who'd taken over his neighborhood "hipsters"—his face twisting into a sneer when he spat the word out. They drove him nuts, but even he had to admit that the revival of his neighborhood, which had been sketchy pre-flood, wasn't a bad thing. It was kind of nice seeing people out walking their dogs or skateboarding or on their bikes after dark down there—before the flood it was a ghost town once the sun went down. Crime had been pretty rife, too. Rory rented one side of a shotgun, and his place had been robbed a couple of times back then, his car vandalized and broken into. But now the houses were being renovated and painted, lawns and gardens planted. Coffee shops and new restaurants and bars were being opened at a manic pace, drawing even more people to the neighborhood. Parking was now an issue—another issue that drove Rory nuts. "Nothing like coming home from the grocery store with a trunk full of bags and not being able to park closer than three blocks from your house," he complained.

The CBD (Central Business District) was also going through the same kind of renaissance. Like the Bywater, driving through there at night pre-flood had always been weird, like driving through some deserted postapocalyptic world. Every time I looked in my rearview mirror I expected to see Mad Max coming up behind me. But now there was a grocery store in what used to be the Sewell Cadillac dealership, abandoned warehouses were being turned into luxury condos, hotels and new condo buildings were being built, the streets were being torn up and repaired, and there were all kinds of new restaurants and clubs. There was actually a nightlife in the CBD now, and I couldn't see that as a completely bad thing.

There were, of course, people like Myrna Lovejoy, who came to New Orleans for what they called "the authentic experience," but then wanted to complain and change things. Those were the people the locals wished would pack up their carpetbags and leave again—and eventually they would. Another city would become the hip new happening place for the authentic Bohemian lifestyle they sought, and they would flock there with their granola and porkpie hats and bicycles and tattoos and piercings.

Unless, of course, their trust funds ran out first, and then who knew what they would do?

That wasn't fair—a lot of the new young people who were moving to the city were coming to work, and they loved the city just as much as the locals did.

I rang the buzzer on the enormous front gate to what Paige jokingly referred to sometimes as Chateau Laborde. The house was gorgeous, a Greek revival–style two-story mansion with Doric columns and a balcony no one used on the second level. The fence was black wrought iron, and the gate was six feet high. The house was painted coral, giving it a Caribbean feel. In the summer the flower beds in front of the porch were festooned with color. There was an enormous side yard, a two-car garage at the end of the lengthy driveway, and a huge carriage house in the back. The yard between the driveway and the house was littered with statuary of nude Greek gods, and there was also the obligatory fountain.

The front gate buzzed, and I went inside. The downstairs shutters were closed. I didn't see Blaine's SUV parked either on the street or in the driveway, so he had already left for the day. His partner Venus Casanova had been renting the carriage house since her home in New Orleans East had been completely destroyed by the flood, but I didn't see her SUV either. Todd's silver Mercedes was clearly visible in the driveway, though—so he was home. I rang the doorbell and shivered. The wind was picking up and getting colder. The sun was hidden by gray clouds that filled the sky. The damp in the air hinted at rain. I could see a shadowy movement through the tinted glass, and the door opened.

"Chanse," Todd Laborde said coldly, without smiling. He stepped aside so I could enter. "I figured you'd be stopping by this morning. Come in."

Todd was a good-looking man in his late fifties, maybe his early sixties. I suspected his blond hair was colored to cover the gray, and he wore it in what used to be called a Caesar—combing the bangs forward to hide his receding hairline. He was shorter than me, maybe about five-ten, since he was a little taller than Blaine. His forehead was unlined and immovable, and I suspected he'd had some fillers added to his remarkably unlined face as well. His blue eyes were sharp. He was in very good physical condition—Blaine told me Todd went to the gym five days a week without fail. His shoulders, chest, and biceps strained his electric blue silk shirt, which seemed maybe a size smaller than it should have been. He was wearing tight charcoal gray slacks and a matching tie. He moved to the doorway to the front room and glanced at his watch. "Come on in and have a seat. Would you like some coffee? I have some time before I have to be at the gallery."

"I don't want to keep you," I replied, sitting down on the overstuffed white sofa. "I'll try to make this quick."

"Let me get the coffee," he said with a slight shake of his head. He paused at the door. "Bill called me yesterday, after you'd left Belle Riviere. I knew I'd be hearing from you.

And really, we can take as much time as we need." He smiled faintly. "I would hope my staff can handle opening the gallery without me there, otherwise I am overpaying them." He turned and I heard his footsteps receding down the hallway.

I shook my jacket off, folding it and laying it down on the sofa beside me. The house was absurdly warm, and I'd already started sweating. It had to be at least eighty degrees in there. It felt like I was in a hothouse. I'd never felt comfortable in Chateau Laborde. Todd was one of those gay men whose idea of the perfect home was one that looked like a museum, rather than a place to be comfortable and relax, where you could forget about all the stress and worries outside. Everything here had a place, and everything was in its place. Over the fireplace mantel was an abstract painting in citrus hues in a simple black metal frame. Placed perfectly on the mantel shelf were several small sculptures, each an equal distance from the others. There was no dust evident anywhere. The hardwood floors shone like the surface of a mirror. To give credit where it was due, at least the furniture was all modern. Todd hadn't followed the stereotypical New Orleans design trend to use antiques in order to make the house look like you'd stepped back in time to pre–Civil War days. Blaine had told me Todd had hired an interior designer from New York to come down and do the house, but Todd had insisted on approving everything in the house and its placement.

I've often wondered, standing in the homes of wealthy gay men in New Orleans and looking around at the Audubon prints and wingback chairs, where the myth that all gay men had exquisite taste had come from.

But Todd's taste was impeccable. The décor was beautiful, if a little too museum-like and pristine for me.

Todd walked back in carrying a silver tray with a silver coffee service resting on it. He set the tray down on the black iron and glass coffee table in front of the sofa, filled two mugs with steaming-hot coffee, and gestured for me to be seated. I added cream and sweetener to one of the mugs and sat down in one of the chairs facing the sofa. The coffee was very strong and bitter. Todd sat down at one end of the sofa, resting against one of the arms. "Thank you for seeing Bill," he said, after sipping his coffee. "I know you did it as a favor for Blaine." He set the cup and saucer down on the side table. "I've known Bill for many years. He was one of the original investors in my gallery." He gave me a strained smile. "I've of course bought out all of my investors since then, but Bill took a chance on me, and we've remained close. I never forget someone who does me a good turn."

Did you sleep with him? Is that why he invested in you? I wanted to ask, but it wasn't any of my business and it had no bearing on the present case. "Bill and Tom seemed very nice," I replied, slowly and carefully. "I have to say, though, I am curious about their not having insured the paintings. That seemed off to me. I can certainly understand why the parish sheriff would question their story. Is taking possession of the paintings before the provenance was settled and the sale completed a normal business practice in the art world?"

"It's not something *I* would ever allow." Todd pursed his lips slightly. "You don't ever let art out of the gallery until the final sale has closed and the work is insured. I won't let anything that expensive leave my gallery without it being insured by the buyer. But Myrna Lovejoy—well, let's just say she has a rather interesting approach to selling art." He picked up his cup and took another sip. "But Bill really wanted those paintings. And he'd worked with Myrna before, so her, um, unorthodox methods didn't seem to be a concern to him." Todd shrugged slightly. "It's his money."

"Did you see the paintings?"

He shook his head slightly. "No." He exhaled. "Look, Chanse, honestly? Something about this entire thing seems off to me. I've never known Bill to skirt legality, ethics, anything like that. He's always been extremely honest in all of his dealings with me." He gave me a knowing look. "Sure, people who have money sometimes have a corresponding lack of ethics. But not Bill. I would have never suspected Bill of being a willing participant in anything remotely shady." He tilted his head to the side briefly, raising his eyebrows nonchalantly. "Tom, on the other hand…" Artfully he allowed his voice to trail off.

"You don't know him well?"

"Bill has had a series of younger men in his life—he's always had a thing for young men. He calls them *protégés*, which gives it an aura of, oh, I don't know, authenticity? Legitimacy? He always ends up setting them up in business of some sort, and some of them have done very well for themselves." He pointedly looked into his coffee cup. "And before you ask, no, I wasn't a protégé of his. It was always strictly a business relationship between us. As for the others… sometimes things didn't work out the way he'd hoped or how he'd wanted, if you understand my meaning. I can't say that about Tom—I don't know him well enough to have an opinion one way or the other about him. How did you read him?"

It was my turn to shrug. "He seemed to be on the up-and-up."

"They always do, don't they?" His tone was only slightly patronizing. "This whole thing—taking paintings before paying for them or without provenance, not insuring them—this is not normal operating procedure for a man like Bill Marren. I have to wonder how much of that is Tom's influence? He's a very sexy young man." He pursed his lips again. "Then again, Myrna Lovejoy also has a rather unsavory reputation in the art world, so…" Again with the little shrug.

"What do you mean by unsavory?"

"One hears things. But nothing concrete, you know. Just gossip." He refilled his cup. "She had a reputation in Manhattan for cutting corners, promoting artists who weren't quite there yet, selling art before she had the right to sell it. You know, little things." He glanced at his watch, a Tag Heuer. "Oh, dear, I'm going to have to cut this short—we're hanging a new installation today, so I have to be there early." He rose. "Not that I don't trust my staff—I have some of the best in the business working for me, of course—but I prefer to be there to make sure everything is just so."

I stood up and held out my hand. He hesitated for just a slight moment before taking it and shaking it vigorously. "Thank you for doing this, Chanse. I owe you one."

"Thank you, Todd." He walked me to the door. Once I was standing on the porch, he said, "One last thing, though. I don't trust Myrna Lovejoy." He reached into his pocket and handed me a business card. "She can tell you more about Myrna and her business practices."

I looked at the card. It was ivory, a heavy vellum, with the name *Serena Castlemaine* in raised letters with a phone number underneath it. Before I could ask anything, Todd shut the door, leaving me standing there on the porch.

Chapter Four

I checked my email on my phone as I walked back across Coliseum Square.

The air was even damper and the wind more piercing than earlier, so I walked a lot faster than I had on the way to Todd's. I'd stupidly not worn a stocking cap, so my head was cold and my ears hurt. My nose was starting to drip a little bit. I was shivering by the time I got my front door open, and I headed straight for the thermostat. The heater kicked on immediately, and I flipped the switch for the ceiling fan. I've been told that in the winter if you reverse the normal direction of the fan's turning, it pushes the heat down and keeps it from rising to the ceiling. *Every little bit helps*, I thought as I went into the kitchen. I dumped the old pot of coffee and started another one. My teeth were chattering. I thought about turning on the oven and opening the door, letting that warm the apartment. As soon as there was enough coffee in the pot, I filled my mug and walked back into the living room just as rain started pelting the windows.

Before I got too cold to keep looking and had slipped my phone back into my jacket pocket, I'd noticed there were several emails from Abby, with attachments. I grabbed my blue wool blanket off the couch and draped it over my legs as I touched the keyboard to wake up my computer. The vent on the floor next to my desk was blowing hot dry air. It felt good. I opened the web browser and clicked on the shortcut to my email account. There were the usual sales emails and other junk, which I deleted quickly. The oldest email from Abby didn't have an attachment—all that was inside was a link. I clicked on it, and it took me to the *New York Times* piece about Myrna Lovejoy. I read through it again quickly—it was actually worse than I remembered. There was the bit about "riding her bicycle in pajamas" and how no one "batted an eye"; the kale quote actually began with the condescending observation that "New Orleans isn't very cosmopolitan"; how fun it was to go to local eateries and run into "famous celebrities"; and on and on.

Yes, it was very hard to understand why the locals had been so offended.

I sighed and bookmarked the page in case I needed to reference it later. Abby's next email had several attachments, and the subject line "Reports." Each attachment was named: MYRNA AND COLLIER LOVEJOY, WILLIAM MARREN, and THOMAS JOHN ZIEBELL. I downloaded them all before clicking on the THOMAS JOHN ZIEBELL file.

As always, Abby began her report with basic facts: date of birth, parents' names, place of birth, names of siblings. Tom had two older brothers and a younger half sister, product of his father's second marriage. He'd been born in Boston and gone to private Catholic schools until he graduated from high school. There was a several-year gap between his high school graduation and when he enrolled in a Rhode Island junior college. After getting an associates degree in communication there, he move on to the University of Connecticut. He'd pulled a double major, graduating with degrees in pre-law and arts administration. He'd gotten an entry-level job at a small art museum in Boston and had lived in the suburb of Quincy. He left the job after a few years, enrolling at the LSU law school. He had finished last summer. There was again a slight gap from when he left the job at the museum to when he enrolled at LSU. Abby had also appended a list of his addresses—after he left the museum his mailing address was given as an apartment on the Upper West Side of Manhattan. Around the time he enrolled at LSU, his address had changed—to Belle Riviere.

His job history also had several gaps—ones that corresponded to the gaps in his schooling. *What were you doing, Tom?* I wondered.

There was no marriage information listed, but I didn't think there would be. There were also current addresses listed for his siblings, all of whom were married and still lived in the same neighborhood they'd grown up in. His mother had died during his senior year of high school; there was an address in Boston listed for his father as well as the date of the remarriage, two years after the death of Tom's mother. I stared at the addresses. I'd never been to Boston and didn't know much about the city. Tom's brothers had blue-collar, union jobs. So did his father. The brothers hadn't gone to college.

I wondered about that gap between high school and the junior college. I checked the address history. Tom had moved out of his parents' home shortly after graduation into an apartment, also in Boston. But no source of income was listed for that period. *How were you paying the rent? How did you end up going to junior college in Rhode Island?*

I bit my lower lip. *Maybe there's a history of being a boy toy. Bill might not be his first sugar daddy.*

I still couldn't shake the feeling I knew him from somewhere. I could picture him so clearly in my mind—in a darkened room with dim, yellowing lighting shining on his pale, sweaty skin as he leaned against the black wall, just wearing those sweaty white boxer briefs. But where was that? Where had I seen him before? Where was that room?

Could it have been porn?

I dismissed that thought. Tom was very hot, no doubt, but his muscularity was more athletic than porn-star like. Porn stars were ripped with very little body fat, if any. Tom wasn't built like that. There probably was some porn with guys like Tom in it—there was porn for any and all tastes—but the only kind I'd ever seen had the ripped boys.

It was frustrating.

Finally I gave up and opened the LOVEJOY document.

This report was a lot longer and more detailed than the one on Tom. I expected as much. Tom wasn't as public a figure as the Lovejoys. They clearly craved the limelight and apparently had employed a press agent when they still lived in New York. Since he worked in show business, it was to be expected. The report ended with a lengthy list of links to newspaper and magazine articles where one or both of them had been mentioned; it went on for several pages. I whistled softly as I scrolled through it. It must have taken Abby hours to compile all this information. She also provided a link to the Lovejoy Gallery's current website. I went back to the top and started reading.

Collier and Myrna had been married for almost twenty years. Myrna's maiden name was McDonnell, and she was originally from Biloxi. *That's odd*, I thought, remembering the article in the *New York Times*. If she grew up in Biloxi, she had to be relatively familiar with New Orleans; why would she act like it was someplace she'd never been before? Her family had moved to Rochester, New York, when she was a teenager, and she had a younger brother who'd died of cancer when she was in her early twenties. The parents apparently still lived in Rochester. She'd done her undergraduate work at SUNY on scholarship and gotten a scholarship for graduate school at Columbia. She married Collier right after she finished graduate school; they had a fifteen-year-old son named Cooper. They were both in their mid forties and were the epitome of the American dream—coming from nothing and achieving success.

I had to give it to Myrna—she was a hustler. Right out of college and a newlywed, she got a job working in a tony gallery in Manhattan. She established a reputation in the New York art scene in a very short period of time. It was amazing how quickly Collier and Myrna became part of the glitterati. They were always seen at the best clubs, the best parties, and the best restaurants, always managing to get their pictures taken with big names. Myrna had even appeared on a season of *Grande Dames of Manhattan*. *Grande Dames* was a horrific series of reality television shows about spoiled social-climbing women in various cities around the country. New Orleans had even gotten a franchise but only filmed one season, which never aired. Myrna hadn't been a cast member, merely a regular credited as "friend of the Grande Dames." That gig had only lasted one season. According to the articles Abby had looked up and condensed, Myrna had not gone over well with the audience; the viewers *hated* her. There had even been a Facebook campaign to get Myrna fired.

In an interview with a fan website dedicated to the shows, Myrna claimed, "I had to close my Twitter and Facebook accounts and hire security guards for my home and my gallery. I was getting *death threats*. Come on, people—it's a goddamned reality show! I got the bitch edit! Let it rest already!"

There was also a quote from *New Yorker* magazine (with a link) when Myrna closed her gallery permanently a few years later, where she blamed the show for destroying her business: "I lost many of my clients because of that stupid show and the way I was edited," she said. "But nothing can keep me down for long because I'm a survivor. Collier and I are kind of burnt out on Manhattan anyway, and he got a very lucrative buy-out offer from his agency. We both fell in love with New Orleans when we visited there for Jazz Fest last year, and we're going to buy some decayed, ruined mansion and renovate it, help get the city back on its feet after the horrors of Katrina. New Orleans is resilient and so am I...so it only makes sense for us to rebuild our lives there. I may even open another gallery—there's a vibrant arts scene in New Orleans, and I want to get in on the ground floor. New Orleans is one of the few *authentic* places left in the country."

Authentic. It made me want to slap her. And again, no mention of her Gulf Coast roots, which was interesting.

Collier Lovejoy was from rural Kansas, some small town in the middle of nowhere called Admire. The town was so small that other Kansans, per an article in *New York* magazine, didn't know it was a town or where it was located. Collier managed to earn a scholarship to the University of Kansas, and like Myrna, got a scholarship for graduate school at Columbia. He had left Kansas and never looked back again. His parents were both dead, and he'd been an only child—both of his parents had worked at a beef processing plant in the county seat. He downplayed his past as much as he could, also like Myrna. *Ashamed of their pasts*, I thought with a knowing nod. I wasn't exactly proud of where I was from either, but I never denied I was born and raised in Cottonwood Wells, Texas.

While getting his master's Collier had interned at several major publishing houses, and once his master's degree was in hand he went to work for a small literary agency. Within three years he had moved on to a major literary agency, representing best-selling authors and making a ridiculously good living. A lot of their friends credited Myrna as a full partner in Sam's drive to the top. They'd had a lovely apartment on the Upper West Side, with a great view. The Lovejoys seemed to have it all—he made partner at the Johnson Harris Agency, and she had her gallery. They got their names in the society pages all the time, mixing with the Beautiful People of Manhattan. They were at every important Broadway opening, every major gallery show, and had even finagled an invitation to the Met Gala one year.

I rubbed my chin. I found it really hard to believe the fallout from her appearing on a reality television show on a basic cable network had been enough to force them out of Manhattan. I vaguely remembered Abby telling me something…

Collier had, indeed, been bought out of the Johnson Harris office. There was a link to an article about it, but there was no real information there, no details. Collier was quoted as saying he was "feeling a bit burnt out with the publishing industry" and so decided to simply leave the business entirely rather than "giving my clients short shrift." He also said he was "looking forward to finding new challenges in life."

Right beneath this Abby closed with this: *Chanse, according to this gossip site, Collier Lovejoy was fired from his agency after the senior partners were made aware that Myrna was sleeping with not only prospective clients for Collier, but another one of the senior partners. That senior partner, Steve Marwood, was married—his wife divorced him and apparently took him to the cleaners—and he, too, was bought out of the firm. There were also rumors that Myrna's affair with Steve Marwood was what got Collier his partnership in the first place. He was apparently a terrible agent—he lost the Johnson Harris Agency any number of high-profile clients to the point where they would only assign him clients they could afford to lose. Steve Marwood apparently also protected Collier and kept him from being fired—how good is Myrna in bed, you think? Or maybe it was blackmail...anyway, once Collier was bought out of the agency, the Marwood divorce happened and he too got bought out. Myrna also got a pretty good price for her gallery business and the building, which she apparently owned. They also sold their apartment in Manhattan for a pretty nice profit. They bought a house on Sixth Street in the Garden District here, and she is leasing a building on Magazine Street for her gallery in the Arts District, close to the World War II Museum and Todd Laborde's big gallery on Camp Street. I didn't provide a link to the gossip site because there's no confirmation, it's all just rumor—but I doubt the gossip site would have gone with the story if there wasn't some truth to it, and neither the Lovejoys nor the Marwoods even bothered to do any spin or take any legal action against the site. The court sealed the Marwood divorce settlement and the transcripts, but Jephtha is working on getting access* (another one of those things I'd prefer not to know about) *but Steve Marwood's ex-wife now lives in Palm Beach in Florida, and I am still working on tracking him down. I will update you as soon as I get any confirmation on the gossip site and a location for Steve Marwood.*

And that was the end of the report.

I pushed my chair back and stood up. The apartment was warmer, but there was still some cold and damp in the air. There was still the report on Bill Marren to read, but I was tired of sitting at the computer. It would keep until later. The information about the Marwoods was interesting and established a pattern of unethical conduct for the Lovejoys, but it didn't really pertain to my investigation. There was probably no reason to look into them any further. Their damage was in the past, and it was highly unlikely Myrna Lovejoy or her husband was still involved with them in any way. Besides, it had nothing to do with the theft of the paintings. If I talked to either of the Marwoods, all they would be able to do was shed some light on the Lovejoys' characters—that might come in handy, of course, but they were hardly unbiased sources.

It's been my experience that women whose husbands cheated rarely have anything insightful to say about the mistress who ruined their marriage.

I needed to talk to Myrna herself. I thought about calling and making an appointment but decided it was probably best to try to catch her off guard, without giving her a chance to come up with explanations and excuses. She was probably expecting to hear from me anyway—surely Bill had told her he'd hired me.

I got dressed, going for a professional look: blood-red button-down shirt, silver silk tie with matching blood-red circles, black slacks, and my black camelhair jacket. I suspected Myrna was the type of woman—her piece in the *New York Times* notwithstanding—who was impressed by men in suits wearing power ties. If I dressed the way I usually do—black sweater and blue jeans—she wouldn't give me the time of day. I checked the address of her gallery one last time to be certain, then walked out my front door.

There was a lot of traffic on Camp Street, like always. It was still cold, but at least it had stopped raining. I brought a small umbrella along just in case. The sky was still gray, and the dark clouds were moving faster. I shivered and crossed the corner at Melpomene. I tried to walk as little as possible since the accident, but I still felt good. I'd tucked the Vicodin bottle into one of my jacket pockets to be on the safe side.

As I walked downtown I couldn't help but think about how much Camp Street had changed since I'd moved there. After taking the job with the NOPD and my basic training at the Louisiana Police Academy, I'd rented a studio apartment in a carriage house in the French Quarter. (That's what the rental agent had called it; I knew it was a slave quarter. There were still holes in the old bricks where the manacles had been mounted.) I'd lived there the entire two years I worked for the NOPD, using my off time to cruise the gay bars only a few blocks from my gate and look for love (lust) wherever I could find it. I tired of the bullshit politics in the police department pretty fast and left to start my own agency after two years. I also left the Quarter, finding my apartment in the then-sketchy lower Garden District neighborhood. There used to be an on-ramp for I-90 to the bridge to the West Bank. A lot of old-timers felt the Camp Street on-ramp was responsible for the decline in the neighborhood over the years. For years the ruins of the ramp, two lanes of concrete rising into the air until it came to an abrupt halt about ten feet up, ending in jagged edges of concrete and rusted metal jutting out, stood as a testament to the ruination of the neighborhood. It was finally jackhammered into oblivion and the pieces taken away. Palm trees now lined the neutral ground between Camp and Coliseum Streets, and even in this area between Melpomene and Calliope the houses were coming back, renovated and painted and looking better than they had in years. The beautiful old Coliseum Theater had been torn down after a fire had ravaged the inside. It was a shame. I'd always hoped the gentrification of the neighborhood would lead to someone renovating the theater and reopening it. The old-style Prytania Theatre uptown was still operating, so I'd always thought the Coliseum could survive as well. It would have been nice to be able to walk to see a movie.

The Lovejoy Gallery was on Magazine Street just past Julia. I walked past the World War II Museum on my way and reminded myself again I should visit it at some point. Julia Street was still torn up—Magazine narrowed to one lane at the intersection and continued as one lane until it reached the corner at St. Joseph. A lot of streets in the city were being torn up—a lot of the federal money allocated after the flood needed to be used up or returned, and apparently the mayor was determined to use every cent of it. There was a restaurant called the Peche Seafood Grill on the riverside of the street—I'd never noticed it before. It was hard keeping up with all the changes in the city over the last few years. Restaurants and bars had always come and gone in New Orleans, but not at the rate they had since the flood.

All this gentrification had to be a good thing, right? New business meant jobs and an increase in tax revenues for the city.

Maybe I should start reading the newspapers or watching the news.

I was a creature of habit and rarely tried places I'd never been to before. Rory was a self-admitted foodie and loved dragging me to some new restaurant I didn't even know existed. I had to admit he had excellent taste in food—I'd never had a bad meal with him. Of course, a bad restaurant wouldn't last long in New Orleans. That had been true even before the flood. Like everything else about New Orleans, the restaurant scene had changed so much over the last few years it was hardly recognizable. I'd recently driven up Magazine Street on my way uptown and noticed all kinds of food places we'd never had before—Thai, Polynesian, Ethiopian, etc.

Change was good, right?

The gallery was between Julia and Girod Streets. I seemed to remember the building had once been a furniture shop. I stood on the sidewalk in front, looking at it. There were enormous windows on either side of the door, tinted dark to keep the sun's glare out, but I could see statues on columns and enormous paintings hanging inside. In bright yellow neon, the word *Lovejoy* was spelled out in cursive in the window just above the door. Other than that, there wasn't the slightest indication that it was a gallery. There were no hours listed on the door. I stood there for a moment, took a deep breath and walked in.

It was freezing inside, and I shivered involuntarily. There was a receptionist's desk right there by the front door, but no one was manning it. There were no signs of life anywhere in the big room, actually, other than the Fleetwood Mac music playing softly through hidden speakers. There wasn't a bell or anything to ring. I glanced around. On a pedestal designed to look like a Grecian column sat a blue glass ball. It was maybe a foot around, and if I were so inclined, I could just pick it up and walk out with it. I wasn't so inclined—even after checking the little card on the pedestal informing me it was called *Blue Glass Ball* and had been "sculpted" by someone named Jane Meakin, and the gallery thought a collector should pay $3,500 for it. I took out my phone and took a picture surreptitiously with the camera before slipping it back into my jacket pocket. Before I could take another step a female voice said from behind me, "Oh, a million pardons! I had no idea you were here waiting. I hope you didn't have to wait long?"

I turned around and saw a familiar-looking face. She was tall and slender, wearing a navy blue blazer with a matching skirt. Her coral blouse was silk, and a long rope of pearls hung around her neck. Her blond hair was pulled back into a French braid and she smelled of expensive perfume. Her face was tastefully made up. Her navy blue shoes had massive stiletto heels.

As I tried to remember where I knew her from, her eyes narrowed and she tilted her head to one side. "I know you from somewhere…" Her forehead wrinkled in concentration. She snapped her fingers. "You were the detective who helped me out when Kenny Musgrave was murdered! During the evacuation for Hurricane Ginevra!" She smiled. "At the Allegra Gallery?"

Of course. I'd met her when I'd gone by the Allegra Gallery to interview him as a potential witness in another murder. The next day when the city was being evacuated, she'd found his body in his office. Unable to get through to the police during the madness of a mandatory evacuation and not knowing what else to do, she'd called me. "Meredith Cole, right?"

She held up her left hand. Her nails were perfectly manicured, but I couldn't miss the diamond ring and the wedding band beside it on her ring fingers. "Meredith Channing now." She held out her slender hand for me to shake. An expensive watch was at her wrist. "I always meant to call you to say thank you afterward, but…" Her voice trailed off.

I waved away her concerns. "No need, Meredith." I gave her my winningest smile. "I don't mind, really. Just glad I could help."

"You're very kind, but really, I don't know what I would have done that day if you hadn't turned up." She glanced over at the glass ball. "Are you interested in that?"

"No, but I am amazed that someone thinks it's worth thirty-five hundred dollars."

"Things are worth what people will pay for them." She barked out a laugh and then looked over her shoulder. She lowered her voice. "My boss—the gallery owner—is amazing. She could sell ice to eskimos." She shrugged. "Are you here to look at art…?"

"No. I'd actually like to talk to your boss. Is she in?"

She shook her head. "No, and it's weird. She had an appointment earlier this morning—she'd lined up a serious sucker, thought she'd be able to move a bunch of this crap"— she waved her hand tiredly at the displays—"to this *actor*"— her voice dripped with scorn—"here to make some TV show.

He bought some big house on Esplanade and wants to fill it up with art." She rolled her eyes. "Myrna never showed. I tried calling her cell and her landline, with no luck at all. That's not like her." Her eyes widened. "You don't think she's dead?"

I bit my lower lip. "I doubt it, Meredith." I tried to make a joke of it. "What are the odds that you'd work for two gallery owners who turn up dead when I show up?"

She barked out another nervous laugh. "This is New Orleans, Mr. MacLeod. Anything can happen here."

She had a point. "Maybe you could help me, now that I think about it."

"I'd be happy to." She fidgeted nervously. "Seriously, it's not like her not to pick up her cell phone. She'd answer it during sex, I think." She made a face, as though to say *New Yorkers*. "I don't know that I necessarily agree with her tactics…she can talk a good game about art, but she doesn't really know anything about it." She drew herself up a bit proudly. "I have a master's degree in both art history and art appreciation from Ole Miss. Art is more than commerce." She laughed dispiritedly. "But I needed a job, so here I am. Jobs for my degrees aren't exactly falling off trees. The original dipso duo."

"I don't want to get you in trouble—"

"Thank you, but I'm a big girl. If helping you would get me into trouble with Myrna, I can always say no."

"All right. I've been hired by Bill Marren about the theft of some paintings—"

She held up her hand. "*That* whole situation is very strange. Definitely set off some alarm bells with me." She sat down behind her desk and leaned back casually in her chair, crossing her long legs at the ankles. "For one thing, that particular art sale didn't come through the gallery." Both of her eyebrows went up, and the corners of her mouth twitched. "That in itself isn't unusual; of course, gallery owners often sell work they aren't currently displaying. How much do you know about how this whole thing works?"

"I spoke with Todd Laborde this morning, so he gave me a bit of an overview."

"It isn't unusual, like I said, for a gallery owner to sell works they've never displayed." She shrugged, her shoulders going up maybe an inch before relaxing again. "A gallery owner really works as an agent for an artist, and of course whenever an owner represents an artist, they create a catalogue. A good gallery keeps files on what their clients like, and when you run across some work you think the client will like, obviously you get in touch with them." She waved her hand at the computer screen. "I'm very good at that sort of thing—and of course, when so-and-so came to his unfortunate end, I may have kept his client list. They were mostly *my* clients in the first place. But I don't know anyone who'd want that ball. Anyway, no, those paintings were never displayed here, were never put into inventory. One day they were there, in the storeroom, in their crates. I asked Myrna about them—if they were going to be hung, who was the artist, et cetera—and she told me not to worry about them, they were already sold, and Bill Marren would be sending someone to pick them up in a van, that afternoon." She nodded. "A very handsome, well-built young man named Tom something or another came by and got them that very day, signed for them, loaded them up into the van, and that was the last I saw of them."

"Was Bill Marren a regular customer?"

"Not of ours." She shrugged. "I thought he primarily bought from Todd Laborde. We've sent him any number of invitations to shows here, but he's never come. The young man—that Tom—he has, of course. I recognized him. Very charming. I don't know that I trust him, though."

"Anything in particular?"

"No." She shook her head. "Do you want to look at the file?" She winked. "You've got my curiosity going." She went behind the desk and retrieved a set of keys from her purse. "I've got the key to Myrna's office. Won't take a second."

"You sure? I don't want you to get in trouble."

She shook her head. "If you won't tell, I won't. Be back in a sec." Her heels clacked across the floor, and she opened a door in the rear of the gallery. She used her foot to click the doorstop into place and went down the hallway. She unlocked a door and screamed.

I ran across the room and down the hallway.

A man was sitting in the chair behind the desk, his eyes wide open and staring at us.

The bullet hole in his chest explained why his shirt was soaked in blood.

Chapter Five

It started raining while we were waiting for the police to arrive. Enormous drops of water pelted and battered the enormous plate glass windows lining the street wall of the gallery. Cars passing by on Magazine had their headlights on and were driving so slowly they barely seemed to be moving.

It was almost like nature was putting an exclamation point to finding the dead body.

I'd somehow managed to get Meredith out of the office without touching anything. Once she stopped screaming, I'd taken her by both hands and started talking to her quietly, got her turned around, and led her back out into the main room of the gallery. I sat her down at the desk, got her a cup of coffee, and retrieved her coat from the coat tree in the small kitchenette at the end of the short hallway. Her teeth were chattering and she was shivering by the time I got back to her. She was going into shock. I draped the coat around her shoulders and pressed her hands around the hot mug of coffee. "Drink," I instructed, and she obeyed without question. I got up and turned the lock on the front door, flipping the switch on the neon Closed sign. I called Venus on my cell phone to report the body, speaking very quietly, before heading back to check on Meredith. I knelt down on the floor in front of her, holding both of her hands in mine, rubbing my thumbs on her inner wrists. I'd always heard that helped with people on the verge of shock. She had almost drunk all of the coffee, and she wasn't shivering anymore. Some of her color came back as I knelt there, rubbing her wrists. "The police are on their way," I half whispered, aware that I wasn't going to be able to keep kneeling there for much longer. My back was starting to ache a bit, and my thighs were burning.

I'd been out of the gym far too long.

She pulled free of my hands and gave me a heartbreakingly sad smile. "Thanks, Chanse. I—I think I'll be okay now. I appreciate it, you're very kind." She held out the empty coffee mug to me. "Would you mind getting one more cup? I think I just need one more and I'll be fine." She blew out a long breath and shook her head. "I guess you shouldn't have made that joke about dead bodies, huh?"

When I came back with her coffee she asked, "Do you ever get used to it? Seeing death, I mean." She gave a brittle laugh. "I suppose it's like anything else, you see it enough you get desensitized, right? Obviously morticians and coroners— obviously it doesn't bother them."

"I've never gotten used to it," I said, not kneeling again because I wasn't sure I'd be able to get back up. I bit my lower lip. "That's not true, I suppose. It doesn't affect me the way it used to, and I don't know if I like knowing that, you know?" I closed my eyes. Maybe it was because I had actually killed before, but always in self-defense. "I gather that was Collier Lovejoy?"

She nodded. "Yeah." She swallowed and closed her eyes. Her skin took on a slightly greenish tone, and she gagged. I grabbed the little trash can and held it in front of her as the coffee came back up. I handed her the box of Kleenex tissue sitting next to her phone. She took it from me, wiping at her eyes and at the corners of her mouth. She gave me a wan smile. "Sorry. Good thing I didn't have breakfast this morning." She took a couple of breaths. "I'm okay now." She stood up and held on to the edge of the desk for a moment. "Would you mind if I went to the bathroom and brushed my teeth?" She sounded like a child asking for permission after already being put to bed.

"Of course. Just don't look in the office."

She closed her eyes and nodded. I watched her walk across the room, her heels clacking on the floor. She gave Myrna's office door a wide berth and pointedly looked away as she went past it. She disappeared from sight for a few moments, and when she came back she was carrying a plastic bottle of water in her right hand.

I moved the garbage can around to the other side of the desk as she approached. She looked better. Her makeup was a bit smudged—she'd clearly splashed cold water on her face, as there were little drops on her eyebrows, but she gave me a brave smile as she sank back down into her chair. "Better."

"I'm so sorry you had to find him like that, Meredith. Did you know him well?"

"I knew him. I don't know if I'd say well. We weren't friends. I mean, I'm the hired help, and that's a line people like the Lovejoys never cross, if you know what I mean."

I did. I knew plenty of people like that. The social strata in a city like New Orleans have built up over generations, and it wasn't as easy to move up a level as it was to move down. Barbara Castlemaine might invite me to her parties on occasion, but I never fooled myself that she viewed me as anything more than an employee whose company she enjoyed from time to time. No matter how often we sat around in her parlor drinking champagne and gossiping, I never forgot that we were not on the same level.

She took a sip from the water bottle. "I don't think the Lovejoys had many friends, really." She frowned. "People were socially polite to them—they certainly knew a lot of people. All the openings here were packed. That piece in the *New York Times* didn't do either of them any favors, if you know what I mean. She was doing major damage control once that came out. People were *pissed*. But you know she was good at spin." She rubbed her forehead. "She claimed things she said were twisted, taken out of context, you know what I mean. It was all bullshit, of course she said all of those things. She really had a low opinion of New Orleans, and the locals. But she just saw everyone as a sucker to be fleeced." She gestured to the artwork in the gallery. "She wasn't interested in art. She was interested in making money, which is fine. I just have a different opinion about art, is all. If the job market was any better I would have quit." She sighed. "I've been looking, there just isn't anything out there." She swallowed and recapped her water. "I suppose now I'll have to flip burgers or something."

"What did you think of Collier?"

"He wasn't as bad as she is, you know? I'm not sure how to put it…Everything she said or did was calculated and phony. Collier was—he didn't seem as phony as Myrna. He seemed naturally nice, like he didn't have to work at it the way she did. Do you know what I mean?"

"Yeah, I think so."

"Myrna was different, but she was a saleswoman, you know? She could talk to anyone, put them at ease, make them feel at home here, like she was their friend and was doing them this enormous favor by selling them art at these low prices." She rolled her eyes. "I guess she was just better at being phony than he is—was." Her eyes got wide. "I should probably try to call her—" She reached for her purse.

I gently grabbed her wrist to stop her. "I think it would

probably be better if the police let her know, Meredith," I said softly.

She resisted me for just a moment before letting her arm go limp. "Yes, you're probably right." Her eyes filled with tears. "This is horrible, absolutely horrible. Myrna's going to be destroyed, just devastated."

"They had a good marriage?"

"Oh, yes, it was pretty obvious if you ever saw them together how much they adored each other. And Cooper—" She broke off again, her hand flying up to her lips. "*Cooper.* Oh, that poor boy. That poor, poor boy." She smiled, using a tissue to dab at her eyes. "Such a nice kid, Chanse. I mean, no matter what I may think of Myrna and her business practices, that is one sweet boy. I always say you can tell the parents by the child, you know? And he's so nice, and smart. Really good-looking, straight A's at Newman, plays football. Myrna and Collier adore—*adored*—him." She drummed her fingernails on the desktop. "Listen at me, rambling on like some crazy bitch, right? Oh, what is taking the police so long? I'm sorry, Chanse, I—I know I'm acting like a fool."

"It's all right, Meredith," I said, managing to keep my voice calm and soothing. "In this case, you're allowed. I'd be more concerned if you didn't react to this kind of shock."

One of the reasons I left the police force in the first place and started my own business is because I got tired of seeing death. Car accidents, fires, suicides, accidental shootings, domestic disputes, bar fights—after two years I'd had enough and turned in my badge. I'd never regretted the decision. But as a private eye, I still came across more death than the average person. I knew by focusing on Meredith I was warding off my own shock, my body's reaction. "It's okay. Keep talking."

"Thanks for letting me ramble on like an utter fool," she replied, shaking her head. Some of her hair had come loose from the French braid, wispy tendrils bouncing around her face. "I'm sorry, really." She gave me a wan smile. "Was I this bad the last time?"

"You're much better this time," I said, giving her a smile and a pat on the shoulder. She rewarded me with a smile just as a police car pulled up to the curb outside. I stood up and my back rewarded me with a sharp jolt of pain. *Oh, not now, for Christ's sake,* I thought as I put my hands up and moved to the front window. The throbbing was getting stronger. The crime lab van also came screeching up, going up onto the curb. Once it stopped moving, doors began opening and lab techs in raincoats started getting out with their equipment. I walked back over to the door and unlocked it, pulling it open and holding up my hands so the cops could see I wasn't a threat. "I called it in," I said to the two uniformed officers as they came inside. I gestured in Meredith's direction with my head. "She works here. The victim is the gallery owner's husband. The body's back in the owner's office, in the hallway back there. The door's open. The body's been there for some time, maybe overnight."

The younger officer, a white woman with all of her hair tucked up inside her cap, flipped open a notebook and pulled a pen out of her jacket pocket. She was short, barely over five feet tall, with pale skin and a slender figure the uniform didn't flatter. Her name was A. LATRELLE. Her eyes were dark brown, framed by long curly lashes. She wasn't wearing makeup, and water from her yellow rain slicker was dripping onto the floor. Her partner, an older black man with a thick, stocky body, drew his gun from its holster and headed for the back of the gallery. "And you are?" she asked, both of her eyebrows going up. Her eyes flicked up and down, giving me a suspicious once-over.

"Chanse MacLeod. I'm a private eye. My ID is in my wallet, in my back pocket." I turned slightly to the side to let her see it before reaching back and pulling it out of my pocket. I flipped it open. My private eye license was on the right side, my driver's license on the left.

"Private eye?" She frowned after writing my name and driver's license number down. "What are you doing here? Did a case bring you to the Lovejoy Gallery?" Unasked was *and does your investigation have something to do with why there's a dead body here?*

I didn't want to explain anything to her. Venus and Blaine were on their way, and I'd just have to explain it all over again to them. But I didn't want to be flagged as uncooperative, either. "I was hired yesterday to find some missing paintings," I said, opening the door again so the crime scene techs could bring their equipment in. "The paintings were purchased from here—my client bought them from Myrna Lovejoy, or rather, she acted as the agent for the previous owner. My client doesn't know who the original owner was, so I came by here see if Myrna Lovejoy would tell me. There was some question about the provenance—the past ownership of the paintings. The last thing in the world I wanted to do was stumble over her husband's body." I quickly described how Meredith and I had wound up finding the body. "I've never seen him before," I concluded. "It was Ms. Cole who identified him."

"And where is Mrs. Lovejoy?" She frowned. "Has she tried to reach her since—" She paused.

"She hasn't tried since we found the body. When I arrived, Ms. Cole mentioned that she had tried to reach Mrs. Lovejoy this morning—but it would be best if Ms. Cole told you her story about this morning, right?" I gave her what I hoped was my most reassuring smile. "After we found the body, Ms. Cole was shaken up, understandably. She wanted to try to reach Mrs. Lovejoy again, but I told her it would probably be better if the police were the ones who broke the news to Mrs. Lovejoy."

Office Latrelle nodded and flipped the notebook closed. "All right. Have a seat, and don't go anywhere, all right? The detectives are going to want to talk to you."

I took a seat. She walked over and started interviewing Meredith, but I was far enough away so that I couldn't hear anything they were saying. I glanced at my watch. God only knew how long I was going to be stuck here. I glanced over at Office Latrelle. She was intently questioning Meredith, writing down her answers, nodding every once in a while at something Meredith told her. She was paying no attention to me. I slipped my phone out of my jacket pocket and sent a quick text to Abby: *Collier Lovejoy murdered at the gallery probably last night Myrna not answering her phone Son is at Newman any way you can get over there?*

Less than a minute later I got her answer: *I would but am in Redemption Parish remember?*

I cursed under my breath. Cooper might know where Myrna was—but it was strange Myrna hadn't noticed her husband hadn't come home last night. It would have been great to question Myrna before the police got to her, but it couldn't be helped. I shook my head. I couldn't believe I'd forgotten Abby was in Redemption Parish for the morning. The meds were definitely fucking with my memory. I texted back *no problem, I'll figure it out.*

I decided to check my emails and read the report she'd prepared on Bill Marren to pass the time when a black SUV I recognized pulled up outside, parking behind the crime lab van. Both doors opened, two enormous black and gold Saints umbrellas opening on either side of the SUV before Venus and Blaine climbed down. It was still pouring outside, and they hurriedly crossed the sidewalk. Venus made a face when she opened the gallery door and saw me. She shut her umbrella and shook it out as she came inside. She strolled over to me with an eyebrow arched. "Again?" she asked, putting her hands on her hips. "I'm starting to think of you as the angel of death, my friend."

I hadn't known Venus when I worked on the force, but I knew who she was. Now in her late fifties, she was a bit of a legend with the New Orleans Police Department. She was the first woman of color to make detective, and she was tougher than most of her male colleagues. An athlete, she'd put herself through college on a basketball scholarship and won an Olympic medal as an alternate on the women's team. She'd majored in criminal justice. She was New Orleans born and bred, growing up in the East, and after college she came back home to join the department. She'd married a lawyer and raised two daughters—also athletes—while working as a beat cop. Once the girls were in school she made detective. She'd divorced her husband after her youngest daughter went off to college, keeping the big house in a gated community in New Orleans East as part of her divorce settlement. The flood had, of course, destroyed the house completely, and she'd been living in the carriage house behind Blaine and Todd's house ever since.

She was a tall woman, and you'd never guess her age from looking at her smooth, unwrinkled face. She had strong features, cheekbones that could cut glass, and a slim, muscular body with a small waist and long, well-muscled legs she liked to show off with stiletto heels that added a couple of inches to her six feet. Her hair was cut close to the scalp. There was some gray in there now, but that was the only indication of her age. She was wearing a long gray trench coat, belted but unbuttoned. Underneath I could see a white silk blouse over black wool slacks. A black leather shoulder bag hung over her left arm, and she held a cup of Starbucks coffee in her right hand. She had a reputation for honesty and not putting up with any crap from anyone. She'd pushed a lot of buttons on the force when she moved up to detective—there were still plenty of assholes who objected to her gender and her race. But she'd ignored the nastiness, outlasting and outsmarting the assholes who wanted her gone. She earned the grudging respect of even the biggest misogynist racists in the NOPD through her hard work and dedication to the job. There were still some rumors about her being a lesbian, which she just laughed off, saying, "If the worst thing they can find to say about me is I'm a lesbian, well, that says more about them than it does me. If I was a lesbian there'd be no question about it because there's nothing wrong with being one."

I shrugged. "I swear, this time I had no clue what I was walking into, Venus. I just came by to talk to Myrna Lovejoy."

"Yeah, you always say that." Venus rolled her eyes as she put the coffee down on the little table next to the chair I was sitting on. She fished her notepad out of her shoulder bag. There was an expensive pen clipped to it. I knew Venus was an honest cop, but she had a definite taste for the finer things. Paige told me once that Venus had taken her husband to the cleaners in the divorce—he'd gotten his secretary pregnant and was willing to do pretty much anything to get free to marry her. She glanced over to where Blaine was talking to the cop who'd been interviewing Meredith. She lowered her voice. "You think this has something to do with Bill Warren and those damned paintings stolen from Belle Riviere?"

"I honestly don't know." I replied. *Of course* Blaine had told her about the Belle Riviere case. If Blaine hadn't, Todd would have. "But it seems like a pretty big coincidence, don't you think? The paintings are stolen, and there's a murder in the gallery that originally sold them?" Venus liked coincidences even less than I did.

The look on my face made her laugh. "Yeah, I know all about the robbery. I was there when Todd asked Blaine to have you go out there and talk to them." She shook her head. "Just between you and me, Blaine and I have done a little checking into it ourselves, you know—unofficially." She glanced over her shoulder at Blaine again and lowered her voice even more. "Let's meet up later at my place for drinks, we can swap stories, okay? I was going to call you later anyway—Blaine and I can tell you what we know…this isn't the place for it, though. But something's seriously rotten in Redemption Parish."

"Shit—I sent Abby up there today to nose around," I replied, wincing as another bolt of pain shot out from my lower back. "She's not in any danger up there, is she?"

She hissed through her teeth. "She should be okay, but if she asks the wrong person the wrong question…" She let her voice trail off for a moment. "No, get that look off your face! I was fucking with you." She shook her head and barked out a little laugh. "Seriously, though, Abby's not a fool, Chanse— you of all people should know that. She's not going to get herself into trouble, she knows how to take care of herself." She patted me on the shoulder. "Let me go check on the lab techs and get a view of the crime scene. Don't go anywhere, okay?" She looked at me. "Take a pain pill, buddy, if your back's bothering you that bad."

I nodded as she walked away, her heels clicking across the floor as she headed to the hallway. I glanced over at Blaine, now talking to Meredith with a sympathetic look on his face. Venus was right; if I was going to have to stay here and give a full statement, I needed a pain pill. I'd just dry-swallowed a Vicodin when my phone started vibrating in my pocket. I pulled it out and didn't recognize the number on the screen, but I recognized the area code. *Redemption Parish*. Thinking it might be Abby, I answered. "MacLeod."

"Chanse! This is Tom Ziebell," he said cheerfully. "Glad I caught you. I'm on my way into the city, and was wondering if maybe we could meet for dinner? I want to talk to you some more about the paintings and everything. Bill—well, Bill didn't want me to tell you about my problems with the sheriff's department yesterday because he thinks I'm overreacting and the two things aren't related. But I can't help but feel they are, you know? I figure you should at least know about what's going on up here, make up your own mind if the two cases are related. No matter what Bill says, the way the sheriff is treating us is definitely motivated by homophobia. Anyway. What do you say, are you free around, say, eight? I have some business but I should be free by then."

"Yeah, sure. Um—"

"I met your partner this morning. She's your *business* partner, right?" His emphasis on the adjective caught me a bit off guard.

"Yes." Was he *flirting* with me? I shook my head. He was a client, and he was already involved with someone. It must be the meds messing with my perceptions again.

"She's sharp. And pretty." He laughed. "She thinks I'm right to be suspicious of Sheriff Parlange. I can tell you all about him over dinner."

"Yes, well, Tom, I'm actually at the Lovejoy Gallery right now." Might as well tell him, get it out in the open—he was going to find out soon enough anyway. "I came by here to talk to Myrna. Have you or Bill talked to her since I was out at Belle Riviere yesterday?"

"Bill talked to her last night, let her know you'd be wanting to meet with her and that it was okay with us if she talked to you," he replied, his tone questioning. "Is Myrna refusing to talk to you about the paintings? Do you need me to talk to her?"

I bit my lower lip. "I haven't seen Myrna, Tom. Her assistant here at the gallery can't seem to reach her, either. Do you know about what time Bill talked to her?"

"It was around seven, I think, right before we had dinner. Why?"

I exhaled. "No one seems to be able to find her today, and her husband—Collier—well, he's been shot. He's dead, Tom. Sometime last night, here at the gallery, in her office—someone shot and killed him. The police are here now."

There was a long silence before he finally let out a low whistle. "Holy shit. This isn't good."

"No, it's not," I replied, wondering if Tom could prove he hadn't come into the city last night. *He's your client. Why would he want to kill Myrna's husband? What was his motive?*

Just because I didn't know what his motive was didn't mean he didn't have one.

Hell, for that matter, *Bill* could have driven in and killed Collier.

There was another long silence. "Should Bill and I be worried?" he asked quietly. "Should we talk to a lawyer?"

"I don't know if you need a lawyer, but it might not be a bad idea," I said honestly. "I don't know if this has anything to do with your case or not. I don't know enough about the Lovejoys to know. They could have had any number of enemies. But you and Bill had business dealings with them"—*that seem a little bit odd to me*—"and now Collier's dead and the paintings y'all bought from them are missing. So, yeah, it might not be a bad idea to talk to a lawyer."

"All right," he said quietly. "I'll make us a reservation at Coquette for eight. We can talk then." He disconnected the call.

I stared at my phone for a few moments before putting it back into my pocket. *He wants to talk to me about the case in a public place—that doesn't make any sense*, I thought. *But maybe that just shows he doesn't feel like he has anything to hide.*

Was he flirting with me?

Venus came walking back toward me, a concerned look on her face. She pulled up a chair and sat down next to me, her notepad in her hand. "All right, let me know how you came to be here, how you came to find the body, and so on."

"I actually didn't find the body—that was Meredith." I took a deep breath and told her about my morning, finishing up with me calling to report the body. "You know all about the robbery at Belle Riviere, right?"

"Yeah." She nodded, scratching her forehead with the back end of her pen. "It's peculiar, to say the least. I don't have a lot of respect for the Redemption Parish Sheriff's Department, though, but that's another story." She looked at the window, which was still being pelted with huge drops of continuous rain, and sighed. "The case Ziebell is working on with that law firm? Suing the Redemption Parish sheriff? It's pretty nasty."

"I don't even know what it's about," I admitted. "Abby's up there looking into it today. You really don't think she's in any danger, do you?"

Venus barked out a mirthless laugh. "I'm more worried about the sheriff's department, frankly."

"What about this?" I gestured to the morgue personnel who were removing the body on a stretcher out to the crime lab van.

"Just between you and me, I'd say he was killed late last

night, sometime between nine and midnight, most likely." She raised an eyebrow slightly. "One shot, right through the heart. Killed instantly. We'll pull the security camera footage, and we'll be looking through that. Your girl"—she gestured with her head to Meredith—"had to disarm the alarm this morning, so whoever killed him knew how to set the alarm. That narrows the field of suspects down to a small number. The Lovejoys, Meredith, and there was another part-time employee, name of"—she checked her notepad for a moment— "Leslea Lowenstein. According to the schedule I checked, this Lowenstein woman wasn't working this week." She shrugged slightly. "But she knew the alarm code and had a set of keys to the gallery."

"There were only two employees? That seems odd in a gallery this size."

"Apparently, the gallery itself was only open to walk-ins from eleven to five every day except Sunday, when it's closed. Most of the art was seen by appointment only." Venus flipped her notepad closed and tucked it into a pocket. "Seems like an odd way to do business, but what do I know? I'm not an art dealer. That's not how Todd does things but maybe it's a New York thing, who knows? Appointment only makes it seem more exclusive, maybe that's something rich people respond to." She sighed. "The most important thing to do now is track down Myrna Lovejoy. She's still not answering her cell phone, and no one's answering the landline. I guess Blaine and I are going to have to head over there."

"Is someone going to be letting the son know?"

She tapped her pen against the side of her forehead. "If we don't raise Myrna soon, yeah, we're going to have to send someone over to Newman and pull him out of class. Christ, what a mess." She stood up. "You want us to drop you on our way uptown?"

"Yeah, that would be great." The throbbing in my back was getting worse. The Vicodin didn't seem to be doing the trick—I needed to lie down for a while with the heating pad.

Stupid fucking back.

CHAPTER SIX

The combination of my cell phone ringing and someone pounding on my front door woke me up out of a Vicodin-induced sleep.

I sat up groggily. I vaguely remembered Venus and Blaine dropping me off at my apartment—they'd given me a ride because it was still pouring. I'd swallowed another Vicodin during the drive back as the pain started getting worse again. My back aching and throbbing to the point I could barely fit my key into the dead bolt, I'd somehow managed to make it to the couch. The heating pad was now cold against my back. The pain had receded to the usual dull throb I was used to and could handle without having to take anything else to manage it.

"Chanse! I know you're in there!" Abby shouted, pounding on the door some more as my phone stopped ringing.

"Coming! Calm the fuck down already!" I shouted groggily as I wiped at my eyes. Abby's face grinned at me from the screen of my phone before it faded away and the "missed call" message popped up on the screen. I picked up my keys from where I'd tossed them on the coffee table and stood up, staggered to the front door, unlocked the dead bolt, and pulled the door open. "Jesus fucking Christ, Abby, I was asleep." It was still pouring rain outside, and a cold wind blasted around her into my apartment.

"'Bout fucking time," Abby groused, brushing past me on her way in. She tossed her umbrella into the brass umbrella stand just inside the front door. I closed the door and turned the key in the dead bolt. I could smell hot grease. "I brought you some food—I figured you probably weren't remembering to eat." She plopped herself down on the couch and tossed a greasy brown paper sack onto the coffee table. She shivered. "Fuck, it is cold in here, dude."

I walked over to the thermostat and flipped the switch over to "heat." I looked over at the cable box. 4:15 p.m. I'd slept for almost four hours.

"You got any Cokes?" she asked, pulling bags and sandwiches wrapped in white butcher paper out of the bag. "I assumed you had some."

"Yeah," I replied, smiling faintly to myself as I walked into the kitchen area. *I must be in really bad shape if Abby's buying me meals.*

Abby always did her best to make sure she never paid for food.

"You owe me fifteen bucks," she called as I retrieved two plastic bottles of Coke from the lower shelf of my refrigerator— which was ridiculously empty.

I need to buy groceries sooner rather than later, I thought as I walked back into the living room, wincing a bit as I handed her one of the cold bottles and sat down on the far end of the couch. I picked up the heating pad controls, pressed the "high" button, and placed it inside my sweater against my lower back. I eased back onto the couch.

"Back bothering you again?" she asked sympathetically as she handed me one of the greasy paper-wrapped sandwiches and an even greasier waxed paper bag of onion rings. Steam rose from both as I set them down on the end table. I tore the tape open and unrolled the sandwich, spilling deep-fried beer-battered shrimp out from either side of the French bread. "Sorry I woke you up, but you need to eat something."

My stomach growled. "I had to take another Vicodin earlier and it knocked me out." I popped one of the hot shrimp in my mouth and chewed it thoroughly before swallowing. I was now so hungry I felt weak.

"Dude, if the Vicodin isn't working you need to take the Oxy," she replied. "I'm sorry but there is just no reason in this day and age to suffer when there's medication that can put you out of your misery." She shook her head. "Call your doctor and get something stronger if you have to. You don't have to prove how tough you are, Chanse."

"The last thing in the world I need right now is an addiction problem." I tore the corner off one of the ketchup packets and squeezed some onto an enormous, hot onion ring. I blew on it for a moment to cool it down before folding it so it would fit into my mouth. As soon as I started chewing it I realized I hadn't eaten since lunch the previous day, before heading out for Belle Riviere. *Not good, Chanse*, I thought, making another mental note to remind myself to eat regularly. That was another part of the problem with the pills—they took away my appetite, and I needed food to help heal the damned injury in the first place. I ate another onion ring.

"Are you going to do the cortisone shot?" she asked casually, unwrapping her oyster po'boy and pointedly not looking at me. "You really need to consider it, Chanse. You can't keep on like this." She looked up at me finally. "I mean, do what you want—it's your back, not mine, after all—but don't you want the pain to stop?" She shuddered. "I try to not tell people what to do, but seriously. It's not fun for me to see you suffer, boss."

She'd been the number one advocate of me having the cortisone shots ever since I made the mistake of mentioning it to her. My doctor at the pain management clinic had presented it as an option almost from the beginning, but the idea of having a needle stuck into my spine wasn't appealing. I've never been much of a fan of needles and shots to begin with. And no matter how unlikely the possibility, no matter how much reassurance I was given that the procedure was safe— any risk of further spinal damage was too much.

This wasn't a winnable argument, though. I was well aware that my position didn't make sense, so I changed the subject. "How was your trip out to Redemption Parish? Find out anything good?"

She rolled her eyes. "You know, I grew up in Placquemines, but I never go back there so I forget how backward things can be out in the parishes. There were a couple of times when I was worried I'd have some severe flashbacks, but I toughed it out. Good thing I did, too, because the trip was *very* informative."

Abby had grown up very blue collar in Placquemines Parish. She came from a long line of shrimpers ("I was related to practically everyone in the damned parish. The Grosjeans were known for their fertility and their Catholicism—a dangerous combination if there ever was one") and from childhood had been working whenever she wasn't in school. After she graduated from high school she helped out on her dad's boat and waited tables at a local diner. She left home at nineteen when her father took a second wife she didn't like. She moved to New Orleans and got a job waiting tables at a diner in the lower Quarter. She got tired very quickly of being groped and abused by drunk tourists who would then stiff her on the tip. That was when she made the decision to, as she put it, "put my body to work for me."

Abby had been on the drill team all through high school.

Even now, in her late twenties, she still had the compact, strong and sexy body of a cheerleader. She was maybe five-three or five-four, about 105 pounds, and carried little excess weight. Her waist was tiny, but she was very well developed in the chest. She scored a gig dancing at the Catbox Club, a strip joint on the sleazy end of Bourbon Street where she made more money in one night than she did waiting tables in a week. She'd been dancing there a couple of years, socking away her money to help pay for college, when she met the love of her life, Jephtha Carriere. Jephtha had always had a thing for strippers, who tended to use the tall, gangly computer genius for as much as they could get out of him before tossing him aside like a used tissue. They fell hard for each other, and Jephtha encouraged her to go to college. She moved in with him and enrolled at the University of New Orleans. She kept dancing while majoring in theater and pre-law. She was good at her job ("just because you're a stripper doesn't mean you can't take pride in your work"), and her theater background combined with her cheerleading bumps-and-grinds made her one of the club's hottest and most popular dancers. She knew how to work the audience as well as how to use makeup, wigs, and costumes to change up her look.

Jephtha had been working for me before he met Abby. At first I was a little skeptical of her, but she won me over. I'd asked her once to use her disguise skills to help me out on a case, and she took to private eye work like it was the work she was meant to do. She was accepted into Loyola University's law school but got certified as a private eye, and I hired her. She went to law school part-time for a while, but put her ambitions of being a lawyer on hold for a while. She still danced as a fill-in at the Catbox Club every once in a while ("to keep my hand in," was what she said about it, but it was really to keep close to the other dancers because "they're excellent sources"). I started farming out more and more of my work to her as she proved to be a valuable asset over and over again. She was so skilled at disguise there were times I didn't recognize her myself. After she'd worked for me for about a year I'd made her a full partner in the business. She was currently taking a couple of classes at Loyola, but she was in no rush to get her degree. "I know I can make more money as a lawyer," she once told me, after a couple of glasses of wine and a joint, "but I've noticed almost every lawyer we ever deal with is a sleazeball, so—" She shrugged. "I never feel sleazy when I'm dancing at the Catbox Club, but being a lawyer? I don't know."

The law's loss was my gain.

"Go on, don't stop there, what did you find out?" I encouraged her. I took the top piece of French bread off my po'boy and liberally applied ketchup to the steaming-hot shrimp. The smell was intoxicating, and I almost felt faint with hunger. I closed the sandwich and took a big bite. I didn't even try to hold in the moan of pleasure as the tastes exploded in my mouth.

Abby rolled her expressive hazel eyes and finished chewing, wiping crumbs from the slightly stale French bread off her chin. "Well, for one thing, that parish seat, Avignon?" She pronounced it the Louisiana way, *Avenon*, rather than the French *Ah-vee-NYOH*. "What a shithole. I mean, *seriously*. That place makes Plaquemines look like the Garden District." She dragged an onion ring through the puddle of ketchup she'd made on the butcher paper her sandwich had been wrapped in. "Well, okay, I'm exaggerating a bit. It's a cute little town, picturesque downtown with a little square park right in front of the courthouse, mostly antique stores"—she made air quotes as she said *antique stores*—"a little diner, your typical little Mayberry in Louisiana type little town, you have to cross a covered bridge over a bayou to even get into the city limits, blah blah blah. You know, the kind of place that looks really nice and charming on the surface but underneath it's all rotting and disgusting? Like one of those towns where soaps are set?"

"I get what you mean." Cottonwood Wells, the small town in East Texas where I'd grown up, was like that—everyone went to church on Sunday but the ones who were the most church-proud were the biggest sinners of them all.

"Well, Plaquemines Parish was like that, too," she conceded with a slight shrug. "But yeah, the courthouse in Avignon reeks to high heaven of corruption. That is one place I wouldn't want to cross the sheriff."

"Oh?"

"They have a newspaper, if you want to call it that. It's a daily, but there isn't really much to it. They have a storefront on the square, just on the other side from the courthouse." She made a face. "I stuck my head in, see if I could find any dirt over there." She gave me a crooked smile. "When in doubt, always track down the social columnist. They always know where the bodies are buried in small towns."

I shifted in my seat. The pain was starting to pick up again. I winced and hoped she didn't notice. "And?" I prompted.

"I pretended I was there working on a story for *Crescent City*." She smirked. *Crescent City* was the magazine where my oldest and best friend, Paige Tourneur, worked as editor-in-chief. Abby and Paige had worked it out that Abby could pretend to be working for the magazine if she ever needed a cover story, and if anyone ever called to check up on her, Paige and/or her assistant would lie for her. It was genius—I would have never thought of it myself. Another great example of how Abby constantly proved her worth to me. "The society columnist is this enormous woman who could stand to miss a few meals, if you know what I mean," she said with all the cruelty of youth. "She was nice, but a horrible snob. You can imagine how excited Mrs. Celeste Topham of the Redemption Parish Tophams, who go back in the parish to before the Civil War, was to talk to someone from an important magazine from *New Orleans*." She said this in a thick drawl, mimicking the unfortunate Mrs. Topham's way of speaking. "She was more than happy to have a cup of coffee with me and tell me anything and everything I needed to know about"—she lowered her voice and rolled her eyes—"those 'confirmed bachelors' at Belle Riviere."

I tried to keep the pain I was starting to feel off my face. "She didn't say 'confirmed bachelors,' did she?"

"She most certainly did." Her eyes danced with amusement. "Bless her heart, Mrs. Topham had the most impressive manners, but she's a terrible gossip. She thinks it's a terrible waste that young Mr. Tom Ziebell is going the way of old Mr. Marren, because there are any number of beautiful and eligible young women in Redemption Parish would make him a good wife." She rolled her eyes. "The women's movement certainly never made it to Avignon. She did show me a picture of young Mr. Ziebell, and I have to agree that it's a shame he's been taken out of the gene pool." She clucked her tongue. "But seriously, you can't imagine how hard it was keeping a straight face while I listened to her go on and on! I can't believe anyone—especially a woman—could talk and think like that still in this day and age. Although to be fair, the poor dear was probably in her sixties and that's just how she was raised. Mrs. Topham, you see, and her circle, believed that when Belle Riviere was renovated, they would start having parties again like in the old days. Belle Riviere is the showplace of Redemption Parish...but not only has Mr. Marren *not* thrown any parties, he doesn't seem terribly interested in letting anyone in to see the place or being part of the Garden Tour in the spring—which Mrs. Topham herself organizes. Mr. Marren doesn't bother to return her calls."

"That probably doesn't sit well with Mrs. Topham."

"You bet your ass it doesn't. But when I asked about the lawsuit, she wouldn't share any details of the case itself with me. All she said was it was just another example of someone wanting something for nothing, and Sheriff Parlange would be completely justified in arresting the whole lot of them."

"Even though she thinks young Mr. Ziebell would be a catch from some of the belles in the parish?"

"Oh, she doesn't blame *him* for anything." She laughed. "You see, she believes that Ed Byrnes, senior partner of the law firm suing the parish, is just using the case to make Sheriff Parlange look bad and further his own political ambitions, and he's just using that poor old colored woman." She scrunched up her face like she'd smelled something foul. "And yes, she did say 'old colored woman.' I suppose I should be glad she didn't use the n-word." She sighed. "Anyway, once I'd gotten everything out of her I could on that score, I asked her about the robbery. She claims that's Ed Byrnes using old Mr. Marren to again make Sheriff Parlange look bad. Everyone, it seems, is out to get Sheriff Parlange, who's just a good Christian man doing the best job he can for the people of the parish."

"Methinks the lady doth protest too much." I winced as I shifted again. I was going to have to take another pill.

"Right? She also made it very clear that he runs the parish. No one gets elected to office without Sheriff Parlange's support. He's got the whole parish locked up tighter than a drum." She dragged another onion ring through the remains of the ketchup puddle. "I didn't think that kind of thing still existed in the modern world, but it clearly does in Redemption Parish."

"Interesting."

"So, I thanked her for her time and told her I'd call her if I needed anything else, and walked over to the courthouse, where I found myself a deputy who looked like he had trouble getting laid—it was really just a matter of picking one, you know, like shooting fish in a fucking barrel—and got him to join me for some coffee at the diner." She took another bite of her sandwich, chewing noisily. "Deputy Sheriff Clay Perlange himself. He just happens to be a cousin of Sheriff Parlange's wife. Nepotism is the only way that douchebag could get a job in law enforcement. Anyway—the homophobia is strong in this one, believe you me." She smiled at me, an evil glint in her eye. "I switched tactics. I was still there doing a story for *Crescent City*, but with him, I acted like I was looking to dig up some dirt on Bill Marren. I told him that there were some questionable dealings with an art dealer in New Orleans I was looking into. Talk about priming the pump!" She scowled. "He also never looked at my face, if you know what I mean. Why any man would think a woman would think it flattering to have him talk to her boobs is beyond me. Deputy Clay Perlange is the kind of man who expects his women to be deferential and wait on him hand and foot—and trust me, he was no fucking prize." She shuddered. "But good ole Deputy Perlange couldn't spill dirt fast enough on the Marren-Ziebell household at Belle Riviere." She took a big pull on the Coke bottle. She leaned back on the sofa, stifling a belch from the carbonation. "Man, living in Orleans Parish we forget sometimes how nasty the bigots can be, you know?"

I nodded, choosing not to mention there were still plenty of homophobic bigots in New Orleans.

"I can't remember the last time I heard someone say *fag*," she went on, opening another ketchup packet before grabbing a couple of onion rings and folding them in half before dipping them in the replenished puddle, "but Deputy Perlange—'call me

Clay, pretty lady'—dropped the word into casual conversation like it was no big deal, like decent people still say it. 'Them fags out at Belle Riviere' was how he referred to them. Them fags. I wanted to slap the snot out of him. I get no credit for restraint." She chewed the onion rings and swallowed. "But to be fair, Chanse, much as I hate to be—clearly the sheriff's department wasn't about to lift a finger to help 'them fags' in any case—it really *does* sound like it was an inside job. I can't for the life of me figure out how someone else could get in there to steal the paintings." She smiled wickedly at me. "He promised to email me the crime scene photos, and there were no fingerprints in the place that weren't accounted for—either they belonged to Bill and Tom or someone on their staff. And the alarm hadn't been set? Really? Who *does* that?" She shook her head, then focused on her sandwich for a moment. "You were out there. The entire estate is surrounded by that brick wall. You have to go over the damned wall to even get into the place, and back over it to get out. There's a code to open the gate, sure—but you'd have to know the code or someone has to let you in. They *had* to go in and out through the gate, Chanse. I mean, doesn't it stink to you, too? And the *only* thing taken was those three Anschler paintings, nothing else—and there were plenty of other valuable paintings in that studio. Why go to all that trouble to only steal three paintings when you could clean out the whole place?"

"Could the paintings have been rolled up? Maybe someone went over the fence. And if the other paintings were framed…"

"The Anschler paintings not only were framed, Chanse, they were supposedly still in the crates. And the crates were gone, too." She shook her head. "They were too big and bulky for one person to take, let alone go over the fence with them. And no one in the main house heard a car or a truck or anything.

So how was it done, Chanse? I don't think the paintings were ever there. They couldn't have been stolen, so the only logical answer is they weren't there to begin with."

"But why would they report them stolen, then?"

"It really doesn't make any sense. None of it does, Chanse. Why would they report them stolen, and then hire us?" She shook her head. "Seriously, Chanse—*why* would Tom not have turned on the alarm? And why is Bill so cavalier about the whole thing?"

"Cavalier?"

She gave me a look. "Chanse, what would you do if your boy toy didn't turn on the alarm and you were robbed? And were lucky it wasn't worse? Would you pat him on the head and say everything's okay, don't worry about it?" She laughed. "Hardly!"

"You met him, didn't you? What did you think?" When her jaw dropped I waved my hand. "No, I'm not psychic. He called me. We're meeting later tonight. He mentioned meeting you."

"He's hot," she admitted with a rueful smile. "I can see why the old man paid for him to go to law school." She exhaled. "Oh, I suppose that's bitchy, wasn't it? He's good-looking, yes, but he's smart and charming and funny." She wiggled her eyebrows at me. "He kind of charmed me."

"He has that effect on people." I popped the last stray shrimp that had escaped from my po'boy into my mouth and relaxed back into the couch. I'd eaten too much and could feel the lethargic state of deep-fried breading coming on. "What was this case he thinks is behind everything?"

She blew a raspberry. "Yes, Deputy Dawg wasn't too forthcoming about *that* one, believe you me." She smiled. "I stopped by the parish newspaper office to talk about it. Again, it was like Mayberry, with racism. Though come to think of it, it was kind of odd there weren't any black people in Mayberry, wasn't it?" She laughed. "Anyway, the story is this. There's an older black woman who lived in Avignon, she works mainly cleaning people's houses. Nice, older lady who isn't really very educated. Everyone calls her Miss Mamie—her name is Mamie Jackson. Mamie's been taking care of her great-granddaughter LaToya pretty much ever since LaToya was a baby—her mother's in jail, armed robbery or something, and Miss Mamie's son won't have anything to do with his daughter or her baby. So Miss Mamie, she has to be in her early seventies maybe?—anyway, Miss Mamie is raising LaToya and gets some assistance, because Miss Mamie doesn't really make all that much money cleaning houses. Well, LaToya's a bit wild. Long story short, the sheriffs went out to arrest LaToya, and Miss Mamie kind of got in the way. The sheriff's story is Miss Mamie tried to assault one of his deputies, the deputy shook loose, and Miss Mamie fell and hit her head. Miss Mamie is in a coma, and the firm Tom works for is suing the sheriff. LaToya claims they beat her—and frankly, from the sounds of her injuries, there's no way she was injured in a fall." She blew out her breath in frustration. "Tom is pretty sure a jury trial wouldn't do any good—the people of Redemption Parish would never rule against the sheriff—so they are looking to sue in federal court, claiming Miss Mamie's civil rights were violated."

I frowned. "I can't believe that hasn't made the news in New Orleans."

"I said the same thing to Tom, but he said that nobody in New Orleans is interested in anything that happens in Redemption Parish, despite its proximity to the city." She made a face. "He's said he's tried to get the newspapers and TV stations here to cover the story but no one will."

"But if it becomes a federal trial, it'll be held in New

Orleans, won't it?" I tried to think but couldn't remember how federal courts worked. "But yes, I can see why the sheriff might want to bury this case…Would it be possible for the sheriff to have somehow gotten the code for the alarm?" I drummed my fingers on my knee. The heating pad was starting to cool down again, so I pressed the button to get it started again.

She picked up the garbage, crumpled it all up, and shoved it into the greasy bag she'd taken it out of. She walked into the kitchen, stuffed the bag into the garbage can, and walked back out. "What do you want me to do now, boss? Do you think Collier Lovejoy's murder is tied into all of this?"

I grinned. One of the reasons I was grateful to have her working for me was she had a fine reasoning brain and was fiercely intelligent. Even though we were full partners, she still deferred to me on investigations we worked together. At first, it annoyed me because I thought she was either deferring to me as a man (as if she would ever do that) or because of age. But when I finally asked her about it, she just shrugged and said, "I think of you as the senior partner. It's your business and you brought me in. If you don't want me to be respectful, I won't be." She then rewarded me with a grin so evil it sent chills down my spine.

I never asked again.

"Well, the painter had ties to New Orleans and his daughter came here after the war," I said. "I'd like to track Myrna down, see what she has to say about the provenance, maybe we can go about finding out about the paintings through the back door… find out what happened to them by tracing the estate of the daughter?" I rubbed my chin. "I could swear, though, that Bill told me the daughter"—I reached for my notebook, flipped it open to my notes and found her name—"Rachel Anschler left all of her artwork to the New Orleans Museum of Art."

She was typing on her phone as I spoke. "I should find out

her local connections, right?" she asked as her thumbs flew over the phone screen. "Don't you know someone who works at NOMA? Didn't Rory take you to some parties there?"

As a Delesdernier, Rory knew practically everyone in the greater New Orleans metropolitan area. His parents had been major area philanthropists ever since his father retired from politics when Rory was just a child. As a result, Rory got invited to practically every party imaginable in the city. "I think the connection at NOMA wasn't Rory but his mother." I thought about it for a moment. Rosalie Delesdernier and I had always gotten along. I never got the sense that Rosalie was uncomfortable around me or had a problem with Rory's being gay. It was his father I was unsure about. Charley Delesdernier had spent most of his adult life in politics in one way or another. He was used to glad-handing people and being phony. There was always a sense of false *bonhomie* and I was never really sure where I stood with him. I had always been invited to all family holiday events, but didn't feel comfortable enough to go.

I'd always felt like a part of Paul's family, which was another indication Rory and I had been doomed to failure.

"I'll call Rosalie, see if she knows anything," I said. My back was starting to twinge again. I suppressed a moan.

"Are you all right? You look kind of green."

I winced as I stood up. "My back—I need to go lie down, I think."

She got up and headed for the door. "I'll see what I can find out about the local Anschler connection and let you know, okay?"

I nodded, biting my lip. I closed the door behind her and turned the dead bolt.

I groped my way down the hallway to the bedroom and collapsed into bed.

CHAPTER SEVEN

Coquette was on the uptown/riverside corner of Washington and Magazine.

It was dark when I turned off Prytania toward the river on Washington, which is considered a main street because it has stoplights at the intersections where it crosses major streets. But unlike Louisiana and Jackson, Washington is an incredibly narrow two-lane street with potholes and low branches from massive live oaks. Parking is permitted on both sides of the street, so sometimes it's impossible for two cars to drive past each other, especially when you're trying to avoid a pothole so enormous it could break your front axle.

I grinned as I passed one of the city's finest restaurants, Commander's Palace—because on the other side of the street from it sits Lafayette Cemetery Number One. I've always found it amusing that one of the city's most renowned and famous restaurants has a lovely view of a graveyard.

The food *is* pretty spectacular there, though.

I grabbed a parking space on Washington in front of a Greek revival mansion sitting behind an enormous black wrought iron fence. My back was under control—back to the usual dull throb, but I gasped as I got out of the car as the wind blasted me and almost took my Saints cap off my head. It was very dark out; there was no moon in the sky, so it was velvety purple with pinpoints of sparkling lights strewn across it. The huge live oaks blocked what little light was coming from the street lamps. The flickering gas lights on the porches of the mansions cast weird shadows across the tilted sidewalk as the wind rustled the leaves and branches overhead. Some windows still had their twinkling Christmas lights taped to their frames while others were dark and shuttered. It was easy to see why people thought New Orleans was a haunted city and why so many authors wrote books about witches and vampires and werewolves and demons that were set here. I shoved my hands deep into the pockets of my long black trench coat, aware that anyone glancing out an upper window in one of the houses and seeing me would think I looked like some kind of supernatural creature. The thought made me smile even though the wind was chapping my lips and turning my cheeks to ice as I walked the half block or so to Magazine Street.

I could see the building that houses Coquette. It used to be an auto parts store or a hardware store in its past, I couldn't really remember anything other than there used to be a big orange sign over the doorway. I avoid Magazine Street as much as possible—it's a two-lane business street that runs from Canal Street to Riverbend. The traffic is always horrendous, as I'd learned when I first moved to New Orleans. Back then, there were stretches of the street that were abandoned with tumbledown buildings. Other blocks had been filled with junk shops masquerading as "antique" stores. But Magazine, like so many other parts of the city, had changed over the years. Now it was a major shopping district with amazing restaurants and coffee shops interspersed between higher-end boutiques and shops. Back when I first moved to New Orleans, a restaurant like Coquette on that corner wouldn't have lasted a year. I'd only eaten there once, with Rory, his sister Rachel, and her husband Quentin. I'd been surprised by how good the food had been—but then a bad restaurant in New Orleans wouldn't last a week.

After Abby had left, I'd taken a Vicodin and lain down for a while until the pain had subsided. I'd spent the rest of the day going back and forth from my desk and my bed, carrying the damned heating pad back and forth with me. The Vicodin made it a lot harder to do the research I needed to do on my computer, as my mind kept wandering and I found myself following links that had nothing to do with what I was trying to find out, as anyone browsing the Internet is wont to do. Rosalie Delesdernier had been more than happy to give me the number of her friend at NOMA, a woman named Harley Walters who worked as the museum's development director. It had been hard to get off the phone. Rosalie was feeling particularly talkative, more so than usual. When I finally made my excuses so I could hang up, she said, "Be *sure* you use my name with Harley." She sighed. "It's been lovely chatting with you, Chanse. I really have missed you. I was really hoping… oh, never mind, it's none of my business, is it? But don't be a stranger, Chanse. Maybe we could have lunch or coffee sometime? Just because things didn't work out with you and Rory doesn't mean we can't still be friends."

"Thank you, yes, I'd like that," I said before disconnecting the call. My mind started wandering down the Rory path—*Why haven't I heard from him since I canceled out on him? Maybe I should call him*—and was even in the process of calling before I caught myself.

You know it's never going to work. You both know it. That's why you broke up.

I sighed and called Harley Walters's number at the museum instead. After three rings it went to voicemail. I left her a brief message, mentioning that I'd gotten her number from Rosalie and that I was calling about the Rachel Anschler endowment. She hadn't called back by the time I left the house to go meet Tom. I'd also put in a call to Serena Castlemaine's number, on the card Todd had given me, but it had gone straight to voicemail as well. She was not only a cousin of my primary source of revenue, Barbara Castlemaine, but she'd also become friends with my best friend, Paige. I'd mentioned all three names in my message, but she hadn't called me back either. One of the great drawbacks of being a private eye is people don't want to call you back. I find it much more effective to just show up at their offices or homes, taking the chance they'd be there and available to talk.

Clearly, that was what I was going to have to do with both women.

I finally allowed myself to send Rory a text, apologizing again for having to break our date, but he couldn't be bothered to respond, either.

He was undoubtedly pissed, and it was probably for the best anyway. Neither one of us was going to move on if we kept seeing each other and sleeping together on occasion.

A clean and total break was best for both of us.

But that was easier said than done.

I crossed Magazine when the light changed, and climbed up the steps to Coquette. I shivered as I stepped into the warm air inside the restaurant. The hostess, a pretty and petite young woman with a smile that appeared genuine, came walking toward me with a menu in her hands just as I noticed Tom. He was sitting at a table back near the door to the staircase leading upstairs to the private party room.

"I'm meeting someone," I said before she could ask me anything, "and I've just spotted him, thank you."

"Go right ahead, sir, and enjoy your meal," she said, slightly bowing her head to me.

I walked past her in the warmth, unbuttoning my coat and removing my hat. Tom saw me coming and stood, a smile lighting up his face. "Hey, so glad you could make it," he said as he stuck out his hand.

I smiled back as I shook his hand. He was wearing a black wool blazer, a pale yellow shirt unbuttoned at the neck, and a pair of matching pleated black slacks. He'd slicked his hair down, but the curls were starting to come back at the ends. His eyes twinkled in the dim restaurant light. His outfit was extremely flattering, tailored to show off his broad shoulders. There were spots of color in his cheek. He held my hand for a second too long, then removed his jacket and draped it over the back of his chair.

"I took the liberty of ordering a bottle of wine," he said, sitting back down, and scooted his chair back under the table. "I hope you don't mind red?"

All I know about wine is there are two different colors, and that white goes with fish and chicken. I folded my trench coat and draped it over one of the extra chairs at our table. "No, that's fine." I returned his smile as I sat down in my chair. My feet brushed against his legs as I pulled my chair into the table, and I apologized, shifting a bit in my chair.

"No problem," he said as he filled my glass for me. "I hope you like it."

I raised the glass to my lips and took a sip. It was tart and full-bodied, with just a hint of a wood flavor to it. "It's excellent." I set it back down on the table and took a sip of water. I'd taken another Vicodin before leaving the house to help me get me through dinner, and downing a lot of liquor on top of it was probably not the best idea.

Especially since I was driving.

Maybe I should have taken a cab, I thought, taking another sip of the wine. It *was* a good red, whatever it was. I picked up the menu and started looking through the entrees.

"Thank you again for joining me," Tom said, looking up from his menu with his ever-present smile on his thick lips. "Some friends recommended this place to me, and I've been wanting to try it for a while, but I really don't like eating alone." He shook his head, the light brown curls bouncing a bit on the sides of his face. "People always look at you when you're alone, like they feel sorry for you. I hate that."

I shrugged. "I've never really thought about it that much."

"You don't care what people think, do you?" He tilted his head to one side as he watched my face. "I kind of sensed that when we met the other day. It's a great quality. I try not to, and I've gotten better about it, but I still find myself worrying about what people think." He rolled his eyes dramatically. "Maybe someday."

"It's incredibly freeing," I replied, deciding to have the red snapper. It's what I'd had the other time I'd eaten there, and I was nothing if not a creature of habit. "So, what brought you into town today?"

"I had some business at the federal courthouse." He made a face and set his menu down. "I had to drop off some paperwork to the judge for a case my firm is working on."

"Is this the case that's put you on the outs with the Redemption Parish Sheriff's Department?"

He nodded. "Yes. It was a very flagrant abuse of our client's civil rights—not to mention police brutality. Nothing makes me angrier than cops who think they're above the law they're sworn to serve." The red color in his cheeks darkened. "Redemption Parish—the situation there is really bad—I don't know if you're aware of what it's like there. It's like the old South. The sheriff runs the entire parish like it's his personal fiefdom, like he's a dictator or something. He controls everything there. No one can get elected without his approval—and he definitely has his price. He has his sticky fingers in everything that goes on in the parish. It's a level of corruption you'd think wouldn't be possible today, but there we are in Redemption Parish with our own petty version of Boss Tweed—although I imagine he sees himself as more of a Leander Perez." Leander Perez had been the longtime boss of Placquemines and St. Bernard Parishes. Tom shook his head. "As if the corruption isn't bad enough, the way he and his men have treated this poor woman is really abominable." He leaned across the table. "The firm thinks this case is the key to bringing him down, like pulling a thread that unravels everything. Bill doesn't seem to get it, or doesn't want to. He thinks I should resign from the firm, find another place to clerk. Maybe he's right. I don't know." He sighed and leaned back in his chair. "Anyway, when Sheriff Parlange and his men basically accused us of faking the robbery, I knew we couldn't back down. If we let him get away with this, there's no telling what he would do next. That's why I wanted to bring you in on the robbery case." He refilled his wineglass. "Bill doesn't really care one way or the other. He's willing to just take the loss." His mouth twisted. "Must be nice to be able to throw away a couple of million, right?"

"So, are you all responsible legally for the paintings, or is Myrna Lovejoy? Doesn't *she* have insurance?"

"She does, but she's been, like we said the other day, oddly uncooperative." He scratched the side of his face. "Maybe Parlange's gotten to her."

"Do you think the sheriff could be behind the robbery?"

"Nothing he could do would surprise me, frankly, Chanse." He made a steeple with his fingers. "He has his fingers in so many things. It's entirely possible he could have pressured the alarm company to give him our pass code." He sipped his wine. "Bill would rather believe I was stupid enough to forget to set the alarm that night. I don't make mistakes like that, Chanse."

"Is he afraid of Sheriff Parlange, do you think?"

Before he could answer, our waitress came by. We both ordered the red snapper. After she walked away, he replied, "I suppose it's possible. I've never known Bill to be afraid of anyone before, though—he actually has always seemed to thrive on this sort of thing, if you know what I mean? He doesn't like to back down. I've never seen him back down. It's part of the reason why he's been so successful. He's smart and he's relentless. So to see him be so lackadaisical, so unconcerned, about this mess and the things Sheriff Parlange has said to us? Usually Bill would have a team of lawyers breathing down his neck and slapped him with a multimillion-dollar slander suit. You cross Bill, he doesn't rest until he's completely destroyed you. He leaves scorched earth behind—that's the way he's always operated. I'm frankly baffled that he's pretty much washed his hands of this whole thing and left it up to me to handle it. He doesn't even like to talk about it."

"Maybe Sheriff Parlange has something on him?" I buttered a piece of bread. "Have you thought of that?"

He stared at me for a moment, blinking, like I was crazy. Then he started laughing. "I'm sorry," he finally said after getting a hold of himself. "I know it's rude, to laugh, and I'm sorry. Please forgive me. But what could the sheriff have on someone like Bill? It's absurd."

I swallowed and picked up another roll. "I don't know, Tom. But I have to consider every possibility. Maybe the robbery and the lawsuit aren't related. Maybe it's just a coincidence that Collier Lovejoy was murdered last night." I tilted my head to one side. "But you know, the common denominator in all three of these things is *you*."

His jaw dropped. He blinked, unable to do anything other than stare at me.

I shrugged. "Anything you want to tell me?"

He spluttered for a moment. "I don't know how you could—I didn't have—how can you tie me to Collier Lovejoy's murder? I barely *knew* the man. And I wasn't in the city last night. I was at Belle Riviere all night."

I took another sip of my wine. I was starting to feel a little buzzed and a little mellow around the edges, which had to be a combination of the wine with the Vicodin. I put the glass down and shook my head to try to clear it a bit. "I wasn't accusing you of killing him, Tom. What I was saying is that *you* are the common thread in all three cases. *You're* the link between them, like it or not. Bill's not involved in the lawsuit, for example, but you are."

"Christ," he breathed.

"That's how the cops are going to look at it, you know. They look for commonalities. Nobody believes in coincidences." I picked up my glass of water and took a drink. "I don't know what motive you might have had for killing Collier, but you're a lawyer. You know they don't have to have a motive to convict. They're going to take a long, hard look at everyone involved with Collier and Myrna. This whole thing with the paintings is going to look pretty fucking weird to the homicide detectives. It looks kind of weird to me, too, if you want me to be completely honest." *Shut up, slow down, shut up, the wine and Vicodin are impairing your judgment, shut the fuck up already.*

"Oh." He gulped down the rest of his glass and refilled it. "I suppose you're right," he said after another moment of awkward silence, just as I was about to say something to fill it.

"I mean, it should have occurred to me already."

"Why? Why would it?" I asked, taking another drink from my water glass. *Damn, the wine is really fucking with me,* I thought, hoping diluting it somehow would help. "It's my experience that most people don't consider themselves to be suspects in crimes, especially when they're innocent." I smiled at him. "Your reaction pretty much clears you, at least in my mind. You didn't know Collier well?"

"I don't—*didn't*—know either of them well." He rested his elbows on the table and leaned forward. "Bill knew them, of course, from New York. That's how I knew them—through Bill. Bill was the one who bought the paintings, made all the arrangements with Myrna."

"And you swear you turned on the alarm that night?"

"I would be willing to swear in court that I did, but I must not have." He sighed. "It's the only explanation."

"How do you think the thieves got inside the gate?"

"I don't know." He scratched his chin. "But they did."

"If they got inside the gate, they had to have had the code, right?" I tilted my head and shrugged. "If they could get the gate code, is it really such a stretch to think they could have gotten their hands on the alarm code as well? How many employees are there at Belle Riviere?"

"The only person who has the code is our housekeeper, LaDonna. You met her yesterday."

"And you trust her?"

"Yes." He laughed. "If LaDonna wasn't honest, she could have robbed us blind by now."

I should have checked her out already. I swore at myself. *The pain pills are messing with my ability to do my job properly. Maybe I should just turn the whole case over to Abby and butt out.* I changed the topic. "How did you and Bill meet?"

"He hired me." He said it without any shame, without

blushing. "I worked as an escort while I was attending the University of Connecticut. He saw my online ad and hired me." A smile played at the corner of his lips. "Does that lower your opinion of me? I'm not ashamed of my past, Chanse."

"No." It would have when I was younger, but I wasn't the same judgmental fool that I used to be. "Is that how you paid for college?"

He bit his lower lip and exhaled. "Yes. I did some modeling work, too. I didn't see anything wrong with it, still don't, actually. I generally don't share the information with people. Not because I'm ashamed, but because people can be so judgmental." He gave me a hint of a smile. "I still care what people think."

"You modeled?" I took another drink of the wine, setting the glass down, remembering as I swallowed that I hadn't intended to drink any more. "Maybe that's why you look familiar to me."

"Are you into wrestling? Because that's the only way you'd know me from that. That was the only kind of modeling I really did."

Wrestling.

A wave of nausea washed over me.

But that could just have been the Vicodin and the wine.

Of course.

I could see him very clearly in my mind, leaning against the black wall in the white square-cuts, his body covered in sweat. I cleared my throat. "Did you know two guys whose stage names were Cody Dallas and Jude Jensen?"

"Yes." His eyes widened in surprise.

"Your stage name was Jamie West, wasn't it?" I closed my eyes. I could feel my heart pounding in my ears.

My ex, Paul, had done wrestling videos under the name Cody Dallas.

It had eventually gotten him killed.

I gripped the arms of my chair and took some deep breaths.

Paul.

"Yes, I was Jamie West," I heard Tom saying. His voice sounded delighted. "So you were a fan?"

My heart was pounding, and I could feel my underarms getting wet with sweat, and beads of water formed on my forehead. I hadn't thought about Paul in years.

Paul was my first boyfriend. My first real boyfriend. I'd never been involved with anyone before seriously. My "friends-with-benefits" arrangement with Blaine was the closest I got to having a relationship with another man. Everything else had just been sex—guys I met in the bath house for clandestine couplings in the shadows, guys I picked up in bars whose names I'd never bothered to learn, whose phone numbers I threw away as soon as my front door closed behind them in the morning. I'd met him one night when he was high on Ecstasy. I'd seen him earlier that day at my gym, working out in pale blue cotton shorts and a matching tank top. His body was amazing. The whole time I worked out I kept finding my glance drifting back to him as he went through an intense workout, as his tank top got progressively more and more wet and clingy. There was no fat on his body anywhere. His entire body was perfectly proportioned, from the broad shoulders narrowing down in a V to the ridiculously small waist, the perfectly shaped butt and strong, thickly muscled legs. That night I'd gone cruising in the Quarter gay bars, only to see him, dancing in a pair of jeans with his shirt off on the stage at Oz around one in the morning. His carved and defined torso was beaded with sweat, as was the waistband of his jeans. I myself had a pretty healthy buzz going from a combination of beer, tequila shots, and marijuana. He'd gone home with me that night. He turned out to be a flight attendant who'd just moved to New Orleans. We started slow, but over the course of a year I fell in love with him. We were in the stage where we had started to talk about moving in together, going to the next level, when I found out about his past as a video wrestler and a nude model through another case I was working.

I hadn't handled it well, to say the least.

"Chanse?"

I took another drink of my wine. My hand was shaking. "Not a fan per se," I said. My voice sounded rough, harsh, distant, like I was talking in a wind tunnel or something. "I have seen some of your work."

"Like I said, I'm not ashamed of how I paid for college."

"I'm not judging you."

"It sounds like it." He broke off and we both smiled at our waitress as she placed our plates in front of us, asked if we needed anything else, and disappeared when we both said no. "I grew up very blue collar. We didn't have a spare cent. I was an athlete in high school, football and wrestling and baseball. I knew the only way I'd get to college was a scholarship, but I wasn't talented enough to get one. And when my dad found out I was gay my senior year, he threw me out." He grimaced. "I stayed with a friend's family until I graduated and got a job as a personal trainer at a gym in the city. But it wasn't something I wanted to do the rest of my life. And when I saw an ad in the gay paper in Boston looking for experienced wrestlers, I answered it. It was good money, and the guys were great. It was like I finally found a family, you know?"

"Do you have a relationship with your family now?"

He shook his head. "My mom died when I was a teenager, and my dad remarried, has a daughter with the new wife. He took early retirement and they live in Florida somewhere now. I talk to my brothers, but not my dad. He can go fuck himself."

His face colored again. "So, that's how I paid for college. Making wrestling videos and escorting. That's how I met Bill. He hired me. I was close to graduating. He hired me a few times, and then he offered me the opportunity to become one of his protégés. I would have been crazy to say no—and I can see by the look on your face you're wondering if we still have a sexual relationship. The answer is no."

"No?" I took a bite of the red snapper. It was fucking incredible and melted in my mouth.

"No," he replied firmly. "Bill is a good guy, Chanse. He's had a long list of protégés, young men he thought had potential. He mentors them, helps with school expenses, and then launches them out into the world." He refilled his glass and topped off mine. "Once I pass the bar exam, I'll have to move out of Belle Riviere and find another place to live. My 'free ride' will be over, and I'm fine with that. Bill and I haven't had a sexual relationship since I agreed to become one of his protégés."

"And Bill has no residual feelings for you?"

"No." He frowned. "Bill is a very special person, but sometimes…sometimes I wonder about him, you know? He doesn't really talk about his past very much, but Bill doesn't want to have a partner, you know what I mean? He prefers to hire someone for his sexual needs, and I guess he gets his emotional needs filled by his protégés." He shrugged his big shoulders. "I've met some of his former protégés. It's a pretty impressive list of men, you know."

"I'm sure." I put the wine glass back down. *Stop drinking, you dumbass*, I reminded myself for the umpteenth time since I'd first sat down. I was feeling it; I was starting to slur my speech, and that wasn't a good sign. I was going to have to take a cab home. Even though it wasn't very far, I didn't trust myself to drive my car.

"Are you all right?"

"Fine. I shouldn't have the wine, it's not mixing well with the medication I'm taking." I heard the words come tumbling out, all slurred and running together as I detailed my car accident and the damage to my back. *Yes, you should definitely tell your client that you're not at a hundred percent.* Of course as soon as I said that I heard myself explaining that I had a partner named Abby who did most of the legwork and so forth, on and on and on. *Shut the fuck up, Chanse!*

"I wanted to make sure you knew there was nothing going on with Bill and me," I heard him saying from what sounded like a thousand miles away. He was smiling at me. "I hope you don't mind my saying you're a very attractive man." He slipped a black American Express card on the bill tray, which our waitress swept away. "And I don't think you're in any condition to drive home."

My tongue felt very thick in my mouth. "I'm going to call a cab."

"Nonsense. I can drive you." He signed the charge slip and pushed his chair back. "Can you walk?"

I pushed my chair back and stood up. I felt a bit wobbly— my head was so wasted I couldn't really focus, but I could stand. I could walk without staggering. I put my coat on and walked out the front door. The cold air was bracing as I stood, waiting for him to lead me along Washington Avenue. He unlocked a Mercedes and helped me into the passenger seat.

I vaguely remember telling him how to get to my house. The blackness was crowding in on the edges of my vision and my brain as I got out of the car and fumbled for my keys.

I remember him helping me inside, and then everything else was lost in a fog.

CHAPTER EIGHT

It was four in the morning when I woke up with my back in agony.

It felt like I had been stabbed in the lower back with a red-hot poker that was now being twisted slowly. I was gasping, barely able to breathe, as I reached out for my nightstand. I kept my prescription bottles there for just such an emergency.

I groped around in the dark, not caring which bottle I grabbed, only caring about making the fucking pain go the fuck away. The pain was so intense I would have done anything in that moment for relief. I was vaguely aware of the red numbers glowing on the digital clock as I finally managed to close my hand on one of the bottles. My hands were shaking so badly I could barely get the goddamned child-proof cap off. I swore under my breath as I fished out a pill with my index finger. I dry-swallowed it, tears running down my face, and took a deep breath. I was now wide-awake, and any chance of going back to sleep was negligible until the pain went away.

As I ground my teeth together, waiting for whatever pill I'd just taken to kick in, I became vaguely aware of someone snoring softly beside me in my bed. *Who the hell is that?* flashed through my mind before the pain crowded it right out again. This attack was one of the worst I'd had so far. In that moment I would have sold my soul to the devil to make my back stop hurting. I clenched my hands into fists so hard I could feel the nails cutting into the skin of my palms. I focused on my breathing—*it's always about the breathing*—making sure to inhale as deeply as possible, holding it for a moment before letting it all out and starting over again.

I was never sure if the breathing worked or was simply a way to distract the mind from the pain. But on the other hand, I'd been panting so rapidly it was also possible I could hyperventilate, and that wouldn't help at all. So I focused on controlling my breathing since I couldn't control the pain.

It felt like hours before the pain began to subside, but a glance at the clock showed it hadn't been more than three minutes.

Funny how pain can affect time, I thought, turning my head to look at the person sharing my bed. I had no idea who it was, but logic—now that my brain was capable of thinking logically again—told me it had to be Tom Ziebell. I racked my brain, trying to remember what happened the night before, with no luck. I couldn't remember anything past dinner, no matter how hard I strained my brain. The Vicodin/red wine combination had apparently erased everything from that point on.

Note to self, abstain completely when on pain meds. This is why the prescriptions come with a warning about drinking. I just hope I didn't make a complete jackass out of myself. But he's still here—so that has to be a good sign, right? At least I know I didn't turn into a drooling idiot.

I could feel the edges of my brain starting to get fuzzy, which meant I'd taken an Oxy. *Just as well*, I thought, *it'll probably put me back to sleep in a moment.*

I rolled over onto my side, carefully so I didn't jar my back, to get a look at him. My eyes had adjusted to the dark somewhat, so I could make out his shoulders and the back of his head. His body was an amorphous outline underneath the blankets.

How fucked up was I? What did we do?

It had been years since I'd woken up in my bed after a blackout with a stranger in my bed. When I'd first moved to New Orleans, it had been an almost nightly event. I'd grown up in a repressive, deeply religious small town in East Texas, firmly believing my attraction to other men was going to send me straight to hell, do not pass go, do not collect two hundred dollars. Getting a football scholarship to LSU got me the hell out of Cottonwood Wells, but I was pretty naïve. Every once in a while I would drive down to the French Quarter and cruise the gay section looking for sex. I didn't drink while I was in college very much—mostly I smoked pot—so when I graduated and got the job with the New Orleans Police Department I discovered the great joy of blunting the edges with alcohol. I got an apartment on Dumaine Street between Chartres and Royal, and I used to lose myself in the gay bars every night I could. Despite being a cop, I wasn't worried about having to pee in a cup—as long as I didn't discharge my gun in the line of duty and stayed within the rules while on the job, no one was going to question me about anything. I took anything and everything I could get my hands on—Ecstasy, Special K, pot, poppers, meth, coke—and washed it down with a steady diet of vodka-cranberries, heavy on the vodka. The parade of strangers who passed through my bed ran the entire gamut of types. I didn't discriminate against twinks or gym queens or circuit boys or leather daddies or bears or whoever caught my fancy at whatever bar I was at that night. Even though Blaine and I had gone through the police academy training program together, I hadn't known he was gay until I ran into him one night on the dance floor at the Parade. I'd started moving away from that kind of life when I moved out of the Quarter. After I started dating Paul we'd go dancing together every once in a while, but he didn't drink anything other than water. When I was with him I didn't get blackout wasted, and we always came home together alone. After he died, and after the flood, there was a couple of lost years when I was crazy—well, *crazier*, at any rate—and I once again lost myself in drugs, alcohol, and an endless parade of nameless, faceless male bodies. Rory had helped me come back into myself, get some sort of control over my life.

And now I was single again, waking up in bed next to someone I barely knew with no idea what had happened or how he got there.

I was just thinking about getting out of bed to set the coffeemaker for later that morning when an alarm started going off from his side of the bed. I recognized it—my phone had the same alarm setting. He moaned and shifted a bit. The sound stopped and he sat up in the bed without saying anything. He moved delicately and carefully, clearly worried about waking me up.

"I'm awake," I said into the darkness, reaching for the pull chain on the nightstand lamp. I tugged on it and the lamp's weak yellow light illuminated the bed and everything lower, casting shadows into the corners. His back was hairless, the skin remarkably smooth, the muscles in his shoulders and upper back rippling as he turned from side to side. There was a small mole on his right shoulder blade.

He turned and smiled at me. His hair was pointing out in every direction from his head; his big round heavy-lidded eyes were half-closed. "Didn't mean to wake you, sorry." He yawned and shivered. "Man, it's cold in here."

"I was already awake," I replied, my tongue starting to

feel a bit thicker. "Had to take a pain pill. There's a robe over there on the chair if you want it. Sorry about the cold, there never seems to be any point in turning the heat on. I can get up and turn the heater on, if you want me to."

He started to laugh but it was cut off by another yawn. "That's okay—you don't need to get up." He got out of bed and walked barefoot over to the chair. He was just wearing a pair of red silk boxers. His skin was very pale, his thickly muscled legs dusted with light brown hair. He slipped my robe on and sat back down on the edge of the bed. "Thanks for letting me stay over," he said, fighting off another yawn. He put one of his big hands on the blankets over my right leg. "I was too tired and buzzed to drive out to Belle Riviere last night." He covered his thick lips as he yawned again. "Sorry."

I sat up, reaching for the sweatpants I always kept on the floor beside the bed. I slid them up my legs. Everything was starting to blur a bit on the edges. I closed my eyes for a moment and took a few breaths. "I'm the one who owes you an apology," I said, pulling my ratty old LSU sweatshirt over my head. "I shouldn't have had that wine after taking a Vicodin. Did you have to carry me out of Coquette?"

He laughed. "No, but you were having some problems for sure. I imagine everyone in the place thought you were drunk out of your mind."

"Great." I slipped my feet into my house shoes and walked over to my closet. I reached up onto the top shelf and got down the pair Rory used to wear when he slept over. "Here, put these on. No sense in freezing your feet. I'll go start some coffee for you and turn the heat on. It doesn't take long for the place to get warmer. You're welcome to shower, if you want." I shrugged. "By the time the coffee's ready and you get out of the shower, it should be bearable."

"You sure?" He yawned again. "I can just shower when I get home, but it would help wake me up." He rubbed his upper arms. "And coffee sounds too good to be true."

"Seriously, I don't mind—it's the least I can do since you got me home safely." I stifled a yawn of my own. My legs were starting to tingle from the Oxy. If I didn't start moving around I was going to fall back asleep—and I had to let him out. *The problem with having a dead bolt that only locks and unlocks with a key*, I thought, standing up a little shakily. "I'd loan you some clothes, too, but I don't think they'd fit you."

He grinned back at me. "I'm good—I'll just stop by the house on my way to the office and change." He yawned and stretched again, the robe falling open to reveal his strong torso. There was a small patch of light brown hair in the center of his chest and a trail of them running from his navel to the waistband of his boxers. "I don't have to be in the office till around seven. I'll even have time for breakfast."

If that was supposed to be a hint, it fell on deaf ears. I didn't owe him that much.

"Let me get in and out of the bathroom first," I said. I switched the thermostat to heat before walking into the bathroom and brushing my teeth. My scalp felt like it was crawling—another effect of the Oxy, and I was vaguely aware I looked a little blurry in the bathroom mirror. I splashed some hot water on my face. I found a spare toothbrush in one of the vanity drawers and handed it to him with a cheery smile. "Here you go."

"Thanks." He brushed his lips against my cheek as he walked past me into the bathroom.

I headed into the kitchen and got the coffeemaker started, then popped an English muffin into the toaster as I heard the shower start. I stood over the vent, letting hot air blow up my legs while I waited for the muffin to pop up and enough coffee to gather in the pot for a cup. I smeared peanut butter on the hot muffin and wolfed it down, washing it down with the coffee. The apartment was starting to warm up, but the floor was still so cold I could feel it through the soles of my house shoes.

I walked back into the bedroom, shaking my head. *How do you ask someone if anything happened last night?* In the old days when this sort of thing happened I just always assumed something had, and I'd never been wrong. I didn't miss those days in the least.

I found my cell phone in my jacket pocket—completely dead, of course. I carried it back into the living room and plugged it in. While it charged up to enough juice to come on, I poured myself another cup of coffee and sat down on the couch. I was still a bit foggy, but the coffee was helping. I wasn't going to be falling back to sleep any time soon, so I might as well get some work done.

When my phone came back up, I moaned. I had about six missed calls from Venus and three from Blaine—and scores of text messages wondering where the hell I was.

"Shit," I said, remembering Venus telling me to meet them last night at the Avenue Pub so we could compare notes about the Lovejoy murder. I'd completely forgotten about it.

They were probably pissed at me, and they had every right to be.

And instead of meeting them, you were having sex with a suspect. Maybe.

I leaned back on the couch with another moan. The stupid painkillers were seriously fucking with my brain. The aftermath of the flood—the combination of PTSD and Xanax—had proved lethal to my once-flawless memory. The years after the flood were sketchy. Those years almost didn't seem real, like they'd happened to someone else. I remembered some of my cases—especially the one where I almost took the law into my own hands and killed someone—through a gauzy shroud, like my brain had smeared Vaseline over my memories and thoughts. I'd had so many panic attacks, taken so many pills, drank too much. It had taken me years to finally realize I was on a dangerous road. The last thing in the world I needed was another fucking addiction.

The cortisone shot was looking better and better.

I heard the shower shut off. "How do you take your coffee?" I called out as I walked back down the hallway, making a mental note to call both Blaine and Venus back. They usually were up by six, which wasn't that far off.

"Black's fine," Tom said, sticking his head back out the door. His hair was wet, the drops of water hanging from the ends of his curls.

He was *really* adorable. And sexy.

I wouldn't mind having sex with him—I would just prefer to have it happen when I'd be able to remember it.

I was relatively certain it would be memorable.

I filled a mug and handed it to him through the doorway. He was blow-drying his hair with the little portable Rory had kept here. I stood there and watched him for a moment as he sipped his coffee and smiled back at me. He seemed like a nice guy, but—

He's a suspect in a murder and a robbery, dumbass. Keep your head on straight.

He was also incredibly attractive. He was smart, was studying for the bar, had an amazing body and a sort of similar background to mine. That smile was irresistible. I tore myself away from staring at him and gathered his clothes from the floor on the other side of the bed, neatly folded them, and carried them back to the bathroom, where I handed them to him as he was running a brush through the unruly curls. After walking back into the kitchen for more coffee, I sat on the couch to wait for him.

I stared up at the enormous black-and-white print mounted on the wall several feet above my television. I'd taken it down after the flood, when I thought I'd come to terms with losing Paul the way I had and stopped blaming myself for it. It was from his days in college when he did some nude modeling. He was sitting on the edge of a chair, with his back to the camera. One hand was running through his dark curly hair, and he was slightly turning toward the camera, so that his upturned face was in profile. Every muscle was tensed and flexed, veins bulging in his arms, a slight shadow falling across the whiteness of his untanned buttocks. Paul had been so beautiful, so perfectly formed, that sometimes looking at him took my breath away. He was black Irish—both of his parents were born in Ireland, both still had heavy brogues I could listen to all day. His hair had been bluish-black and curly, his eyes a startling wintry ice blue. The photograph had hung in his apartment uptown, and after he died his mother had given it to me.

I'd originally hung it in penance, so I would always remember what my selfishness and inflexibility, my horrible temper, had cost me. Every time I looked at it, it reminded me to try to be a better person, to not be the insanely jealous possessive prick who'd lost Paul.

When I finally realized, in the weeks after the flood, that I wasn't to blame, that it wasn't my fault, that I wasn't the center of the universe and everything bad happened as punishment for my sins, I'd taken it down and put it in the closet.

It was a gorgeous print—Rory was the one who convinced me to rehang it. "For one thing, it's a beautiful piece of art by a top photographer," he'd pointed out, "and it's of someone you loved, who was really important to you. Why would you want to forget him? And now you're at the point where you can remember him and smile, right? You don't still blame yourself, do you?"

He'd been right, even if I hadn't been willing to listen to him or believe him when he said it. It took another couple of weeks before I could steel myself to seeing the image every time I walked into my living room—but he'd been right about that, the way he'd been right about so many other things. He'd been good for me on so many levels…it was a shame it hadn't worked out the way either of us had hoped. I hadn't thought I'd be able to get close to someone again after Paul's death. Even after accepting I wasn't to blame, I still didn't believe I deserved to be happy. Rory had helped me realize that I did deserve some happiness.

For a while, we had made each other happy.

And the picture was beautiful.

Frowning, I picked up my phone again and scrolled through the list of recent calls. I was a little surprised to see there was nothing from Rory—no texts, no calls, nothing.

Did you really expect he'd call to check on you? You need to call him and apologize for bailing on him the other night. It was last minute—even if it couldn't be helped—and you owe him that much at least. He deserves better than that. Isn't that what finally drove the final wedge between us? Because you refused to let yourself be happy?

I sighed. Apologies had never been easy for me, so I tended to avoid them. But I was getting too old for that kind of behavior. I needed to be an adult for once. Rory deserved better than that from me.

I got up and turned the heater down. The floor was still ice cold but the apartment was getting that hot, dry stuffy feel that I hated. I sat back down on the couch and started checking my emails on my phone. I still hadn't read Abby's report on

Bill Marren—but that needed to wait until Tom was gone. A few moments later, Tom came walking into the living room. His jacket was over his arm, his tie draped around his neck. He sat down in the easy chair and set his coffee cup down on the table. He smiled at me. "Thanks for letting me shower and stay the night."

"It's the least I could do."

"Seriously, though. I was pretty tired myself." He yawned. "I might not have made it home last night. I appreciate it."

"Well, I probably owe you an apology as well as thanks," I said hesitantly, taking another sip of my own coffee. "I shouldn't have had wine on top of the pain meds. I'm sorry you had to deal with that, and thank you for making sure I got home safely."

His smile grew wider. "It was my pleasure, Chanse. I'm only sorry you were so messed up that we couldn't"—he gestured with his head back in the direction of the bedroom—"have some fun, you know? I hope we can get together again sometime."

"That would be nice." *Even though you're a suspect. What the fuck am I saying here?* I was attracted to him, that was true.

"I hope you really mean that." Tom crossed his legs. "I really like you. I want to get to know you better." He hesitated for just a moment. "I'm just going to put my cards out on the table, Chanse. I really think you're attractive, and you seem to have a great personality. You're maybe a bit guarded…I want to get to know you better because I want to get to know the person behind that shield you have up." He looked up at the photo of Paul. "I didn't know Paul well, but he was a great guy. If you two were involved, that means you had to be a great guy, too, because I don't believe Paul would have been involved with an asshole. So I hope you'll agree to have dinner with me again." He pulled out his phone and fiddled with it a bit. "I think I'm going to have to be in town again in a couple of days. Would you be up for having dinner again?"

"Sure." *Why not? What could it hurt?*

He's a suspect, dumbass, that's what it could hurt. No matter how fucking hot you think he is.

"Great. I'll pick you up this time, make it a proper date." He frowned. "Do you need me to take you back to your car?"

"I took another pill before you woke up. That's why I was awake, the pain woke me up." I shook my head. "I can have Abby swing by and take me to the car later this morning."

"If you're sure—then I'll be on my way." He stood up, and we walked over to the door. I slipped the dead bolt key in and turned it. He paused for just a moment, then went up on his toes and brushed his lips against my cheek. I resisted the urge to take him in my arms and really kiss him good-bye.

He smiled at me. "Thanks again. And the next time I sleep over, we're not just going to sleep." He winked, went down the steps and out the gate.

I waited until he drove off before shutting the door and locking it.

I got another cup of coffee and sat down at my computer. I checked my emails, but there was nothing that couldn't wait for a few days. I started to open Abby's report but felt my edges starting to spin out of focus again. *No, probably best to read that when I'm not drugged.*

Instead, I pulled up a search engine, typed "Top Rope Productions" into it, and the first link that came up was the website I remembered looking up after Paul had confessed his past to me all those years ago. I clicked on the link and the website came up. I clicked the box stating I was twenty-one and hit enter. The page loaded, and there was a hot young muscleboy smiling at me, with thumbnail shots of six additional ones to the side. *Max Coleman gets taught a lesson in Belly Busters 14!* the headline screamed at me. There was a search engine in the upper right hand corner, and my fingers trembled as I typed the name I never thought I'd look for again: CODY DALLAS.

I hit return and a list of DVDs came up. And sure enough, there was the one I'd seen, *Mat Studs 8*. I clicked on it and the first of five matches on the DVD came up.

And there he was, Tom Ziebell, in a skimpy pair of tight white bikini-style trunks, smiling at the camera.

The caption under his name read Jamie West.

I sat down hard in my chair and took another drink of coffee.

What a fucking bizarre coincidence.

Cody Dallas, of course, was my former boyfriend, Paul Maxwell.

I could feel my heart racing in my chest.

I looked back up at the picture over the mantel.

There had been a time when I didn't think I'd be able to not think about him, not remember that horrible fight we'd had the last time we'd seen each other or the way he looked when the police and I had found him in that psycho's house, battered and dying and unconscious, in Bay St. Louis, or the horrible days that followed, as machines kept him alive in the ICU at Touro Infirmary.

Or the really terrible day when his parents finally decided to turn the machines off and allow his organs to be harvested. I'd sleepwalked through my life the next year, getting involved with one of Paul's other wrestling buddies, Jude from Dallas, and that was where I'd evacuated when it had become apparent that Katrina was coming to New Orleans. When I'd come back to New Orleans, when I began coping with everything with medication and therapy, I'd slowly started to get over what

I now referred to obliquely as the Time of Troubles. I'd met Rory when I was back on my feet again, starting to live and ready to get on with my life.

But that didn't work out so well, did it? You fucked that up with your inability to commit, to admit that you wanted to spend the rest of your life with him.

Maybe—maybe I wasn't as over the whole Paul situation as I had thought?

But Tom made me feel the way I used to feel with Paul—the way I hadn't felt with Rory. Rory and I had been able to go slow because even though he was cute and had a nice enough body, the attraction wasn't there the way it had been with Paul.

The way it now was with Tom, whether I wanted to admit it or not.

I got some more coffee and did a search on the Top Rope site for Jamie West. He'd done quite a few matches for them. *Mat Studs, Belly Busters, Ring Battles, Demolition*—he'd appeared in almost every series they had. There even was a *Starring* tape, in which he appeared in every match. I clicked through the photo galleries. He always wore the same white square-cut trunks and wrestled barefoot, even in his ring matches. Jude had explained some of the terminology to me—it looked like Tom/Jamie had been what they called a "heel," a wrestler who always won his matches and sometimes cheated in order to win. I could hear Jude's voice in my head, explaining, "Some guys just look like villains, you know, and others look like good guys. Paul was a good guy, what they call a *face*, who's good-looking and a good wrestler and always fights fair. He'll lose sometimes to someone who cheats, but if he does they have to give him a rematch so good can triumph over evil."

Jude. I closed my eyes and remembered Jude. I hadn't

thought about him in years. He'd been so good to me after Paul died, after the flood…and I had treated him pretty badly.

Rory's not the only person you owe an apology to, I thought.

Calling to apologize would also give me a chance to ask him what he knew about Tom.

It wouldn't hurt to do some checking on him, would it?

I got up and walked over to the hallway closet, sliding the doors open and reaching up onto the shelf. I pulled down the small box where I kept my mementoes of Paul, opened the lid, and pulled out the DVD case.

Mat Studs 8.

It wouldn't hurt to have a look at Tom in action, would it? And he never had to know I'd watched it, did he?

I walked back into the living room and loaded the disc into my DVD player.

I sat back down on the coach, turned the television on, and clicked play on the DVD remote.

CHAPTER NINE

The dulcet tones of Lady Gaga and Beyoncé singing "Telephone" dragged me out of a deep, drugged sleep.

I opened my eyes and reached for my phone. It was daylight, and I was sprawled out on the couch. My throat and eyes were dry. The apartment was hot, stuffy, and dry from the heater running. It was still going as I wiped at my eyes with my free hand. The caller ID said Blaine Tujague, and his smiling face stared at me from the phone's screen. I yawned and slid my finger across the screen to accept the call, but it was too late—it had already gone to voicemail. It was also after eight in the morning. I sat up, yawning. The TV screen had gone back to blue with the brand logo of the DVD player floating around lazily from corner to corner. I was still feeling groggy, my mind fuzzy as I stood up. I walked into the bathroom and brushed the new gunk off my teeth, splashed some hot water into my face, and called Blaine back as I put a cup of the lukewarm leftover coffee from earlier into the microwave.

"Did I wake you?" was how Blaine answered his phone. "Sleeping beauty?" His voice was teasing, the way it always was. Part of his charm was his happy-go-lucky nature. Blaine was only somber when he absolutely had to be.

Most of the time it was adorable. When I'd just woken up and was still sleepy, not so much.

"What's up?" I managed to slur out as the microwave dinged.

"Wanted to make sure you were alive, for one thing." He went on cheerfully. "Since you never showed last night and you never answered our texts or returned our calls. You do, however, sound like shit this morning."

I took a big swallow of the coffee. Reheated always tasted odd, but it would have to do for now. "Yeah, sorry about that, I got kind of sidetracked," I said, dumped the filter and refilling it with coffee grounds. I poured out the dregs of the old pot and filled it with water. "And then I took a Vicodin and drank wine on top of it." I stifled another yawn as I dumped the pot full of water into the reservoir, replaced the pot on the burner, and hit the brew button. "I was pretty wasted—I had to be helped home." And then I remembered my car was still parked on Washington Avenue, and swore under my breath. Hopefully Abby would be able to take me down to pick it up.

Or you could walk, it wouldn't kill you to get some exercise even if it is cold outside.

"Dude, mixing painkillers and liquor is a really bad idea," Blaine said quietly.

"I know, I wasn't thinking." I shook my head, taking another drink from the reheated coffee and grimacing. It was undrinkable, so I poured it out. "I was having dinner with a client—"

He started laughing. "Chance, I don't want to tell you how to run your business, but it's not a good idea to get so wasted in front of a client that he has to help you home."

"Fuck you, Blaine," I replied companionably. There was enough coffee brewed for a cup. I filled my cup with relief and walked back into the living room. "Any news on the Collier Lovejoy murder? Or do you just want to compare notes?"

"Are you too sleepy to walk across the park?" Blaine teased. "Seriously, put some clothes on and come over. Venus went out and got some muffins and donuts. We can have a nice healthy breakfast and some coffee while we talk."

"Sounds good," I replied. "Be there shortly." I hung up the phone and scrolled through the list of recents. There was nothing from Rory—neither call nor text. *Quit putting it off and call him—you owe him a real-time apology.*

I sighed and walked back down the hallway to the bedroom to get dressed.

Twenty minutes later, I walked across Coliseum Square to Blaine and Todd's place. Venus must have been watching for me from one of the front windows because she came out as I crossed the street to meet me at the gate, which she unlocked and opened. "What the fuck, man?" she asked with a stern shake of her head. "You don't respond to texts messages, you don't return calls, you don't show up—just not cool, man, making us worry like that. Your meds again?"

"Yeah." I stepped inside and she swung the gate closed behind me. I followed her up the front steps and inside the front door. The house was overheated, and I shook my leather jacket off. "Didn't Blaine tell you? One of my clients called and invited me to dinner and I completely spaced about meeting you guys. My bad, and then I drank wine on top of taking a Vicodin and it really fucked me up. My client had to help me home." I shook my head and gave her a crooked smile. "Besides, the murder investigation is *your* headache, not mine."

"Yes, well, your case is mixed up with ours, whether you like it or not." Blaine appeared in the doorway to the front sitting room. "And Myrna Lovejoy still hasn't turned up. And that has us both a little concerned."

"She hasn't?" I whistled as I sat down on the couch. There was a tray with a coffee service set out on the coffee table, along with several plates of muffins and donuts. I helped myself to coffee and a blueberry muffin with sugar crystals glittering on it. I looked back and forth from Blaine to Venus. "That's odd. And suspicious. You think she might have plugged her husband and run? What about the kid? What's his name? Cooper?"

"Well, we're not sure what it means. No sign of her at her house, she's not answering her cell phone, and we've got an APB out on her car." Blaine poured himself a cup and leaned back in his chair, crossing his legs. "Cooper is staying with friends in the meantime."

"Poor kid—he must be freaking out." I finished the muffin and reached for another one. My lower back throbbed dully as I leaned forward, not bad enough to warrant a pill. It was a nice little reminder to be careful with how I moved, though.

I noticed Venus's eyes narrow as she watched me. "If something hasn't happened to her, then she's the worst mother in the world." Venus pursed her lips as she watched me. "Cooper is pretty freaked out, as you can imagine." She shook her head. "Seems like a good kid, too. I hate this kind of shit."

"When did he last hear from her?" I asked, narrowing my eyes back at her.

"The last time he saw his parents was two mornings ago before he left for school. They all had breakfast together—he said they always had breakfast and dinner together. When he came home after school there wasn't anyone there, so he packed his bag and went to his friend's house, where he was staying. The plans had been made for a while—they were working on term papers due yesterday." Blaine shrugged his shoulders. "It was convenient for the killer that Cooper wasn't home to miss them that night."

"So you think it was premeditated?" I looked from him to Venus and back again. I refilled my coffee cup. It was going to have to be the last one—I was starting to feel a bit over-caffeinated. But at least the cobwebs in my brain had been swept away.

They exchanged a look. "Well, nothing we can prove yet, but it had to be premeditated," Venus said after a brief pause. "Why else would Collier be there after hours? Meredith Cole said she was the last to leave, when she closed up no one was there. And it was unusual for either one of the Lovejoys to be there late, anyway. She said if they were there when the gallery wasn't open, it was usually *early* rather than late."

"But they had been there late before," I observed, "and if they were ever there after closing time, if she'd already left she can't say they didn't come by later, can she?"

"True," Blaine said. "And the safe hadn't been opened—it doesn't look like there was a burglary, so we can rule that out. But the most telling thing is that Meredith had to turn the alarm system off when she arrived yesterday morning. Whoever killed Collier knew how to turn the system on."

"Why would Myrna do that, though?" I replied. "It doesn't make any sense. If Myrna killed him, why would she turn the alarm system on if she was going to run?"

"That's why I believe something's happened to her." Venus sat down and picked up her coffee cup. "Like you said, it doesn't make any sense unless someone *forced* her to turn the system on when they left. Or she killed her husband and she's the most awful mother since Medea. The kid is really torn up."

"Well, from everything I've heard, she's a pretty awful

person in general," I said, trying to wrap my mind around it all. "So you *don't* think she killed her husband?"

"Well, it's still too early to rule anything out," Blaine replied. "And considering that the security camera recordings are missing for that night—"

"Say what?" I looked back and forth between their faces. "The recordings are gone, too?" So, Myrna most likely *had* to have been there…unless Meredith was involved somehow.

No. I dismissed that. There was no way she was a good enough actress to fake her shock and horror at finding Collier's body.

"The gallery had a top-of-the-line security system," Venus took over the story from Blaine. "Several cameras, positioned so there were no blind spots, including one mounted on the corner of the building and trained on the front door. The DVR machine recording the broadcasts was actually located not in Myrna's office, but in another office—the one where she kept the safe—which, by the way, we still haven't been able to get into. Meredith didn't have the combination. The discs covering the period from nine p.m. the night of the murder to the following morning are missing." She shook her head. "Whoever took the discs knew what they were doing—knew which discs to take. So, we have no idea of who was there that night, or when they showed up, or how long they were there. Meredith Cole claims Myrna had left for the evening just before her, around seven. As we know, Cooper was spending the night at a friend's—and fortunately, his friend's family don't have a problem with him staying longer while we try to locate Collier's sister. Apparently she's the only living relative the kid has, besides his parents."

"So whoever killed Collier knew which discs to take, knew the son wouldn't be home so neither Collier nor Myrna would be missed until either Collier's body was found or until Cooper got home from school the following day and no one was there." I stroked my chin. "And you say Meredith doesn't have the safe combination?"

"No." Blaine refilled his cup. "The safe has a secure drop for envelopes. They don't do much cash business—no one carries that much cash around—so it's usually just checks or credit card slips. Meredith would run the sale, put the signed slips into an envelope, which she would then date and drop into the safe. Myrna took the deposits to the bank in the morning and handled all the banking. If she was on vacation, Meredith would close out the sales and drop the envelopes…and they'd stay in the safe until Myrna came in to the gallery again." He gave me a look. "Of course, it's also possible that someone else knew the alarm code and was familiar enough with the system to take the DVR recordings." He raised his eyebrows. "Another bizarre crime where the alarm was bypassed—sound familiar?"

I nodded. "So we have a robbery at Belle Riviere where the alarm was apparently never turned on, and a murder in New Orleans where the alarm was apparently set, turned off and then back on after the crime was committed, and the security camera footage has disappeared." I exhaled. "The assumption with the robbery at Belle Riviere was that Tom forgot to turn the alarm on, but given this—it's possible that the alarm there was turned off, isn't it? Meredith is certain she armed the system when she left that night?"

Venus nodded. "Meredith swears that she turned the system on—and we're waiting for the records from the security company that installed the system. The records will show when it was disarmed and re-armed that night." She smiled at me, her eyes half-closed.

"Of course." I shook my head, angry at myself for not

thinking about checking with the Belle Riviere security company. I took out my phone and made a quick note, just in case the Vicodin was going to mess with my memory again. "What company installed the gallery's security?"

"Vigilant Eye." Blaine leaned back in his chair and folded his arms.

"That's who installed the system at Belle Riviere." It couldn't be a coincidence. "Where are they based? Here in New Orleans?"

Security was part of the services my business offered, but I didn't have a lot of clients because I had one major client, Crown Oil. Crown Oil was probably about seventy-five to eighty percent of the annual income accrued by MacLeod & Grosjean, LLC. It wasn't a terribly difficult job—the fact my landlady and friend Barbara Castlemaine was majority stockholder and chairman of the board of directors had a lot to do with that—but it was incredibly time consuming. I was in charge of every aspect of their corporate security, from their Internet communications to the security of their domestic oil fields, pipelines, and refineries, as well as general security at their corporate buildings in Dallas and Tulsa. I subcontracted out a lot of the work because it was beyond what I personally could do, but I stayed on top of it. Four times a year I toured their office buildings and all of their properties, testing and upgrading the systems I'd designed for them.

Generally I would only take on local security jobs as a favor to someone, or if I was bored, but as a general rule I referred prospective security clients out to other local businesses I knew and trusted to do good work. Part of being a security consultant was staying current on recent developments in security equipment, and occasionally I went to seminars or sales clinics for companies developing new equipment or improvements on the equipment they already sold. There weren't a lot of us in southeastern Louisiana, and over the years I'd gotten familiar with the competition, particularly in New Orleans.

But I'd never heard of Vigilant Eye, and that was odd. It was very odd, in fact, and I typed a note into my phone to look into them, see whatever I could find out about them.

Well, I'd probably put Jephtha on it, but it was something that needed to be done.

Maybe it was just a coincidence—there weren't many security firms in the area, as I said—but it seemed a bit curious that Vigilant Eye, a business I'd never heard of, had installed the systems at both places involved in this case. It was yet another connection between the burglary at Belle Riviere and Collier's murder, and one that couldn't be overlooked.

"Too many coincidences," Blaine said, and Venus nodded in agreement. They both rose. "Well, buddy, we've got to get moving," Blaine said. "Is there anything you want to share with us?"

I thought for a moment as I stood up and pulled my jacket back on. "No, nothing that has anything to do with the murder. But thanks for the food, coffee, and information." I nodded at them both. "I'll keep you posted if I find out anything." I didn't expect them to reciprocate—they'd already shared more with me about an investigation in progress than they should have. But they knew they could trust me—I wasn't going to jeopardize anything they were doing. And we'd cooperated so many times now it would have seemed weird if they didn't help me out some on this one. I didn't think they'd shared everything they had turned up with me—I was neither stupid nor naïve enough to believe that—but they'd shared what they could.

And they'd given me a really good place to start.

Vigilant Eye.

I went out the front door and waited for Blaine to buzz the gate open from inside. Once it buzzed, I went out and crossed over to the park. I pulled my phone out and send a quick text to Abby: *What are you up to today? Want to meet for lunch, compare notes?* I slipped it back into my pocket and started across the park. It vibrated in my pocket once I reached Camp Street. There was a bunch of traffic, so I pulled it back out again and checked the message while I waited for an opening to cross the street.

But the text wasn't from Abby. It was from Tom.

Thanks again for letting me stay over. I really want to have a real date next time, okay?

Sure, I painstakingly typed out with a shivering finger and hit send. The street was clear, so I went ahead and crossed.

The problem with being a private eye is you tend to become more suspicious of your fellow man and his motivations. It was entirely possible Tom was attracted to me—I was still, despite the accident and lack of quality gym time, in fairly decent shape. My track record with relationships notwithstanding, I liked to think I was a pretty nice guy. I had a good sense of humor and I could make conversation. I wasn't stupid. But this timing seemed suspicious to me. Tom was younger than me by about ten years or so—*so is Rory, remember him?*—but he could also be into older guys, or just didn't pay any attention to age differences.

But the real question was, I realized as I climbed my front steps, *what does he have to gain from flirting with me?*

Distraction? I unlocked my front door. *If he was the one who stole the paintings and killed Collier...*

I locked the front door behind me. I'd forgotten to turn off the heat before I left, so I did so now and plopped down on the sofa. The TV was still on, with the blue screen.

Is it so out of the question? He knew Collier, he was the

one who didn't turn the alarm on the night of the robbery... maybe he wasn't the one who actually did either, but he could be involved...the paintings were worth several million dollars. It wouldn't be the first time someone turned on their mentor— and for several million dollars? Whoever stole the paintings also had to know the passcode to get onto the property, otherwise how did they get in the front gate?

I sat down at my computer and touched the space bar to bring it back to life. The Top Rope website was still up in my browser, open to the search I'd done on the site for Tom aka Jamie West. There he was, smiling at the camera, his strong jaw and curly hair, the muscles clearly defined, the square-cut white trunks I'd remembered. He'd worked as an escort and as a model during the missing years, he'd said, before enrolling in college. He continued doing the same work while in college. I looked at the name in red letters across the page: JAMIE WEST. I opened another tab in my browser and pulled up a search engine, typing the name in and entering it.

Almost immediately a long list of links appeared on the screen in front of me. Some of them were obviously not Tom—but there were a few that I assumed *were* him: Muscleboys4hire.com, Rentboys.net, and one that was just his name. I clicked through them all, one by one. Yes, those were definitely Tom's listings on the hustler-for-hire sites— and they'd never been taken down.

Is he still for hire?

I clicked on his website. The front page had an age restriction; I clicked the box to state I was over twenty-one and entered the site. Once inside, the home page had a huge full-color image of him wearing nothing more than a wet jock strap. There was a page for "live cam"—I clicked on it but the page didn't work—another page for rates, another page for videos, which had a link to the Top Rope site—and cruised around through the galleries for a few moments.

Maybe he just never got around to taking the site or the listings down, I thought, clicking over to check my emails. Nothing new.

I changed into my sweats and went through my yoga workout. By the time I finished and hopped into the shower it was almost ten. I got dressed and checked my phone. I'd missed a call from Abby. I called her back, but it went straight to voicemail. Odd. I went back to my computer and there was no email from her. That was even odder. I was expecting her report from her trip out to Avignon.

That wasn't like her.

I called her cell number again, and when it again clicked over to voicemail, I called Jephtha. His also went to voicemail. I sent her a text asking her to call me again and sat down at the computer again.

I did a search for Benjamin Anschler. There were a lot of links, and a lot of information. I took a deep breath and dove in, following links and reading. Some of the information I already knew—the things that Bill had told me about his life and career. He had married a Jewish girl from New Orleans, Rebecca Goldberg. The Goldbergs had been a pretty prominent family in the Jewish community of New Orleans at one time. Rebecca had died before the war, before the Germans invaded and began exterminating the Jews of the Netherlands. Bill hadn't exaggerated Benjamin's importance as a painter, either. Several universities offered courses on his work; and his paintings, valuable while he was alive, had gone up exponentially in value after his death in the Nazi death camps. Then I saw a link with the headline *Missing Anschler Paintings Nazi Loot?*

I clicked on it and started to read. It was the English translation of an article from a French art magazine:

Benjamin Anschler was one of the most important painters in the Impressionist school before World War II. He was originally from Rotterdam and studied art in Paris at the Sorbonne. He established a strong reputation while studying, and once he began showing his work his importance continued to grow throughout his career. Most of Anschler's art is accounted for in private collections and museums throughout the world. Yet there are three paintings that are missing, and have been missing since the outbreak of war in September 1939. Visitors to Anschler's large home in Amsterdam all can attest to the presence of the paintings in the home; Anschler's arthritis had caused him to cease painting during the late 1920s. These three paintings, which Anschler refused to part with, were considered by witnesses to be his best work, painted through the crippling pain of the arthritis that eventually ended his career.

The paintings were titled "Midnight on the North Sea," a beautiful seascape depicting the full moon in a cloudy purple sky over the rough sea; "Spring Tulips," depicting the massive tulip fields outside the city as they began to bloom in a riot of color under a bright sun; and "Skaters on the Canal," a winterscape of one of the city's many canals, frozen in the dead of winter with skaters going about their business on the ice.

After the German conquest of the Netherlands in 1940, Anschler and his family were placed under house arrest under the anti-Jew laws of the Nazis.

His youngest daughter, Rachel, had left for England shortly before the Germans invaded; the story was she had gone to England to try to secure money for her family to escape before the Nazis came. Anschler and his entire family not only did not escape from the oncoming terror but were victims of it; Rachel Anschler, in her late twenties, was the only Anschler to survive the war. In 1948, unable to remain in Europe with its incredibly painful memories, Rachel immigrated to America, where her mother's family, the Goldbergs, still lived in New Orleans. Rachel Anschler survived everyone in her mother's family as well, as one by one her American relatives died off until she was the sole survivor of both branches of her family. Rachel died of cancer in 1968. She left her entire estate to the New Orleans Museum of Art, creating an endowment to assist young Jewish artists and leaving her extensive art collection to the museum.

However, once her collection was catalogued by the museum, conspicuous by their absence were her father's three paintings from the Amsterdam home.

Stories have circulated that Rachel had gone to England to sell the paintings to raise the money to get her family out of Amsterdam and over to the United States—the sale of the paintings would have raised enough money for them to live on comfortably. Rachel herself never spoke of the paintings, and no one has seen them since an American journalist mentioned them in an article he wrote about Anschler; he viewed the paintings on visiting the Anschler townhouse in the summer of 1939 as the clouds of war began to gather on the horizon in Eastern Europe.

There are also stories that the paintings were looted and removed to Germany, part of an enormous trove of treasure the Nazis "liberated" from the countries they invaded and conquered. While some of this art was recovered after the Nazi surrender, some remains missing to this day. Were the last paintings of Benjamin Anschler a part of the Nazi loot, or did they come to America with his daughter in 1948? No one in New Orleans has seen the paintings, nor were there ever any reports of the paintings being seen in the apartment in London Rachel Anschler lived in during the war.

The mystery of the Anschler paintings remains unsolved to this day. Did Rachel sell them in England to a private collector who has kept the paintings hidden away from the public ever since? Did she bring them with her to America and sell them once she arrived? Rachel refused to be interviewed after the war. She was a recluse, rarely leaving the Goldberg home in the Uptown district of New Orleans. She would speak to no journalists, no biographers, no war or art historians. There's a story that she also destroyed all of her papers, including diaries, journals, and personal correspondence of her father's, in the weeks after her cancer diagnosis; a longtime servant said as much after Ms. Anschler's funeral. Why would she destroy her father's papers? What happened to his final three paintings, which would be worth a minimum of $750,000 apiece in today's market? Why did she refuse to be interviewed about her father, about her family and her childhood?

Perhaps the memories of everything she lost

were too painful for her to relive. We can only guess
to her motives. But whatever her secrets were, she
took them with her to the grave.

I bookmarked the page and stood up.

But rather than answering any questions, the article had done nothing more than add to the mystery.

I could certainly see why Bill wanted the paintings—their value alone, not to mention the provenance would prove, once and for all, what had happened to the paintings and where they had been for almost seventy years, ending a great mystery of the art world.

That is, if Myrna had been able to produce said provenance, and it was valid.

I felt in my coat pocket for the card Todd had given me the previous morning. *Serena Castlemaine*, my landlady's cousin-in-law who had recently moved to New Orleans.

Maybe Serena could provide some answers.

I was just about to dial her number when the phone started ringing, and the damned Beyoncé/Lady Gaga song started up again. Rory had downloaded and set up ringtones for my phone—"Telephone" was the default for most people calling. He'd thought it was funny to set up "Bad Romance" as the ringtone when he called, and whenever my best friend Paige called, the ringtone was "Hips Don't Lie" by Shakira.

Paige found it much less amusing than Rory had thought she would.

But Abby's face was smiling at me from the screen, so I slid my finger across her face and said, "There you are. What's going on?"

"I'm out in Redemption Parish, in Avignon. Barney Fife gave me a call first thing this morning, and I booked out here."

She added, a bit defensively, "I was going to get you my report this morning but then this happened. I did try to call you a little while ago."

"What are you doing out there? What was so important that you went back out?"

"You're going to be hearing from the sheriff's department soon enough." She exhaled. "Chanse, someone murdered Bill Marren last night. Shot him through the heart."

I closed my eyes. "And I'll be hearing from them because?"

"Apparently, you're Tom Ziebell's alibi." She sounded exasperated. "He spent the night with you?"

CHAPTER TEN

Just after crossing the street at the corner of Jackson and Magazine, I started regretting my decision to walk to where I'd left my car.

It wasn't as cold as it had been earlier. It's not unusual during a New Orleans winter for there to be as much as a thirty-degree temperature swing, which can be an enormous pain in the ass. I'd walked outside originally wearing my trench coat, my wool Saints cap, gloves, and a muffler. As soon as I reached the bottom of my front stairs, I'd turned around, gone back inside, and ditched everything but the cap. I even traded in my trench coat for my black leather jacket. The result of this unexpected rise in temperature, combined with the moisture in the air, was a fine mist. It looked like an enormous white cloud had sunk down from the sky, making it almost impossible to see more than five feet in either direction around me. The tops of buildings and trees were invisible, lost in the fog, a downy white that made everything above my head look like it had been wrapped in cotton. The only thing missing was the sound of foghorns moaning on the river less than a mile away. The cars driving past me on Magazine Street had to use their headlights, cautiously crawling along at about fifteen miles per hour. The stoplights were wreathed in the mist, glowing with their shifting colors. Despite the slight chill in the air, the exertion of walking resulted in a cold sweat on the back of my neck and under my jacket. I could feel drops of sweat on the back of my neck, beads forming on my shorn scalp beneath the Saints cap of gold wool pulled down low on my forehead. My underarms and feet were damp and uncomfortable. I was also at the point of no return. That intersection was the midway point of the walk. There wasn't enough of the distance left to make it worth flagging a cab, and it was the same distance to the car as it was to walk back home.

It was times like this when I regretted quitting smoking cigarettes. I usually didn't miss it. Quitting had been a long, on-again off-again process lasting several years. As bothersome as I now found other people's secondhand smoke, I also was well aware that all it would take was one puff and that monkey would be climbing right back on me. I resisted the urge to stop into the deli just past the flag store at the corner.

The walk was helping clear out the remaining cobwebs in my mind. I could tell the Oxycontin I'd taken at four in the morning was beginning to wear off. The smoothed-down edges in my mind were getting sharper again. Unfortunately the dull ache in my lower back was starting to make itself felt again. Every time I put a foot down on the sidewalk, pain arrowed out in every direction from the epicenter. My sinuses were also starting to kick in because of the heavy, moisture-saturated air.

I wiped at my nose and kept walking. I promised myself a cup of coffee at the Starbucks on the corner at Washington and Magazine as a treat.

The carrot always works better than the stick with me.

The clearance of the cobwebs had allowed common sense to creep back in. My initial gut reaction to Bill Marren's murder had been that I needed to get the car and head out to Redemption Parish. Since Sheriff Parlange clearly already had it in for Tom, hanging a murder on him would be the perfect cherry on top of the sundae for the homophobic bastard.

But Abby had talked me out of it.

"There's no sense in you charging out here." In my head, I could see her rolling her expressive eyes as she said it. "Tom doesn't need you to get on your white horse and ride to the rescue, you know. He's a lawyer *and* he works for a law firm—a law firm committed to bringing down Sheriff Parlange, remember? So you're not going to accomplish anything, right? It's not like he's going to have trouble getting a lawyer. If you come rushing out here to give him an alibi, it's going to look funny, you know what I mean? And if Parlange and his office are as homophobic as Tom says they are, it's not like they're going to *believe* you. And you might just make things worse. It's going to be bad enough for these homophobes that his alibi is spending the night with another guy. This guy is the law around here, and there's no one outside of Tom's firm to challenge him. He could arrest you for perjury, Chanse, or anything he wants to, throw your ass in the parish jail, and then what are you going to do? Seriously. The best thing for you to do is wait—let *them* come to *you* to confirm Tom's alibi. If they don't bother to check it out, then we also have a better idea of what we're dealing with out there and can maybe get the state or the feds involved on civil rights violations." She sighed and continued, "So you just stay put and let me find out what I can—I can always do some flirting with Barney Fife again, repulsive as he is."

"You're right," I'd had to admit. I always forget she studied law.

"And besides, the drive might be bad for your back.

Remember the last time you drove out there? And if you have to take one of your pills to deal with it—well, do you want to deal with a corrupt sheriff's office when you're drugged out of your mind, Chanse?"

I really hated it when she was right, which she almost always was. She wasn't above pointing out how often she was right whenever we disagreed on something.

There's nothing more frustrating to me than sitting around and waiting for news. It's not something I'd ever been good at without a distraction of some sort. Working out at the gym used to be my favorite way to take my mind off waiting. Thanks to the fucking car accident, that was no longer an option. So that was why I decided to walk to where I'd left the car last night. I certainly could use the exercise, for one thing, and for another the walk would clear my head.

And maybe letting my mind wander while I walked would help me get some insight on the case.

Damn, I missed going to the gym.

And much as I hate coincidences, I couldn't rule out the possibility that the murders were not connected to the robbery—or even to each other, for that matter. Granted, it wasn't very likely. What were the odds?

Bill Marren had been a very wealthy man, and had been mostly a self-made man. He'd inherited some money from his father, according to the dossier Abby had prepared for me, but nothing close to what his current net worth had been. She hadn't been thorough—I had only asked for an overview of his background to get a sense of who I was dealing with. But without going into every investment or into great detail on some of the ones she did list, it was highly unlikely he could have amassed such a fortune without making enemies. There had to be corners he'd cut, backs he'd stabbed, people he'd climbed over in the pursuit of accumulating so much wealth. And even if he hadn't, even if he'd been completely ethical and fair in his dealings, there were bound to be people who *believed* he'd treated them unfairly.

It was entirely possible that the theft of the paintings and his murder were part of some master revenge plot by some unknown enemy. I stopped at the corner at Second Street, pulled out my phone, and sent Jephtha an email, asking him to put together a thorough report on Bill's business dealings. I dropped the phone back into my pocket and pulled off my cap, wiping my forehead with it. Only a few more blocks to walk, and my head was getting too hot. I put it in same pocket with my phone and started walking again.

Taking Collier Lovejoy's murder out of the picture did help. The only link I could think of between the two murders was Myrna. But even assuming Myrna killed her husband, why would she kill Bill Marren? Who had a reason to kill *both* men? Collier was only peripherally linked to the robbery, through his missing wife. Unless…

Unless Collier Lovejoy wasn't the killer's target.

Maybe the killer had gone to the gallery intending to kill Myrna, and finding Collier there…

The paintings—the robbery had to have something to do with it. It was the only thing that made sense.

So, who *owned* the paintings to begin with? Who'd been trying to sell them? How had Myrna come into possession of them?

I also couldn't just dismiss that the gallery and Belle Riviere had used the same security service—one I'd never heard of, just to make matters even more interesting. I'd texted Jephtha as I walked out my front door to get that ball rolling and he'd responded with an *aye aye sir* text almost immediately. I pulled my phone out of my jacket pocket and typed a note to myself to ask Tom how Bill had come to choose Vigilant Eye.

And where *was* Myrna? I typed in another note to call Meredith Cole again, see if she knew who Myrna's closest friends were.

My phone began braying Lady Gaga and Beyoncé again as I crossed First Street. I didn't recognize the number. "MacLeod," I said as I crossed Third Street.

"Chanse MacLeod? This is Serena Castlemaine, returning your call." The Texas accent was broad and thick, so much so it almost seemed like it had to be put on for effect. "How nice to hear from you! I've heard so much about you." She laughed, a loud raucous sound that almost hurt my ears. "Don't worry, all of it was good. To what do I owe the long-overdue pleasure of hearing from you?"

In spite of myself, I smiled.

I'd never met Serena Castlemaine in person, but New Orleans being what it was, I did know quite a bit about her.

I'd been invited to a party in her honor when she'd first moved to New Orleans about two years ago. My primary client, Crown Oil, was owned almost wholly by the Castlemaine family, and the majority shareholder was my friend Barbara Castlemaine. Barbara had married Serena's cousin, who'd died in a plane crash and left his entire estate to her. Barbara was also my landlady, and one of my first clients. She'd hired me to handle a blackmail problem shortly after I moved into the house on Camp Street. She'd been so pleased with my success that she reduced my rent to practically nothing and hired me as Crown Oil's security consultant. The arrangement had proven very lucrative to me. Barbara was hosting the party at the Palmer House, her enormous historic landmark home in the Garden District, and the object of the party was to introduce Serena to everyone in the city who mattered to Barbara.

Unfortunately, I'd been in Dallas on Crown Oil business and so had missed the party. My best friend Paige had gone, and they'd become friends. Paige actually liked her quite a bit. Serena had originally bought a condo on one of the upper floors of 1 River Place, the expensive and tony high-rise on the riverfront near the convention center and the casino. But she'd since sold that place and bought a place in the Garden District only a couple of blocks from the Palmer House. The house she'd bought also had a bit of unpleasant history—a notorious and unsolved child murder some twenty or thirty years earlier. Paige told me that Serena loved the place and actually relished its notoriety. Paige had gone to Serena's housewarming, and said, "You'd never guess one of New Orleans' most notorious crimes had occurred on the grounds."

"That's good to know," I replied now, trying to match her lively tone. "Listen, ma'am—"

"Call me Serena," she interrupted me. "You're a friend of Paige's and you work for the goddamned family business, so you're practically family already. I can't believe we've not met yet. We have to rectify that! Maybe lunch or drinks or something? Dinner?"

She was like a whirlwind. "That would be nice," I said, keeping my voice measured. "But I'm afraid this is a business call, Serena."

Her tone changed immediately. "What can I do you for, Chanse?"

"I was hoping you might have some free time this morning, or maybe early this afternoon?" Might as well take advantage of her being eager to meet me, I figured. "I'm working on a case—"

"Is it the Collier Lovejoy murder? Please tell me it's the

Collier Lovejoy murder." She blared out that raucous laugh again. "I had drinks with Paige and her fiancé last night, so I know all about it." She lowered her voice to a conspiratorial tone. "Anything I can do to help, you just let me know."

"Really?"

"Crime *fascinates* me," she said, keeping her voice low, like she didn't want to be overheard. "I love reading crime novels, you know. If I hadn't been born with a silver spoon shoved down my throat I probably would have been a cop or a private eye. I hope you don't mind Paige telling me about your case?"

I tried not to smile. "No, of course not, I was just a little surprised, is all." I shouldn't have been surprised Paige knew without me telling her anything about it, of course. New Orleans was a much smaller town than people thought, and gossip was the fuel that drove conversations at every social gathering. And not only was Paige engaged to Blaine's brother, she and Venus were also pretty close friends, going back to Paige's days as the crime reporter for the *Times-Picayune*.

New Orleans was a *very* small town.

"I understand you knew Myrna and Collier?" I went on. "Did you know them before they moved here?"

"Oh, yes, I'm afraid I've bought a lot of art from Myrna over the years. I've known the two of them since—was I a virgin back then?" She laughed again. "No, I met them between my first and second marriages, or was it between the second and third? If it was between the first and second, I was practically a virgin." She laughed again. "I met them in New York…I was a regular customer of the Lovejoy Gallery in Chelsea." She took a deep breath. "You could even say it's *my* fault they moved to New Orleans in the first place. After I moved here from Dallas, I of course told them how marvelous the city is…When were you thinking of coming by?"

"What's convenient for you? I can be there any time."

"Any time?" Again with the loud laugh. "Darling, don't you know a man should *never* put himself at the mercy of a woman?"

I bit back a laugh of my own. "You're doing me the favor."

"That's true, I am, aren't I? Let me check my schedule." She hummed for a moment, and then added, "Well, my massage therapist is coming by at four, and I have dinner plans later, of course. I am not ashamed to admit that I practically am free all day. I'd thought about doing some shopping—I'm not even remotely close to finishing decorating this place, you know, and I need to get a dress for a party I'm going to this weekend, but I can do that any time, really. Do you know where my house is?" She lowered her voice again. "I've managed to buy the old Metoyer place, where the baby beauty queen was murdered twenty or so years ago. You don't need to worry, there aren't any ghosts here! At least none that I've seen, at any rate. Then again, the ghosts are probably terrified of me. What's convenient for you?"

"I can probably be there in about half an hour, give or take, or would that be too soon?" I glanced at my watch. I was only a block from Washington, and the Metoyer house was on Coliseum between Third and Fourth Streets. At most, I was only a couple of blocks from her place. "Does that work for you? I just happen to be in the neighborhood."

"Well, isn't that convenient! Sure, that'll give me time to slap on some war paint, so I won't scare you to death. See you then." She disconnected the call.

I put my phone away with some degree of satisfaction. Paige had told me more than once that Serena loved nothing more than a good gossip session, and apparently she was right.

The light at Washington turned green, so I crossed to the other corner. I could see my car parked up the block with the ubiquitous orange parking ticket under the driver's side wiper blade. The only city employees who did their jobs with any degree of efficiency were the meter maids. I'd paid my weight in gold in parking tickets since moving to New Orleans. I shook my head and went into the Starbucks there on the corner.

It was crowded, which was no surprise. New Orleans had a very strong coffee culture long before the rest of the country caught up—probably because it had been the primary port of entry for the coffee beans from South America for decades. There had been the usual doom-and-gloom stories when Starbucks first came to New Orleans—it would signal the end of an era, the local chains and mom-and-pop coffee shops would close, letting the coffee chain into Orleans Parish would be the beginning of the end of the city's charm and culture, ad nauseam, ad infinitum. (Rather similar to the protests about the opening of the Tchoupitoulas Walmart, and of course none of the dire warnings and predictions had come true.) To be honest, I wasn't even sure where the Starbucks in the city were. I knew there was this one here at the corner of Magazine and Washington, one in Canal Place, and another one on Canal Street near the corner at St. Charles. I wasn't a big fan of coffee shops in the first place. I can make pretty damned good coffee myself at home, and paying about a third of the cost of a big coffee can for just one cup seemed ludicrous to me. And since the Kaldi's on Decatur Street had closed, I rarely visited coffee shops. Much as I hated to admit it, on the few occasions I'd gone into a Starbucks, I'd found myself liking the coffee. Their dark roasts always tasted like the beans had been burned—I'd heard others complain about that, but I rather liked it every once in a while. And I also liked that the condiment table had vanilla powder so I didn't have to pay extra for a shot of vanilla syrup.

There was a short line of the usual Garden District types at the counter. Fit housewives wearing tennis skirts despite the cold. Hipsters in skinny jeans with tattoos on their necks and enormous holes in their ears stretched open by enormous earrings and smelling like they hadn't bathed since Labor Day. A few college students with heavy backpacks hanging from one shoulder were staring at their cellphone screens like they were hypnotized. While I waited my turn I glanced around the large interior. It was the usual, stereotypical crowd of more hipsters, other college students pounding away at the keyboards of their laptops with ear buds firmly in place, and nannies with the children of the wealthy, bored housewives in strollers while they gossiped over lattes.

If not for hints here and there of a corporate presence in coffee mugs and other merchandise, it could be any New Orleans coffee shop.

I thought I saw a familiar head in the back, but before I could make sure it was who I thought it was, it was my turn to order. I ordered a large dark roast with room for cream, which got me an oddly relieved look from the young woman behind the register. She smiled at me gratefully, spun around and filled an enormous cup for me. I gave her cash and added another dollar to the tip caddy beside her register and headed over to the condiment table. I smiled to myself as I added half-and-half and sweetener to the hot dark coffee.

It *was* Paige, sitting by herself and scowling at her laptop.

She didn't notice me. I liberally sprinkled vanilla powder into my drink, stirred it vigorously, and replaced the lid. I walked over to the table where she was sitting, still scowling at her computer screen. "What are you doing here?" I asked, sliding into the chair on the opposite side from her. "What a pleasant surprise." I winced as a dull throb of pain shot up my spine and hoped she didn't notice. I didn't need another lecture about the cortisone shot.

She looked up from her computer screen with a deep sigh. "I have to write this feature story and I just can't wrap my mind around it."

"Really? What's it about?" It wasn't like Paige to have trouble writing anything. She'd once told me that she thought writer's block really was *writer's lazy*.

She rolled her big eyes dramatically. She was wearing colored contact lenses that turned her eyes a deep, rich blue. I hated when she did that. To me, one of her most arresting features was her mismatched eyes—one was green, the other blue. She ran a hand through her curly, blond-streaked red hair and let out a moan. "Trust me, you don't want to know. The real problem is I can't think of any way to make this fucking story interesting in the least." She picked up her coffee cup, took a sip, and made a face as she spat it back into the cup. "And I've let my coffee get cold."

"I'll get you another one," I replied, standing up and taking her cup.

"Thank you." She glared at her laptop as I walked away. She moaned in relief when I returned and placed her fresh cup on the table. "Thanks." She glowered at her computer screen before shutting the laptop. "I don't know why I'm having so much trouble writing this. I can usually do this in my sleep. I can make anything interesting, but I…" She sipped at the steaming-hot coffee. "I couldn't focus in the office, so I decided to try to work at home. When that didn't work, I came here." She rolled her eyes. "Not that this is working any better. What are you doing here? You hate coffee shops."

"I left my car on Washington last night. I had dinner with a client at Coquette last night, and drank wine on top of a Vicodin."

"Not smart." She shook her head and ran a hand through her hair again. The enormous diamond on her ring finger caught the overhead light and flashed fire.

"That engagement ring skirts the very fine line between tasteful and vulgar, you know," I said with a crooked smile.

She raised an eyebrow and held the hand up so the big stone caught the light again. Her fingernails were bitten down—something she only did when she was stressed out. *Definitely* not a good sign. "I'll have you know this was Ryan's grandmother's ring—his grandfather had the diamond specially cut, you know." She examined it again for a moment. "I never thought I'd like a diamond ring, but I have to admit I love this one, old-fashioned as it is. Does that mean I've sold my soul?" She peered at me across the table. "It weighs a fucking ton."

"An heirloom? Why didn't the first wife have it?" For the life of me, I couldn't remember the name of Ryan's first wife. She and Paige got along quite famously.

"She has a name, you know." Paige gave me a sardonic look, pointedly not saying the name so I would have to remember it. "And she did have it. The eldest son gives it to his fiancée." She rolled her eyes. "Family traditions. Lord, what am I getting myself into? Anyway, she gave it back to him so he could give it to me." She blew on it and rubbed it on her purple LSU sweatshirt. "You need to watch the liquor with the painkillers, Judy Garland. That's a surefire way to the emergency room, if you're lucky. If you're not lucky—" She narrowed her eyes and drew an index finger across her throat. "No more, Chanse. You really need to have the cortisone shot." As I started to splutter, she held up a hand to shut me up. "I get it, I do. But everything is a risk, Chanse, and it's certainly no more risky than mixing painkillers with liquor, is it? I don't understand this need you have to suffer when you don't have to. You need to get down from the cross, we need the wood."

"I'm not being a martyr," I replied, feeling my cheeks flush. I knew she was right, but that didn't make it any less annoying.

"Was the client you were having dinner with Bill Marren?" Paige blew on her coffee before taking another drink. "We missed you the other night at dinner. Rory was really disappointed you canceled." Her tone was disapproving. Unspoken were the words *if you'd just have the damned cortisone shot, you wouldn't have these problems.*

"Yeah, well, Rory and I aren't together anymore anyway," I muttered. Paige had not been happy when Rory and I ended our relationship. I'd gotten a lengthy lecture from her about how I was throwing away happiness with both hands, and I needed to get over myself and recognize that I had just as much right to be happy as anyone else. It was a can of worms I didn't want reopened, so I quickly added, "No, I was having dinner with his partner, Tom Ziebell. You interviewed them, didn't you? For the piece on Belle Riviere?"

"Tom Ziebell?" She nodded, pursing her lips. "Yes. The place is gorgeous, of course."

"What did you think of them?"

"Bill Marren was—how should I say it?" She mused, staring off into space for a moment. "He was very public face with me." She smiled. *Public face* was her term for people who act differently in front of the press rather than being themselves. When Paige interviewed people, she liked to, as she put it, "get behind the public face down to the private rage." Her ability to do that was one of the reasons she was so good at her job, and very rarely did her interview subjects hold a grudge against her. She had a likability factor, an ability to put people at their ease that other journalists would kill to have. It was a skill that came to her naturally, and it was, she often said, something that couldn't be taught. You either had it or you didn't. "Very smooth. It wasn't his first time with a reporter, I could tell. And nothing I did or said cracked that veneer one bit. Smooth operator." She made a bit of a face. "And you know I don't trust smooth operators."

"Interesting. What did you think of Tom?"

"Tom? Very good-looking. Almost too good-looking for his own good. I mean, it was pretty obvious he's used to getting by on his looks." She sucked on her lower lip. "Not that there's anything wrong with that, of course, more power to him, but you know that shit doesn't work on me." She grinned at me. "I even told him, 'The twinkling eyes bit won't work on me, pretty boy.' Give him props, though—he had the decency to be self-aware enough to laugh." She sighed. "Another one who is too smooth for his own good." She shrugged. "Granted, I didn't try too hard to crack their façades. It was just a puff piece about the renovation, after all." She raised an eyebrow. "Why all the interest in Tom Ziebell?" A corner of her mouth twitched. "Thinking about crossing the personal/professional line?"

I ignored that. "What do you know about the sheriff in Redemption Parish?"

"Brad Parlange?" She snorted. "A blowhard. He has some pull in Redemption Parish, sure, but he's a nobody outside the parish line. He likes to think he's a player, but he's not. I had thought about doing a story on the beating thing—have you seen the pictures of that poor woman? But Rachel nixed it." Rachel was the publisher of *Crescent City* magazine, she was also Rory's older sister. "Much as I hate to admit it, it's not in our scope. We cover New Orleans, and I can push that to the metro area, but Redemption Parish? None of our readers gives two shits about what goes on there."

I glanced at my watch. "Well, pleasant as this is, I have to run. I'm going to talk to your buddy Serena. Thanks, by the way, for mentioning my case to her the other night."

"You're welcome," Paige replied, blowing me a kiss as she reopened her laptop. "Don't be a stranger, Chanse. And get the goddamned cortisone shot? For all of our sakes? And can we have dinner sometime soon? Rory's not the only one who misses you."

Chapter Eleven

Serena Castlemaine's house was a beautiful old Victorian on Coliseum Street between Second and Third Streets.

It would always be known in New Orleans as the Metoyer house, no matter how long Serena lived there. The Metoyer family had built the place originally, and then of course there was the murder twenty years or so ago in the carriage house on the property. The house wasn't traditional, if the Garden District could be said to have a traditional style. It was three stories high, but the third story was gabled. Three gables faced Chestnut Street, each one set back a little farther than the one to its immediate right. A gallery with a three-foot-high railing ran around the entire second floor. The first gable also had a balcony tucked underneath its roof, with slender French doors leading out to it. The rooms beneath that first gable jutted out of the line of the house, three sided, like an alcove or breakfast nook. The front porch ended at the sides of the front of the house, but side porches were visible on both sides. All the black shutters were open, in stark contrast to the gray painted walls of the house. A five-foot-high black wrought iron fence ran across the front of the lot, so that people walking past on the Chestnut Street sidewalk could get a lovely view of the front of the house and the enormous yard. Several magnificent live oaks were scattered about on the property, but the one closest to the house was clearly dead, its bare branches and gray trunk looming like a tragic ghost alongside the house. The rest of the property line was delineated by a seven-foot brick fence that tilted dangerously here and there.

Paige was right. Just looking at the beautiful old house, you'd never guess one of New Orleans's most notorious crimes had occurred on the grounds. I vaguely remembered the case—most Americans in their late twenties or older couldn't help having some knowledge of it. The story had been all over the news and the tabloids for at least a year. Every so often it would bubble back up, whenever someone involved would die or get married or wind up in the news again for whatever reason. Sometimes it was just the anniversary. One of the major cable news networks had done an exhaustive documentary on the case on the twentieth anniversary a few years ago that had splashed the story back into the public consciousness again.

It was impossible not to feel sorry for the members of the immediate family. All of them had been suspects, with legal "experts" theorizing how each one of them might have done it. I'd always felt sorry for the son—he was eight or nine years older than his sister, and it had to suck to be a teenager suspected of murdering your younger sister.

Part of the reason the story had gained such notoriety was because the mother was a former Miss Louisiana, basically some nobody from one of the more rural parishes who'd then managed to marry into New Orleans high society. If she'd left well enough alone, she might have been accepted, grudgingly, into the city's upper crust. But having a daughter put stars back in Mrs. Metoyer's eyes, and she became a stage mother. Young Delilah Metoyer was put through dance lessons, acting lessons, singing lessons, and the kiddie beauty pageant circuit. She was murdered just before Christmas when she was eight years old.

The murder was still unsolved, and the Metoyer family had shattered under the pressure of all the public scrutiny. The parents eventually divorced, the father had fled New Orleans with his son in tow, and the former pageant queen had finally given up on trying to live down the scandal and have a life in New Orleans. She put the house on the market and left town. The house had stayed unsold for years before Serena fell in love with it and bought it, determined to make it her own.

I parked in front of the house and got out of the car. The mist was clearing and the temperature was dropping, which meant it was going to start raining soon. The gate was open, so I walked through and up the short walk to the porch. Up close, the house was much more enormous than it looked from the street. I rang the bell and stepped back to wait, resisting the urge to look through the window next to the door.

It was very odd that we'd never met in person, despite being one degree of separation from Serena through almost everyone I knew. Of course, I'd heard enough "Serena stories" to write her bio. There was no middle ground with Serena Castlemaine. People either loved her or they hated her. She'd come to town looking to make a splash—and she'd definitely done that. She'd joined the Krewe of Muses, the bawdy and fun ladies' Mardi Gras parade krewe that was all about the shoes and featured walking groups like the Camel-toe High-steppers. She'd given an enormous amount of money to the Audubon Zoo, the Aquarium of the Americas, and the New Orleans Museum of Art—but then had appeared on a local franchise of an enormously successful but trashy reality show that wound up not airing after several members of the cast had been murdered.

Old-line New Orleans society, which all too frequently these days has the position but not the cash, kept Serena at arm's length, despite her almost overly generous philanthropy.

Serena didn't give a shit what people thought of her—which is easy to do when you're sitting on top of an oil fortune. I'd heard a story that a doyenne of one of the city's oldest families had been rude to her at a party and Serena had laughed in her face. Paige quoted her as saying, "I blew any chance at being accepted into high society three divorces ago, and what's more, I don't really have any great desire to put a stick up my ass." As a result, while she'd been invited to join Muses, she hadn't been asked to join the older, more aristocratic ladies' krewe of Iris. She hadn't been rewarded with a regular table at Antoine's or Galatoire's, or been invited to attend the Rex or Comus balls. Blaine's aristocratic mother, Athalie Tujague, liked her, but believed she was still a little "too Texan" for New Orleans society's delicate sensibilities.

What I knew about her I found fascinating. There were the numerous ex-husbands—four in total, everything from another oil heir to a rodeo star to a Saudi prince to a television actor—and numerous affairs, most rumored, some confirmed. There was a story that she'd left Texas because of an affair with a high-powered politician in the state. Depending who you heard the story from and how they felt about Serena, it was anything from "she was run out of the state in disgrace" to "she left Texas so he and his wife could patch up their marriage and save his career."

I didn't know if any of it was true, but I wanted it to be.

A thickset older black woman in a black uniform with a white apron opened the front door. Her face wasn't lined, but there was gray in the hair she'd pulled back into a tight bun at the nape of her neck. "Mr. MacLeod?" she asked in a low, husky, lightly accented voice. When I nodded, she bowed her head slightly and said, "Ms. Serena is expecting you. Please come in." Once I was inside the door, she closed it and said, "May I take your jacket?"

I took my phone out of the pocket, took it off, and handed it to her. "Thank you." It was very warm inside the house, and I felt my sinuses reacting to the hot, dry air.

She draped my jacket over her left arm. "If you'll follow me?" Without waiting for an answer, she turned and started to walk down the hallway.

I followed her, taking it all in. The hallway ran the length of the house. A long red, gold, and black Oriental-style runner went from the front door to the back door. There was a hanging staircase near the back door. To my right, closed pocket doors shut off the rest of the house from this front part. Her housekeeper silently indicated, with an inclination of her head, that I was to go into a lovely sitting room all done in modern style; everything was black metal and glass and gold chrome. The room was painted a dark, vibrant green with gold fleur-de-lis stenciled in patterns on them. The furniture looked jarringly incongruous at first, given the hardwood floors and old-style chandelier and paint. I sat down on the uncomfortable-looking couch, which faced the front windows. The green and gold brocade curtains were closed over them. The couch was much more comfortable than it looked. On the glass and chrome coffee table magazines were fanned out across the center: *Vogue, Vanity Fair, Rolling Stone, Street Talk, Crescent City.* There was a crystal candy dish filled with hard-looking pastel mints to the left of the fanned magazines. To the right was a matching crystal ashtray. The room was overly warm. The ceiling fan wasn't turning, but there was a fire going in the fireplace. Serena clearly didn't like to be cold.

The longer I sat there, the more I began to appreciate the design aesthetic; the contrast of modern simplicity versus the old-fashioned ornateness of the room itself. It was a refreshing change from the wingback chairs and the Audubon prints and the antiques most New Orleans homes were infested with.

The housekeeper entered the room and gave me another slight bow. "Miss Serena said she would be with you shortly. May I offer you some coffee or something to drink? Perhaps some cookies, or would you prefer a piece of cake? It would be no trouble, sir."

"I'm good for now, thank you." I smiled at her. To be honest, servants always make me uncomfortable. I'm not around them very often, but the deference always bothers me.

You can take the man out of the trailer park, apparently, but you can't take the trailer park out of the man.

"Chanse darling!" Serena swept into the room with her face wreathed in smiles. She was much taller than I expected, close to six feet tall in her perfectly white, new-looking Nike training shoes. Her thick blond hair hung in loose, almost studied disarray around her heart-shaped face. She was tanned—a real, golden-brown tan from the sun, not one of those awful brownish-orange tans that came from a bottle or a spray machine and that stained furniture. Her almond-shaped brown eyes had flecks of gold in them and tilted upward at the outside corners. There were hints of dimples in her cheeks, and her chin appeared to be sharp enough to cut glass. Her lips were maybe just a touch too thick for her face, which made me suspect there was some collagen injections involved. Her forehead was also suspiciously smooth and immobile.

She was casually dressed, but further inspection showed the "casual" look was carefully constructed. Her dove-gray sweater was cashmere. A double rope of perfectly matched pearls rested on the impressive shelf formed by her large, full breasts, and the skinny jeans were an expensive style of an expensive brand. Pearl teardrop earrings sparkled at her ears. Her makeup-free look was also not quite as makeup-free as it looked at first glance; there wasn't much of it, but what little there was had been so artfully applied that it did its job perfectly without being noticeable. Her waist was almost ridiculously narrow, but her hips had a lush curve to them that straight men would find irresistible. Her legs were long and shaped well beneath the compressing cotton/Lycra blend of the skinny jeans. A bracelet of thick gold links adorned her right wrist, and an expensive watch encrusted with tiny diamonds sparkled at the other one. Her hands were in perfect proportion to her arms, with long, aristocratic fingers ending in French manicured nails trimmed to just the right length to flatter her hands.

"So lovely to meet you at last! I've heard such lovely things about you from Paige and Barbara and, well, all of the mobs of friends we have in common." She gave me a dazzling smile, exposing pearl-white teeth that were so perfect they couldn't be natural. She threw her head back and barked out her raucous laugh. She laughed with her entire body, holding out her hand to be shaken when she was finished.

I had stood up when she entered the room, and shook her cool, dry hand. Despite her height, her hand disappeared inside mine. "I've heard wonderful things about you, too," I replied, sitting back down on the sofa.

"Have you really?" She gave me a shrewd look before giving me a sly smile. "I'm sure you've heard some horrible things about me as well." She shrugged. "And it's probably all true." She barked out that laugh again. It was infectious, and I couldn't help grinning back at her. She sat down in a chair that looked like black metal and some cushions had been put together before being blown up with dynamite to reshape it. She gracefully moved her right ankle over the left, revealing a gold charm anklet dangling there over the white tennis sock. She peered at me. "My, everyone told me you were good-looking, but I had no idea just how good-looking you are."

I could feel color coming to my face. "Thanks, I think."

"Oh, don't be modest. Modesty is overrated." She leaned back in the chair. "Did Therese offer you anything?"

"I'm good."

"Well, I'd like some coffee." She picked up a cell phone and quickly typed on its screen, her perfectly manicured fingernails clicking on the surface. When she was finished she tossed it onto the coffee table with a clatter. "So you're here to ask me about the Lovejoys? What took you so long?" She arched an eyebrow up, which I wouldn't have thought she could do because of the Botox, which I was apparently wrong about. "Todd of course called me as a courtesy to let me know you'd come sniffing around—those aren't his words, darling, obviously. As I am sure Paige has told you, I'm a bit of a troublemaker. I love to stir the shit." Her eyes twinkled.

"If I didn't know before, I do now." I smiled back at her. Her charm was contagious.

She beamed at me. "I do love gay men, you know, darling. I just know we're going to be close friends."

I tried not to laugh. "So, what can you tell me about the Lovejoys?"

"Well, it is so terribly sad about Collier." The smile disappeared, and the corners of her mouth turned down. "Such a horrible thing to have happen. Myrna must be just *destroyed*. She adored him, you know." She made a face. "People have said terrible things about them over the years, but there was never any doubt in my mind about how much they loved each other. No matter what happened, no matter what went down, they loved each other."

She paused as Therese entered, carrying a silver serving tray with a silver carafe and full coffee service on it. She placed it on a sideboard and turned to us. "If you need anything else…" Her voice trailed off and when neither of us said anything, she walked back out of the room.

Serena rose and walked over to the service, pouring herself a cup. "Are you sure you don't want anything?"

"No, I was just at Starbucks." I shrugged. "I'm good."

"So, how's Myrna holding up? I've called her several times but haven't been able to get through. I just get her voicemail... but then I would imagine she's too shaken to talk to anyone, and getting thousands of calls. She must be prostrate with grief. I thought about running a casserole over there—isn't that what you do when someone dies? Bring food to the family?" She sat back down and sipped her coffee.

"I suppose." I debated with myself for a moment, then decided *what the hell* and plunged forward. "No one's been able to reach Myrna. She's not at home, and no one seems to know where she is. Her son doesn't know where she is, and the police haven't been able to track her down."

"That's not good, is it?" Serena frowned. "That's definitely not like her. If she adored Collier, she basically worshipped the ground Cooper walked on. She would never abandon him for any reason, no matter how grief-stricken she might be." A look of alarm crossed her face. "I'm serious, Chanse—if Cooper doesn't know where she is, she must be in serious trouble. That child was like the second coming of Christ to her." She shook her head. "She had trouble getting pregnant—they even went to fertility experts, thought about getting a surrogate. She wanted a child pretty badly—and then of course just when they started interviewing surrogates she got pregnant. Isn't that always the way?"

I didn't think so, but saw no point in disagreeing with her. "So the marriage was in good shape? They didn't have problems?"

"Well, no marriage is perfect. They had their ups and downs, but Myrna adored that man. You could see it on her face every time she looked at him. It was a little sickening, to be honest, but then again, what do I know? I've tried marriage four times and failed miserably every time. I'm friends with all of my ex-husbands, of course, but I seem to get along better with men as a friend rather than as a spouse. Never again." She shuddered delicately. "No, I'll just take lovers in the future, thank you very much. I always admired Collier and Myrna's relationship, honestly. It was almost like a fairy tale." She laughed. "Nauseating as it sounds, they really did love each other—but some people, of course, didn't think so."

"And why was that?"

She leaned forward, her ropes of pearls clacking against each other. She lowered her voice, like someone was listening and she didn't want them to overhear us. "They had an open marriage—Myrna told me once she and Collier hadn't had sex in years—but they were devoted to each other." She gave another little shrug. "Myrna took lovers. If Collier did, I never knew of any, and Myrna's never lasted long. Collier was more of a best friend to her than anything else, you know." She shook her head slightly. "I always wondered if Collier might not be gay. I guess we'll never know now, of course. Poor man." She picked up a tissue from the box on the end table next to her chair and dabbed carefully at her eyes.

Taken aback by her blunt openness, I blustered, "So how long did you know them?"

"I've known them—knew them—oh, whatever. I met them years ago, when we were all barely more than children." She pulled an electronic cigarette out of a little box on the table and clicked it on. She took a long drag on it before expelling white vapor in a plume. "When I graduated from college and shed my first husband—I was practically a *child bride*, you know, and my family did not approve of my first husband, not that they've approved of any of the others, for that matter, but my father was particularly glad to write a check so Hubby

Number One—he might have been broke, but he was an honest-to-God Italian count but my father was convinced he was a gigolo—could ride off into the sunset—I'm still rather close to Giulio, I'm close to all of my exes, of course—what was I saying? Oh yes, of course, after I got out of college and built my own home, I needed art for it, of course." She smiled. "Art is the only constant lover I've had, you know."

"And that's how you met Myrna? At her father's gallery?"

"Yes, of course. I'd already decided that I was going to be a great collector of art, have lots of affairs and live a grand life full of high drama, then die and leave my vast collection with enough of an endowment to some little museum that could then turn itself into a rival to any of the greats." She took another puff off the cigarette. "Delusions of grandeur have always been a problem for me, Chanse. Anyway, that was how I first met Myrna. I went to New York to buy art, and the Lovejoy Gallery was one of the places any serious art collector had to go to. It was like a pilgrimage. In order to be taken seriously as a collector, you had to impress Myrna's father, Simon Lovejoy. He was quite wonderful, a charming old bastard, and he could sell ice to Eskimos. She was working there while she was finishing her master's, and since we were around the same age, we became fast friends." She exhaled. "I've always suspected her father encouraged her to befriend me, you know—every time he looked at me he saw dollar signs—but I genuinely liked both her and Collier. They were fun, they always knew where the best parties were and could of course get me in. They also never made fun of my accent or that I was from Texas, like so many of those pretentious Manhattan fucks did." She went on, uncrossing her legs and tucking them beneath her on the chair. "I used to go up to New York several times a year when I lived in Dallas. I do buy a lot of art." She gestured at the bare walls of the sitting room. "As you can see, I'm trying to be a bit more minimalist in this room. But I have acquired a wonderful collection." She winked at me. "Our family place in Dallas is quite palatial— my grandfather built the house specifically to be enormous in order to have lots of art to display." She shook her head, the blond hair bouncing around her head. "I majored in art at SMU—Southern Methodist, though I've never been much of a Methodist—and so when I had the chance I started buying new art for the place." She pulled a lock of hair into her mouth and chewed on it for a moment. "I'm always looking for new artists, you see, the unknown artist who's going to be the next big thing. That's part of the fun of being a rich bitch, you know." She drummed her fingers on her leg. "Yes, back then I rather liked Myrna."

"Back then? You don't like her now?"

"I was far more callow, and far less discerning, in my youth." She said this with the utmost seriousness, and once the words hung in the air she exploded with peals of laughter. "No, seriously, though, when I was younger I thought someone who always knew where to get the next line of coke from and owned a gallery in the village was the epitome of cool." She shrugged. "Myrna always knew where the next party was. She really had her finger on the pulse of the city, you know what I mean? She was ahead of the trends, always knew what the next big thing was going to be…and there I was, a rube from Dallas with a degree in art and more money than she knew what to do with." Her eyes narrowed. "Ripe for the plucking, was I." She blew out her breath. "Although I will give Myrna credit—she did know what she was talking about. She advised me what artists were on the rise, or were about to break big… so I got some great, valuable art for far less than it would have cost a few years later."

"So, I gather the two of you had a falling out of some sort?"

She gave me a shrewd look. "Of some sort, yes. That's a rather elegant way of putting it." She started laughing again. "Myrna always had a problem with the truth, you see. She also failed to see it as a character flaw. She liked to tell people what they liked to hear, even if it wasn't true. That always proves problematic in the long run. And then after her father was murdered—that was such a terrible time, can you imagine? She inherited the gallery and took it over. Apparently once she got her hands on the books she was horrified. He'd been losing money hand over fist for years—she thought she was inheriting this great business, a veritable cash cow, only to find out she was maybe one step from the bankruptcy courts. I made the colossal mistake of loaning her money to bail her out of her difficulties." She rolled her eyes dramatically. "And like I said, I wasn't particularly smart back then. I was in the process of divorcing my third husband and feeling particularly vulnerable…I wrote her a check without even thinking twice, or even getting something in writing." She turned the cigarette off and replaced it in the box. "To this day she hasn't paid me back. I won't tell you how much the so-called loan was for—but it was enough to buy this house." She sighed. "I don't wish her ill, you know. I just don't know how she can live with herself, owing me so much money. You can imagine how shocked I was when she decided to relocate here, open another gallery."

"Did you know Bill Marren back then as well?"

"Bill." She smiled, her eyes glinting nastily. "I've heard the police out in the middle of the swamp or wherever that monument to slavery he bought is don't believe his paintings were stolen. Imagine that."

"What do you believe?"

"It's funny," she replied slowly, leaning back in the couch. "Those paintings—original, missing Anschlers, right, isn't that they're supposed to be?"

"Yes."

"Why didn't she offer them to me? I collect him. I have the largest collection of original Anschlers outside of a museum." She shrugged. "And she knew that—she was the one who introduced me to Anschler's work all those years ago in New York. The first painting I bought from her father was an Anschler." She shook her head. "It wouldn't surprise me in the least, Chanse, if those paintings never existed in the first place."

"Never existed?"

"Well, they existed, of course, but it wouldn't be a huge surprise to me to find out that Myrna never had them." She shook her head. "I've heard stories about her selling art to people before she'd been commissioned to actually sell it. And those Anschlers…those paintings…" She hesitated. "You know they disappeared during World War Two?"

"I'd read that, yes."

"I think they were destroyed." Serena's lips set in a firm, disapproving line. "Or lost forever during the war. Anschler's daughter was the only survivor, and you know by the end of her life she was practically broke, right? Living off her New Orleans relatives? Why wouldn't she have sold the paintings then? Why would she have lived like a poor relation when she could have sold those paintings?" She narrowed her eyes. "It doesn't make sense."

"But what would be the point, Serena? *That* doesn't make sense. Why would Myrna pretend to sell paintings she didn't have?"

"Who knows why Myrna does anything?" Serena rolled her eyes. "But the paintings have disappeared again, haven't they?" She smiled smugly. "No provenance, either, I heard, and no insurance. Only a fucking insane idiot wouldn't have insured paintings worth millions, Chanse. And why did Bill take possession of the paintings before he owned them?"

"I wondered about that myself," I replied. "I gather that isn't normal? Todd wouldn't say one way or the other."

"Todd is discreet, which can be a drawback." Serena loaded another cartridge into her electric cigarette and inhaled again. "But no, it's not standard or normal. Myrna and her father both bent the rules, did things other art dealers wouldn't." She smiled at me. "I heard on the news this morning that Bill Marren was shot and killed last night...that's kind of odd, don't you think?"

"Did you know him?"

"I know everybody, Chanse." She exhaled white vapor. "But yes, Bill is a collector, and we've crossed paths any number of times. I suspect Myrna might have, oh, I don't know, been up to something there." She sighed. "I'm not trying to cause trouble for her, despite our little falling out. Myrna, for example, has no idea that I don't think of her as a friend anymore. But ask yourself this, Chanse." She leaned forward again. "Collier's dead, and so is Bill Marren. Several million dollars' worth of paintings have been stolen—paintings that weren't insured, that don't have a provenance. Now, Bill has—*had*—a reputation for not having a lot of scruples when it came to his art."

"You think Myrna was selling art that was Nazi loot?"

"I didn't say that, now did I?" Serena puffed away at her cigarette. "But as soon as I heard about what happened out there at Belle Riviere, well—let's just say I have my own suspicions about those paintings and leave at that, shall we?"

CHAPTER TWELVE

My back was hurting again when I got back into my car and started the engine. The cold seemed to somehow get through my jacket and my sweater, going straight to the epicenter of the pain. I sat there for a moment with my eyes closed, waiting for the heater to start blowing warmth through the vents again. Despite the growing pain trying to push everything else out of my mind, I couldn't stop thinking about what Serena had said. Over and above the pain, the words kept swirling around in a vortex in my mind, leaving steadily more wild theories behind in their wake.

What if the paintings had never existed in the first place?

Had the entire thing been a scam from the beginning?

The paintings had been delivered but not removed from their crates, was what they had told me. The thieves had stolen the crates. What if the paintings had never been inside the crates to begin with? That was why they had to be stolen back before they were opened and discovered to be empty.

I put the car into gear and pulled away from the curb, trying to remember exactly what Tom and Bill had said to me that first morning when I'd gone out to Belle Riviere. I distinctly remembered Tom saying, *We didn't unpack them from their crates because we didn't want to have to re-crate them if the provenance didn't come through.*

So, neither Tom nor Bill had actually verified that the paintings in the crates were actually the long missing Anschlers, which struck me as odd. Wouldn't you make sure that what was delivered was what you actually paid for? Especially when you were going to be paying millions of dollars for them? *Anything* could have been inside those crates.

And again, the crates *could* have been empty. Going with the assumption that Myrna was running a major scam on them—so Bill put several hundred thousand dollars into an escrow account as a deposit against the purchase price, once the provenance came through and the seller proved he or she owned the paintings legally. But if the paintings were "stolen" before they could be insured, it also stood to reason that Bill would not only lose the money in escrow, but would be responsible to the owner of the paintings for their actual value.

With Myrna acting as agent for the owner, it also stood to reason that Bill would have to channel the money to the paintings' owner through her. And if there were no paintings and no actual owner, she'd just made a couple of million dollars.

It was actually a great scam, now that I was thinking about it. It couldn't be pulled on just anyone, though. Myrna could only pull it on someone she had a long-standing business relationship with—someone like Bill Marren.

If the paintings did exist, she could still pull the same scam, bilk a couple of million dollars out of Bill, and then turn around and sell the paintings to someone else.

And maybe the paintings couldn't be insured, or a provenance provided, because the paintings showed as having been stolen somewhere? Or were listed as Nazi war loot?

But if everyone thought the paintings disappeared during the war, and there were no living Anschler heirs, the paintings belonged to the New Orleans Museum of Art.

NOMA sure as hell wouldn't be selling them.

So, the key would be to target art collectors with questionable ethics. Bill Marren clearly fit that description, and there were bound to be any number of others like him.

My phone vibrated in my coat pocket. I had stopped at the light at Magazine and Jackson, so I pulled it out and glanced at the screen. Jephtha's smiling face looked back at me. I'd been distracted by the back pain when I got into the car and had forgotten to activate the Bluetooth, so I flipped on my turn signal and made a left turn onto Jackson, heading toward the river. I pulled over in the first available place I saw. I slid my finger across the screen, hit the speaker icon, and said "MacLeod" as I turned on the Bluetooth button on the steering wheel.

"Hey, Chanse," Jephtha said cheerfully. "You're never going to guess what I found online this morning!"

"And you're right, I can't guess," I replied, shifting a little in my seat in a vain attempt to find some way to sit that would relieve the growing pain in my lower back. The cortisone shot was looking better and better by the minute. "So why don't you just go ahead and tell me?" It came out bitchier than I'd intended.

Stupid fucking pain.

He exhaled with a heavy sigh. "You spoil all my fun," he replied, grumpily. "Not even one guess?"

"Yeah, well, you know it's what I live for." I closed my eyes and reached for the lever to push the seat farther back. Once it was back as far as it would go, I started twisting slowly from side to side, feeling the muscles stretch and pull. "So go ahead and tell me. I'm in the car."

"Yeah, you and Abby both are no fun at all," he grumbled. "You both need to lighten up a bit, you know? Relax and enjoy life a bit."

I couldn't help but grin. Abby and Jephtha had been together for five or six years. They'd met, of course, because he had been a huge patron of the Catbox Club. Jephtha was a genius when it came to computers, the Internet, hacking— you name it. He came from a pretty shitty background—he didn't know who his father was, and saying his mother had an addiction problem was putting it kindly. He'd grown up in the lower Ninth Ward, a bright kid whose schoolwork didn't challenge him. One of this mother's boyfriends had gotten him a laptop when he was a teen, and he discovered his true calling.

Unfortunately for Jephtha, he'd also discovered how easy it was to hack into other people's computers and get their credit card information. He was sixteen when he was finally caught, and he'd pled down to a two-year sentence in juvie. He'd served his sentence for credit card fraud, got his GED while inside, and was released when he was eighteen. The problem was the conviction pretty much meant he couldn't get work doing what he was best at—computer programming. His grandmother had died while he was inside and left him her old camelback double shotgun in the Irish Channel. He got a job working the grill in an uptown bar and spent his free time designing computer games. He'd been doing this for about two years when Paige found him. She was doing a story about the waste of talented youth who'd fucked up as teenagers in New Orleans, and brought him to my attention. He'd learned his lesson about using his powers for evil, and before long I put him on a healthy retainer so he could quit the grill job. He used the extra money to become a big tipper at the Catbox Club—and there were any number of strippers who'd been more than happy to take advantage of the nerdy guy with a good cash supply.

I'd had to intervene a few times to run off some of the more leech-like of them.

Given his track record, I was more than a little suspicious of Abby when she turned up in his life. But once she moved in with him, it was pretty clear she loved him and worshiped the ground he walked on. I wondered sometimes if they were ever going to get married and have some kids. However, the thought of what evil genius their combined genes might create was terrifying, so I avoided thinking about it as much as I could. Jephtha, despite spending two years in juvenile hell (which he never talked about), was still nothing more than a big kid. And I do mean big. He's at least six feet six, and when I first met him was lucky if he weighed one hundred and fifty pounds. Abby's cooking had filled him out to about two hundred pounds or so, but he was still way too thin for his height. He flatly refused to join a gym or hire a trainer. His arms were long, he slouched, and he wore his light brown hair long—sometimes pulled back into a ponytail. He also wore Coke-bottle glasses that magnified his murky brown eyes so they looked like a fly's—but Abby had succeeded in nagging him into wearing contacts most of the time.

The conviction was unfortunate, because when it came to all things computer, he truly was a genius. Oh, sure, he had trouble tying his shoelaces, but park him at a keyboard and he could do anything. The retainer I paid him was sizable, but I was still not paying him what he was truly worth. Had he not gone to jail and become an insurance liability, he'd probably be working for a major software company.

Silicon Valley's loss was my gain.

"So, what did you find?" I prodded. "I don't have all morning."

"Well," he drew the word out into about twenty syllables before continuing, "did you get a chance to read the report Abby and I put together on Bill Marren?"

I cursed under my breath. "No, I haven't."

He sounded a little hurt. "Dude, that was a lot of intense work for both of us. And we did it pretty darned fast, too."

"I know, and it was really thorough—maybe a bit too thorough, you know? I just haven't had the time to sit down and go through it all. It was really good work, though. I will when I get back to the apartment, I promise."

"You need to get the goddamned cortisone shot," he lectured. "It's affecting how you do your job, Chanse, seriously. You would never let a report on a case you're working on go this long before you hurt your back. Especially one that involves murder! Dude, we're both worried about you. Promise me you'll get the damned shot."

"I'm seriously considering it, all right?" I shifted in my seat again. "So tell me—what did you find that's so important?"

"Oh, yes, of course." He cleared his throat. "Well, there were a couple of things in his background that got my antennae twitching. One, he was married when he was young—that in and of itself isn't a big deal, of course, back then lots of gay men stayed closeted and got married because they thought they were supposed to, right?"

"Right."

"But what was interesting was the grounds for his divorce was adultery—and the co-respondent wasn't a man, which you'd automatically assume, right? His wife caught him with another dude and she got a lawyer. But that wasn't the case."

"He cheated on her with a woman?"

"Oh, yeah. The divorce was sealed, which bugged me. It took me a while to crack—"

"I don't want to know this."

He exhaled, "Oh yes, of course, sorry, anyway, I managed to get the name of the woman he was having the affair with— her name was Jane Meakin."

"That name sounds familiar." I frowned.

"That's because she was Myrna Lovejoy's mother." I could almost see the smirk on his face. "And no, he couldn't have been Myrna's father, although I suppose without a DNA test we can't say for sure, but anyway, she wasn't born until several years after the divorce, and her mother had remarried. I also found out that Bill was the one who fronted the money so Myrna's father could open the gallery in New York."

"Interesting." I started tapping my fingers on the steering wheel. The connection between Bill and Myrna was even deeper than I'd thought originally, which meant it would be even easier for her to run a scam on him. He'd known her almost her entire life and had also known her father—had been intimate with her *mother.*

Of course he would trust her! Of course he would take delivery of the paintings before paying for them, before seeing the provenance. He had no reason to not to believe she was being aboveboard with him.

It was all very clever. Collier had to have been in on it as well. But why did she kill him? What had changed?

"Yes, it's very interesting, isn't it?" He exhaled. "And there's another thing I found out as well. I don't know how it fits into anything else that's going on, but Bill's father? He wasn't American—he was British, from Lancashire and educated at Cambridge. He married someone with a bit of money, and worked in investments, built it up into a nice little nest egg to get Bill on his way to being filthy, disgustingly rich. Bill was an only child, by the way, and the family emigrated to the United States in the late 1940s. And get this, it gets even better, believe it or not. Bill's father, Stuart Marren? He was a friend of the Anschler family. He was the London banker who loaned them money and tried to help Rachel get them out of Nazi-occupied Netherlands after the war started and the Nazis invaded."

"What?" I shook my head. I couldn't have heard that right. The Marren-Anschler connection went back that far?

"I thought that would get your attention," Jephtha said smugly. "So there's been a connection between him and these paintings that goes back a lot further than he's been letting on."

"You haven't heard?" I replied. "He was killed last night." I bit my lower lip. *Maybe he found out about the scam? Maybe he confronted Myrna?*

Myrna was getting out of control.

None of this was making sense.

The more I found out, the more confused I was.

"Dude." Jephtha inhaled sharply and was silent for a moment. "That sucks. Do they know who did it?"

"No—no, they don't."

"Do *you* know who did it?"

"No, no, I don't." I almost gasped as a flare of pain shot out from my lower back. I grasped the steering wheel so hard my knuckles turned white. I closed my eyes, not wanting to say anything. The last thing I needed was to hear *I told you so* again about the fucking cortisone shots. I managed to say, "Thanks, man, I need to get going, I promise I'll read the Marren report when I get back home." I didn't give him a chance to say anything before I hung up on him.

I sat there for a moment, still gripping the steering wheel.

It was all there in my head, but I couldn't piece it all

together in a way that made sense to me. There were still too many missing pieces. I took a deep breath and put the car into drive, turned around, and headed back to my apartment. I walked inside and found my pill bottle on the nightstand. I shook out a Vicodin, found my pill cutter in the bathroom, and sliced it in two. After dry-swallowing the half-Vicodin along with two Advils, I sat down at my computer and touched the spacebar to wake it up. The BILL MARREN document was still on my desktop, so I clicked on it. I switched on the heating pad and slid it behind my back while the document loaded. I scanned it quickly. He did have a history of questionable ethics and business practices—always skirting that line between unethical but never crossing into criminal. Jephtha had also tracked down rumors about his methods of art collecting—again, never anything criminally actionable, but certainly questionable ethically.

He would have been easy prey for Myrna's scam…if it was indeed a scam, and I was beginning to believe Serena was right. Myrna had never had the paintings in the first place. The crates had been delivered empty. There was a fireplace in the gallery—that would explain how the crates had been taken out. All the thief would have needed was a claw hammer to pry the crates apart and break them down. The wood could have been burned in the fireplace—and to anyone, it would look like the paintings had been stolen.

I had to hand it to Myrna, it was a fiendishly clever plan.

I was still staring at my computer screen when my cell phone rang again. I didn't recognize the number, but I was pretty sure the number that came up had a Dallas area code.

Jude.

I closed my eyes and answered. "MacLeod."

"Hey, Chanse, it's Jude." His voice sounded guarded, and

in the background I could hear people talking. He was in a public place. "I have to say I never thought I'd hear from you again. I wasn't sure I should call you back or not, to be honest. But finally I was too curious not to, you know?" He laughed hollowly. "What on earth could Chanse MacLeod want from me after all this time? So, today I figured what the hell. How are you? Well, I hope?"

He sounded friendlier than I thought he would, so that had to be a good thing. We hadn't really left things between us very well. "I could be better, thanks for asking. You sound good. I hope you're doing well?"

"Can't complain," he replied. "Well, I can *always* complain, but that's a quirk in my personality."

"Great." I forced out a laugh. "I did have a reason for calling, though."

"I figured you weren't calling up to catch up on things with an ex after—how many years has it been? Christ, I don't think I want to know how long it's been." He sighed. "Look, things just didn't work out with us, but there's no need for us to not be friends. Maybe it was me, maybe it was you, whatever—but I came to terms with it all a long time ago. I'm actually glad you called, Chanse. It's really nice to hear your voice again…we just weren't suited, and you weren't in the right kind of head space anyway." He paused. "What can I help you with?"

"Thanks, Jude." I was touched. "I mean it, really." I did, too—it was nice to know there was an ex out there who *didn't* hate me. "I'm glad you're willing to help me."

"Yeah, well, you never were much for the personal, were you?" He was quiet for a moment. "I'm sorry, I didn't want to go there. Forget I said it. So why *did* you call? I assume you need something?"

"I'm working on a case—"

"Of course you are."

"And I kind of have run across someone you might know, so I thought I'd call you, see what you knew. I was hoping you could give me some perspective on him. I'm not really sure what to make of him, if he can be trusted."

He sighed. "Who?"

"Tom Ziebell."

There was silence on the line. After a few moments, Jude said slowly, "I'm sorry, but I can't help you, Chanse. I don't know him. That name's not even familiar."

"Are you sure?" I prodded. "Think back to your wrestling days, when you did the videos for Top Rope. That's where you'd know him from. You worked together."

"I told you, Chanse, I'm positive I don't know this guy, not even from back then," he said, his voice rising a little. "I mean, it's been a long time, but I remember all the guys I worked with. I'm still in touch with most of them, you know, and I have never heard that name before."

"He wrestled under the name Jamie West?"

There was silence for a moment, then, "Oh, *him*." He barked out a laugh. "I don't know what he's trying to sell you, Chanse, but his name isn't Tom Ziebell. Jamie West's real name was Rand Barragry." He paused. "You need to stay away from that guy, Chanse. Get as far away from him as you can. At the very least, he's a sociopath."

I felt my stomach start twisting. "A sociopath? Are you sure?" The hairs on my arm began standing up.

He sighed. "Look, Chanse, I don't know, it's been twelve years or so since I last saw him, okay? We did a match together once, that's all—but we were at several different tapings together. When I first met him I didn't get a good feeling from him, okay? It was probably one of the worst experiences I had with Top Rope, working with him...I didn't trust him, I didn't like him, and you can't work well with someone taping a wrestling match if you don't trust him, you know? Trust is essential...Sure, he was hot. My God, he was hot. But still..." His voice trailed off.

"Was there anything specific?"

"I don't know, it was a while ago. Let me think." He was quiet for a moment. I could hear the noise behind him, someone's name being called, the whirr and hiss of an espresso machine. He was in a coffee shop. Finally, he went on, "You know, there was just something about him I didn't like, I wasn't comfortable with. He was friendly enough, and good-looking enough, and the body—well, he wouldn't have been filming if he wasn't hot as hell, but..." He hesitated. "After that first trip, where I met him the first time, I had some fraudulent charges on my credit cards, all of them coming from Rhode Island, which I, you know, didn't think anything about. Department store cards, Visa, MasterCard, that sort of thing. I filed disputes with the companies and it was all taken care of. I never thought anything about it. Well, I was talking to Steve—the guy who owns the company—online a couple of weeks later and he mentioned the same thing happened to one of the other guys who was there that weekend—a coincidence? Steve also said some things were missing from his house—nothing major, nothing worth reporting to the police. Come to find out later this kind of thing happened every time Jamie West taped. So Steve decided to fire him, not use him again. I know Paul—" He stopped.

"It's okay, Jude. It's been years." *I can think about him now without it hurting.*

"Well, I'm glad to hear you've finally gotten past that." I

also appreciated him not pointing out that Paul's shadow was part of what ruined things for us, or that I'd used him. Part of Jude's appeal to me back then, when I was drinking too much and blaming myself for Paul's death, was that he'd known Paul and we could talk about him and remember him together.

I was not a good person back then—not that I was much better now.

I need to call Rory and apologize.

"Thank you for saying that, and for not—you know. You deserved to be treated better than that. I am sorry, Jude."

"You don't need to apologize to me for anything, Chanse. Seriously. I wasn't in a good place when we were together, I was insecure and you had your martyr complex. It's not like we had a chance…it was a wonder we managed to stay together as long as we did."

Martyr complex. I still have one, didn't I? If I didn't, I would have the fucking cortisone shot and stop suffering.

He was saying, "After we broke up I met someone, and we've been together ever since. We get over to New Orleans every once in a while…maybe next time we could have dinner or something."

"I'd like that." I meant it, too. "And I'm glad you found someone. You deserve to be happy."

"So do you, Chanse. Do you still have the martyr complex?"

"You don't know the half of it," I muttered.

"I'm sorry, I didn't hear you?"

"I said I'm glad you found someone. You deserve to be happy."

"Yeah, well, I won't argue that point," he said with a laugh. "I think you'll like Clay…Okay, next time we come over to New Orleans we'll get together for dinner. So, where were we before we got sidetracked into the personal drama?

Oh, yes, that crazy fuck Jamie West." He sighed. "The last time I saw him was maybe twelve years ago?"

"Did you say twelve years ago?" Something niggled in my mind—something about the time frame seemed off, didn't fit. But I couldn't put my finger on it.

"Yeah, Paul stopped working for Top Rope around the same time, it was the last time we all worked for Top Rope—well, you know—and that was the last time I saw Rand Barragry. It was after that Steve told me he let him go."

"Rand Barragry?"

"As I said, that was Jamie's real name."

"You're sure?"

"Positive. His name was Rand Barragry." He spelled the last name for me. "I'm looking at my Dropbox account on my laptop—I have pictures stored from my days at Top Rope, and I have one of him, and that's the name it's labeled with." He laughed. "You know how anal I am about things."

I pulled up the report Abby had sent about Tom on my computer. "Thanks, Jude—you've been a big help. I hate to do this, but I kind of have to go now."

"No worries, I do, too—I have to get back to work. I'm glad you called."

"Me, too. Call me the next time you're in town."

"I'd like that. Bye." He hung up.

I stared at the report, reading through it quickly.

It had been in front of my face the whole time.

Paul had stopped working for Top Rope two years before he died. He'd been dead ten years. So that meant "Tom" had been working for Top Rope twelve years ago. But according to the report, he *would have only been seventeen twelve years ago*—and that was the *last* time he'd worked for them. Paul and Jude had both told me they'd taped all of their matches for Top Rope over a period of about three years.

If Tom had started around the same time, he would have only been fourteen when he started.

I would have caught that if my brain hadn't been addled with fucking pain pills.

I pulled up the Internet and typed in "topropevideos.com." And sure enough, there it was on the front page: in order to enter the website you had to verify that you were over twenty-one. There was also a disclaimer that all of the models used in Top Rope Productions were over eighteen, and proof was on file at Top Rope headquarters.

I clicked the box and went inside the site, and there it was—the link to "contact us." I clicked on it, and the mailing address for the company came up, along with an 800 customer service number.

I dialed it.

"Top Rope Productions."

"My name is Chanse MacLeod, and I'm a private investigator in New Orleans, Louisiana. I'm looking for information on someone who used to work as talent for your company—his stage name was Jamie West."

"Let me connect you to someone else." There was a silence, and then another click as someone picked up the line.

"This is Steve, I am the owner here. What are you asking for?"

I reintroduced myself, adding, "I'm looking for information on Jamie West. I'm hoping you can help me."

There was silence, and then a low whistle. "There's a name I'd hoped I'd never hear again. How do I know you are who you say you are? My employment files are confidential."

"I can take a picture of myself with my private eye license and email it to you. I can also scan the license."

"Do that, and I'll call you back."

I did, and five minutes later my phone rang. "MacLeod."

"I got your information, but I don't know this is real."

"Listen, I used to date Paul Maxwell—he wrestled for you under the name Cody Dallas. And I just spoke to Jude Mueller, and he used to wrestle for you as Matt Miller…If you want to give Jude a call to verify I am who I say I am, I'll wait."

Five minutes or so later my phone rang again. "Jude vouched for you, but I have to say, I'm really not comfortable sharing my employment files with you—there are privacy laws, and I don't want to open myself up to litigation."

"We can talk in hypotheticals—although the police may be in touch with you, just a heads up."

"Okay, hypotheticals."

"The man who used to wrestle for you under the name Jamie West now lives in Louisiana and calls himself Tom Ziebell. Was that the name you knew him under?"

"No. And we do have his driver's license and social security card on file. That was *not* the name he was calling himself then."

"And he was over eighteen?"

"We don't use models who are underage. That's why we have the photocopies of his documents on file, just in case someone came back and accused of child porn or whatever it is they call it now."

"Thank you."

There was a pause. "May I ask what this is about?"

"Hypothetically, I can tell you my case is about murder, robbery, and possible fraud."

"Then Jamie West is probably your man." He hung up the phone.

Tom wasn't Tom.

Bill had a connection to Myrna that went back years.

And they were both connected to Benjamin Anschler.

This whole thing stunk to high heaven.

I called Abby, but it went to voicemail.

I stood up. Much as I hated the thought, I was going to have to drive out to Redemption Parish.

CHAPTER THIRTEEN

I found an empty pill bottle for the other half of the Vicodin I'd taken, to bring with me on the drive out there. The half I'd taken had dulled the pain down to a throb, kind of like a minor toothache that was bearable.

I needed to keep my mind clear but I also needed to dull the pain. If it got worse I'd take the other half—but taking a whole one was out of the question until I got back to New Orleans.

Now that I knew Tom wasn't really Tom, I was worried about Abby. I'd tried calling her but it went straight to voicemail—which never happened. I'd also sent her an urgent text, but she hadn't yet responded as I went out the back door and got into the car. I turned the Bluetooth on and tossed the phone into the passenger seat.

I was trying not to panic. There wasn't any reason to think Abby was in any danger. She'd planned on nosing around the sheriff's department in Avignon. She hadn't said anything about going out to Belle Riviere.

But Abby never turned off her phone. She never allowed the battery to run down, either. She could never understand how anyone could ever let a cell phone die, and she even paid extra so it hooked up to a satellite when she was out of her provider's service area so she was never out of touch. She was amazing with it—it was like another limb to her. Her entire life was in that phone.

No, something was definitely off.

I got on the highway, biting my lower lip as I merged into the heavy westbound traffic. I couldn't shake the feeling that Abby was in some kind of danger. She had no idea who she was dealing with.

I could kick myself.

How could I have missed the age thing, how? If anything happens to Abby because I was too fucked up on pills to think clearly...My thinking is impaired. You're always in pain or on some kind of pain pill that fucks with your memory. You should have listened to everyone and gotten the fucking cortisone shot. If anything happens to her because of my stupid martyr complex...

Jude was right. Everyone was right. I *did* have a martyr complex. I never believed I deserved to be happy. It had been so drilled into my head growing up that homosexuality was wrong and a sin—even after coming out, coming to terms with who and what I was, I'd never gotten over that. It was why I'd never had anything lasting with anyone.

And when I'd finally found it with Paul, I'd allowed my own pettiness and stupidity to sabotage the whole thing. And when he was murdered, when he died, I blamed myself and believed I didn't deserve to be happy. I'd fucked things up with Jude. I'd fucked things up with every guy I'd dated since Paul died. I'd kept Rory at arm's length, unable and unwilling to take it any further.

Martyr complex. Yeah, that's definitely what my problem was.

My phone rang, and I answered through the Bluetooth. "MacLeod."

"Chanse, it's Jephtha again." His voice was higher than normal, which wasn't good. His voice always tended to go up a register or two (or three) when he was agitated. "Abby's not responding to anything—every time I call it goes right to voicemail. That's not like her. Have you talked to her?"

Fuck, I said to myself. The last thing I needed was for him to go off the rails. I was also glad I hadn't told him anything I'd found out about Tom. "Jephtha, you need to stay calm," I replied, hoping I could follow my own advice. "I'm on my way out there now. You don't know anything's wrong. Her battery could have died, or she turned it off because…I don't know why, but she might have a good reason."

"Except she never turns her phone off, and she never lets the battery die. You know that." His voice was rising in pitch again. "She has a charger she could plug into the cigarette lighter of her car. She has another that's solar powered. She always has a charger in her purse."

"Seriously, buddy, you need to stay calm." I pressed down on the accelerator so I could pass an eighteen-wheeler in the center lane. "I promise you, as soon as I get off the phone with you, I'll call the sheriff out there and let him know we're worried about her. I'll let him know everything we have on Myrna and the robbery, okay?"

"Yeah, okay. You call me if you hear anything."

"You do the same." I disconnected the call. I didn't tell him I'd already called the sheriff before I left the apartment. Parlange had listened to me—because Venus and Blaine had already contacted him about me, and he was "always willing to cooperate with the New Orleans Police Department." He'd been surprised that I didn't want to discuss the robbery with him, but he'd listened and then told me he'd let his patrol guys know to keep an eye out for her car—which was hard to miss. I'd hoped he'd send someone out to Belle Riviere, but he didn't offer. There was no reason for anyone to go out there and look. There was no reason for me to even be worried she'd gone out there.

I could also hope that the Barney Fife she'd been flirting with would be concerned once he heard she'd dropped off the radar. Maybe he would take a drive out to Belle Riviere just to be on the safe side.

I still hadn't figured out what was going on with the paintings.

All I was sure about was the man I knew as Tom Ziebell was really named Rand Barragry. The quick web search I'd done on Rand Barragry turned up a newspaper report about his death ten years ago—right around the time "Tom" had entered Bill Marren's life.

Well, at least a body had been found in Providence. The corpse was missing his arms and his face had been bashed in. He'd been carrying Rand Barragry's wallet, so the Rhode Island police had simply assumed that was whose body it was. Why run dental records or fingerprint matches when there was ID on the body? I was a former cop, so I knew how easy it was to just close the file and be done with it. All of those cost money, budgets were tight, and there was a lot pressure to close cases quickly.

No one was looking for Tom Ziebell, because Rand Barragry had taken his identity.

It was frightening how smart he was.

He'd undoubtedly murdered Bill Marren, using me as his alibi. I would have been willing to swear he'd come home with me. He'd been there at four in the morning, hadn't he? He'd probably brought me home, put me to bed, gone back out to his car and out to Belle Riviere to kill Bill. Once that was done, he headed back to New Orleans, let himself back into my apartment, and got back into bed with me.

It was a big risk to take—how could he have been sure I wouldn't wake up and realize he was gone?

The whole night was foggy to me.

I'd swear I'd not had more than one glass of wine, maybe two at the most. The whole night was shrouded in fog. Maybe he'd slipped something into my wine? Something that on top of the wine and the Vicodin would put me out long enough for him to commit the murder?

It was an hour and half, give or take, from New Orleans to Belle Riviere. Give him half an hour to commit the crime, and then another ninety minutes back to New Orleans. We'd had dinner at seven. He could have had me back home by nine—I'd have to have Venus and Blaine check the dinner receipt—be out there and back in bed by one in the morning.

It was a risk, but then sociopaths got off on risk, didn't they?

And he was getting bolder. Collier's murder hadn't been as big a risk as Bill's.

There's no reason to be worried about Abby, she's probably nowhere near Belle Riviere.

Hell, if I hadn't figured out the age was wrong I wouldn't have suspected anything amiss with him. So why would Abby? Everyone knew him as Tom Ziebell. I remembered reading that the best way to change your identity was to take over someone else's, apply for a social security number with the name of a dead child...It would have been easy. All he had to do was kill Tom, take his IDs and credit cards, and move away, avoid people who actually knew him.

But the paintings—what was the fucking deal with the paintings? And why did Collier have to be killed as well?

Where was Myrna?

Or was he just killing all of his partners? To keep all the money for himself?

You can never trust a criminal partner because they've already proven they don't care about the law.

And I'd never suspected a thing. Not even when I recognized him from Top Rope. How he must have laughed at me! Although it must have scared the pants off him at first—what were the odds that the detective Bill hired would have known him as Jamie West?

Am I so shallow that I won't suspect a good-looking man?

I didn't like to think so. There was always the excuse that the pain and the meds were fucking with my brain.

Why are you being such a goddamned martyr? Why won't you have the cortisone shot that will make the pain go away? It isn't risky.

Bill had hired me to look into the disappearance of the paintings. Did he suspect his protégé? Did Tom/Rand/whatever the fuck his name was start to wonder if Bill was on to him?

It all came back to the paintings.

Bill's father tried to help the Anschler family during the war. The three missing paintings…

"Call New Orleans Museum of Art," I instructed the Bluetooth. I asked the woman who answered for Haley Flax, and this time I was put right through.

"Haley Flax, Development."

"Ms. Flax, this is Chanse MacLeod, and I'm a private investigator—"

"Yes, I got your messages, I'm sorry to have not called you back." She interrupted me. "It's been crazy around here lately. You were on my list of callbacks for tomorrow, I'm sorry."

"That's all right. The reason I was calling was because I was wondering about an estate settlement? It goes back a number of years. A woman named Rachel Anschler left her estate to the museum?"

"That's very odd." She clicked her tongue. "You know, someone called asking about that bequest recently. I went on vacation and hadn't had time to put the file back…it's here on my desk somewhere."

"Someone called you about the Anschler bequest?" I could feel the hairs on the back of my neck starting to stand up. "Do you remember who?"

"Of course. A woman named Myrna Lovejoy who has a gallery down on Magazine in the Arts District. She called asking about the Anschler bequest." I could hear papers rustling on her desk.

"What did you tell her?"

"She wanted to know about paintings that Ms. Anschler might have bequested to the museum, and I gave her the list. There weren't any paintings, of course…well, there were three, but they were so badly damaged they were irreparable. Ah, yes, here it is." She whistled softly. "There were three paintings, not framed, but rolled up and bound together with twine. They'd been damaged by water, damp, mold…at the time we tried to have the paintings repaired and restored, but the mold and rot had gotten into the canvas…according to my notes, Ms. Anschler had been living in quite an advanced state of poverty. Such a shame, too—the paintings were works of her father's and would have really been worth a fortune, and would have been an excellent addition to our collection here at NOMA."

"Was that common knowledge? About the paintings, I mean?"

"I can't imagine that it was." She hummed a bit, and I could hear papers rustling. "At the time of the bequest, when she died, no one here at NOMA really knew who she actually was. It wasn't until they found some of her father's sketches amongst her things that the connection was made. The state of the paintings—according to the notes here in the file, the director didn't want to make a public announcement unless the paintings could be saved—which of course would have been big news—but since they weren't salvageable..." Her voice trailed off. "I think they figured it wasn't a story anyone would have any interest in."

"Thank you."

"Is there anything else I can help you with?"

"No, thank you." I disconnected the call.

My mind was racing as I drove past the airport exit and out toward the lake marsh bridge. Bill had to have known the paintings had been ruined. He was a friend of the family. So why would he have put up a couple of hundred thousand dollars for paintings he knew didn't exist? Granted, he had more money than God, but one thing I'd noticed about rich people—they could be very tight-fisted, and they watched their money pretty damned closely.

And what had been Myrna's game? She had to have been in on the whole thing with Rand/Tom from the very beginning. What was in it for her? The money?

I called Jephtha back. He answered on the first ring. "I still haven't heard from her, Chanse." His voice had gone up another register. Pretty soon he'd be able to shatter crystal.

"I'm on my way. I'm on the lake bridge now." I tried to keep my voice calm, smooth, one note, to help him level off and not lose his mind completely. "Do you have the financials on the Lovejoys handy?"

"Why do you ask me for reports if you're not going to read them?" He sighed. "The Lovejoys were way over their heads, as you'd know if you'd read the damned reports. They were pretty extended. Credit cards were all maxed out. The money they got for the sale of the gallery and the apartment in New York didn't cover the house here or the gallery space, so they'd opened another line of credit. Bill Marren cosigned that line of credit, by the way—they would have never gotten it on their own, not as overextended as they were. I don't know how they were paying their bills."

"Bill Marren?" That didn't make sense to me. Why would Bill Marren—

Rand.

Rand had somehow managed to get Bill to sign that application, or had forged his name to it. Bill probably had no idea…

And now he was dead.

What were the odds that his will left everything to the man he thought was Tom Ziebell?

"Yeah, I thought that was weird," Jephtha was saying as I flew past the exit to I-59 north and Hammond. "I mean, he cosigned the loan for their house, too."

"Thanks. If you hear from her, call me." I disconnected the call.

So, "Bill" had cosigned the mortgage for the Lovejoy house, and a line of credit for them that was keeping them afloat. He'd also sunk a couple of hundred thousand dollars for paintings he should have known no longer existed.

I tried to remember everything about the day I'd been out there, the day he'd hired me. My back had been hurting, and I'd not been paying as close attention as I should have because of that.

You need to get the fucking cortisone shot.

Collier and Myrna were broke and desperate. They'd had to leave New York under a cloud of disgrace, and they'd come to New Orleans to start over. Bill Marren, a friend of her father's and a longtime client of her gallery in New York, had recently moved to the area—in fact, visiting him at Belle Riviere was what made them decide on New Orleans in the first place. It wouldn't, I suppose, be much of a stretch given their longtime relationship to assume Bill would cosign things for Myrna.

But why would Myrna try to swindle Bill?

Why wouldn't Myrna try to swindle Bill?

"Call Redemption Parish Sheriff's Department," I instructed the Bluetooth as I drove down from the bridge onto dry land. I was getting close to the exit. Someone in the sheriff's office answered and I asked for Sheriff Parlange, giving my name and being put on hold, which forced me to listen to "Friends in Low Places" by Garth Brooks for far longer than was absolutely necessary.

"This is Sheriff Parlange."

"Sheriff, this is Chanse MacLeod again—"

"No one has seen your partner," he interrupted me. "I can't really justify putting out an alert on her just yet."

"I know, and I appreciate what you're doing already—"

He laughed. "Well, just between you and me, she's been flitting around here the last couple of days asking all kinds of questions and getting people all stirred up. One of my deputies kind of has a thing for her now. She's a hell of an investigator, all right."

"What I want to talk to you about now is the robbery at Belle Riviere—the robbery and the murder," I said. "I have some—"

"Now, Mr. MacLeod, I don't want any trouble with you but I have to tell you even before old Mr. Marren was murdered we had some questions about things out there," he replied. "I know Mr. Marren had some questions about our investigation, but I am telling you, I wasn't trying to do anything against the law. I know I have a reputation—my enemies like to spread stories about me. That young fellow of Mr. Marren's thought I was trying to mess up their lawsuit, but this had nothing to do with that." His voice was grim. "I tried to settle that lawsuit any number of times but the lawyers won't have it. Well, that's fine, my boys messed up and they'll have to pay for it. My preference would be not to go to court but it's not up to me. But I don't appreciate that Ziebell boy telling people that I have a vendetta against him because of that lawsuit and we didn't investigate that robbery proper. We did everything by the book, Mr. MacLeod, and I am telling you, no one broke into that place that night. No one. And I told Mr. Marren that himself."

"What?" I couldn't believe what I was hearing.

"I told Mr. Marren when I made my report to him—what day was that? Monday."

The day before they hired me.

"I don't understand. If Bill believed your report—"

"He believed me, all right. He thanked me for my time, even offered to make a donation to my next campaign fund, so you can see why I was so surprised to hear he'd hired a private eye. I went out there on Wednesday night to talk to him, and he told me I didn't have anything to worry about."

"And he was killed later that night." The exit for Avignon was coming up on my right, so I turned on my signal and started slowing down.

"Yes, that's right. He was." His voice was grim. "I understand that you're in a position to give Tom Ziebell an alibi?"

"I wouldn't say that." I replied as I took the off-ramp and turned the signal on for the left turn I was going to make at the bottom of the ramp. "He was in New Orleans that night—we had dinner—but from about nine o'clock until about four in the morning I can't vouch for him." I quickly explained my reaction to the wine, the pain pills, and my suspicions about being drugged. "He was there when I woke up at four in the morning, but to be honest, I don't remember even going home from the restaurant."

He whistled. "Interesting."

I made the left turn and accelerated. I was about a mile from the T where you turned right for Avignon or left for Belle Riviere. "And his name isn't Tom Ziebell. It's Rand Barragry."

"What?"

"You heard me. His real name is Rand Barragry, and he's wanted for petty theft and fraud in Rhode Island. About nine or ten years ago, I believe he murdered Tom Ziebell and took over his identity. You can check with the Providence police—they found a body with Reed Barragry's ID on it, with the face messed up and the arms missing. They didn't bother to verify the ID. But it wasn't Barragry, the body was Tom Ziebell." I explained why the Ziebells hadn't been missing their son.

"I'll be damned."

I slowed for the stop sign. There were no cars coming from either direction. "Like I said, Sheriff, I'm worried about my partner." I made up my mind and turned left and headed for Belle Riviere. "I'm about a mile or so from the plantation house."

"You need to stay away from Belle Riviere—I'll get a car out there."

"I can't wait, Sheriff." I disconnected the call and headed down the river road. The pain in my back was getting worse, but I didn't care. All I cared about was getting there and making sure Abby was okay.

CHAPTER FOURTEEN

The gate at Belle Riviere was open.

I turned into the driveway and put the car in park.

Unsure what to make of the gate not being shut, I glanced up at the left side and saw the security camera was there, pointed at the driveway.

What the hell, I decided, *might as well go on.*

I took a deep breath, resisting the urge to slam the gas pedal all the way down to the floor, and drove slowly through the gate. I was worried, but losing my head wasn't going to solve anything. It certainly wouldn't help Abby—if Abby actually *was* here and in need of help. *She can take care of herself*, I reminded myself as I drove down the long strip of road under the canopy of branches, *probably better than you can take care of your own self, remember? Her brain hasn't been fogged by pain pills for the last few months. She doesn't have a martyr complex. She knows how to handle men, much better than you can, and she's bright and she's alert and she can get herself out of a tight situation. She doesn't need to be rescued.*

But there was always a first time, wasn't there?

I also had to remind myself that I was here on nothing more than a hunch.

As I came out of the trees I could see the parking area in front of the house was empty other than the Mercedes and the Aston Martin. All the shutters were closed on both floors. I stopped, shifted the car into neutral, and thought for a moment.

The house is a crime scene. It wouldn't look right for Tom/Rand/whatever his name is to stay here afterward, in the same house where his mentor was murdered. But both cars are here. I don't see Abby's, though—but that doesn't mean she isn't here and the car isn't parked somewhere else.

Abby's car was hard to miss. It was incredibly conspicuous. It had been Jephtha's grandmother's car originally, part of his inheritance that included the house. It was an old 1988 Oldsmobile Delta Royale 88 that ran like a dream and looked like it should be run through a compactor. Jephtha's grandmother had babied it from the day she bought it, with the end result that it had lasted all these years and still ran. Awful as it looked, it was one of the most comfortable cars I'd ever ridden in. The paint job looked leprous—the blue paint Oldsmobile had used for that year had been defective, bubbling and blistering and peeling away. Jephtha's grandmother had declined to take advantage of the recall to get it repainted, and the more years that passed, the worse the paint looked. The windshield was cracked, and the driver's side mirror was duct-taped to the door to keep it on. The driver's side window crank was also broken, so a screwdriver had been inserted on the inside between the door and the window glass to keep it from sliding down. It had well over two hundred thousand miles on it, and when it was parked on the side of the road it looked like it had been abandoned. Jephtha had bought a new car almost four years ago for her, but she preferred the Oldsmobile. She'd been saying she was going to get a new one for several years now, but somehow never got around to it. If she ever needed to

be inconspicuous, she borrowed Jephtha's navy blue Malibu—
he never drove it anyway.

Relieved that I'd been wrong, I pulled into the parking
lot and whipped the Jeep around in a wide circle, ready to
head back into Avignon. I glanced in my rearview and noticed
something that looked odd. I put my car into park and turned
around to look out the back. The back end of a car was barely
visible behind one of the outbuildings behind the main house.
I realized the building was the gallery, and it looked like the
rear end of the Oldsmobile. I bit my lip and kept driving in a
circle until I was facing the right direction and followed the
drive around the side of the house and headed for the back
building.

As soon as I'd come around the back of the main house I
could see Abby's car, sitting there in plain view. I pulled over
and turned off my engine, retrieved my gun, and moved the
safety off. I got out, closing the door gently so it didn't make
any noise, and started creeping across the back lawn.

*You're being ridiculous. As far as you know nothing's
going on and Abby is fine. But then what is her car doing back
here? She doesn't know that Tom's not who he claims to be,
and Tom doesn't know that I know. For all he knows, she's just
my partner and she's here to help him out. But why is she out
here?*

The wind was howling and the gun was cold in my hand.
In my rush to get out here, I'd forgotten to grab a pair of gloves.
I cursed my stupidity as my nose started to run from the cold.
The frozen, dead grass crunched under my feet.

As I got closer to the gallery, I could see through the
side windows. The shutters were open, of course, and the
lights were on inside. I could hear snatches of music over the
whistling of the wind, but not enough to recognize what it was.
I could see Tom and Abby standing in front of a painting. She

was wearing a red wig, a pleated plaid skirt, knee socks, and a sweater. Glasses perched on the end of her nose, and she was scribbling notes on a notepad as he talked. Tom, wearing only a pair of tight jeans and an extremely tight T-shirt, was pointing at the picture as he talked, pointing things out to her, no doubt.

I sighed in relief and slid the safety back on before depositing the gun back in my coat pocket. She was okay—but I still had to get her out of here.

And where was the car the sheriff had said he was sending?

I climbed the steps to the front porch of the gallery and knocked on the door before turning the knob handle and walking inside.

"Sorry to interrupt," I said quickly.

"Chanse!" Tom's face lit up with a smile. He looked like he hadn't slept much, the bags under his eyes looking deeper, and his eyes appeared to be red and sunken. He crossed the room quickly and threw his arms around me, catching me off guard as he gave me an enormous hug. "It's so nice to see you," he whispered in my ear, tightening his grip on me.

Having no choice, I hugged him back, trying to signal Abby over his shoulder to get the hell out of there as quickly as possible.

She just made a face back at me, not understanding what I was trying to say to her.

"I still can't believe it," Tom said brokenly as he let go and stepped back. His eyes actually welled up with tears. "I can't believe someone killed Bill."

"If you need me to come back another time, Mr. Ziebell, I'd be happy to," Abby said quickly, closing her notepad and slipping it into her enormous purse.

"Oh, no—no, that's fine. I'm sorry." He wiped at his eyes with the tail of his shirt, revealing his flat stomach and the fine brown hairs leading down to his jeans, the muscles of his arms flexing as he did. "Chanse, this is Tiffany Glade from *Crescent City* magazine. She's doing a story on Bill's"—his voice broke again—"art collection. She'd called, of course, before the murder"—he paused, taking a few quick breaths and biting his bottom lip before continuing—"and I thought it would be a nice distraction, take my mind off…you know…" His voice trailed off and he turned away from both of us.

He was quite a good actor. The performance would have been convincing had I not known it was a performance. "Nice to meet you, Ms. Glade," I said, trying to keep my voice normal while gesturing with my head for her to get the hell out of there. "I'm Chanse MacLeod, a private investigator."

She shook her head slightly, giving me a dirty look that clearly meant she wasn't going anywhere and what was more, she wasn't thrilled I wanted her to get out. "A private investigator!" she said, raising her voice. "I've always wanted to meet a private eye. Are you the private eye they hired about the stolen paintings?"

"Yes." I was afraid to make another gesture for fear he would turn around and see me.

"And how's that going? Have you had any luck tracking down the thieves? Do you think the murderer and the thieves are connected somehow?" She gave me a weird look I couldn't interpret. She pulled her phone out of her bag and gestured her head at it as she started typing on it. I pulled out my phone and turned it to vibrate.

What r u doin here? popped up on my phone screen.

Tom turned and faced us both again, wiping at his eyes. "Is there news? Is that why you've come?"

I opened my mouth to answer just as we all heard the sound of a siren in the distance. Tom frowned. "What the hell are they coming back here for?" He looked at me. "You can imagine how nasty they were to me, Chanse. Have they called you? Tiffany, Chanse is my alibi." He shook his head. "I can't believe I even need an alibi. I can't believe anyone would think I would kill Bill, after everything he's done for me. I owe him everything."

"Yes, I'm sure you do," Abby replied, slipping her phone back into her purse. "Do you want me to go?"

"No, if they're coming here to harass me some more, it might be nice to have a reporter here," he said grimly.

If I didn't know already he was a liar, I would have been convinced he was a victim of a conspiracy on the part of the Redemption Parish sheriff. I had to stay calm, wait until the police arrived, not do anything to make him suspect that his cover was blown. I put my hand in my coat pocket and grasped the gun. I didn't want to have to use it, but if I played this right I wouldn't have to. I knew Abby always had hers in her purse as well, but I didn't know how quickly she would be able to get to it. He didn't seem to be armed, thank God.

I just had to keep playing along until Abby was out of there.

I knew I could pull it off. I knew I could play the part of concerned friend and hired detective until I could get out of there and let Sheriff Parlange's people do their thing with him.

He'd killed God only knew how many people already, and he wouldn't let us live if it was to his benefit. I couldn't let on that I was on to him.

He walked over to his desk and sat down in the leather chair behind it. He smiled even as the siren got louder, drawing closer, cocking his head to one side as he looked from me back to her and then back again, the smile on his face getting broader. He opened a desk drawer and pulled out a gun, which he trained on Abby.

"Chanse, why don't you move over and stand next to your partner?" His voice was still pleasant and friendly, the warm smile still on his face. "Do what I say or I will shoot her."

"Tom—"

He fired the gun, startling us both. The bullet went right past Abby and into the wall behind her. "Next time I won't miss. And both of you, put your hands up in the air. Do as I say, Chanse. It doesn't matter to me if I shoot her." The smile never wavered. "Or you, either, for that matter, if it comes down to it."

I complied, walking over and standing next to her.

"Tom—Mr. Ziebell—I don't know what this is about—" Abby started, but he cut her off.

"Don't take me for a fool, because I'm not," Tom said, his smile getting even bigger and more predatory.

Why did I never notice how flat and dead his eyes are? How could I have been so stupid?

"You might be wearing a wig and a disguise, but you're Abby Grosjean," Tom went on, his tone conversational, almost charming. "MacLeod and Grosjean. Do you think I didn't do a lot of research on you both before Bill hired you?"

"Why did you let Bill hire us?"

"I tried to talk him out of it, of course, but it was hard to, once I'd convinced him the sheriff was trying to make the firm look bad, to win the lawsuit." He shrugged. "Bill had already had some run-ins with Parlange already, so it wasn't hard to convince him that the sheriff was up to no good. But he wouldn't let it go."

"Did you think he would?" Abby said, dropping her nasal tone and using her real voice. "He was going to be liable for a couple of million dollars."

"He was going to get the damned things back," Tom replied, making a face. "We were going to sell them back to him for just a couple of hundred thousand dollars." He rolled his eyes. "Myrna and Collier were both such small-timers, really. But when you're desperate…" His voice trailed off. "That's the problem most criminals make, you know. They don't *plan*, they don't think things through, because they wait until they're desperate to commit the crime. *Big* mistake." He laughed. "The thing to do is carefully plan, and always stay calm—something else the two of them couldn't do. You stick to the plan, but leave it flexible enough to adapt to changes. Panicking is the worst thing you can do—that's when you make mistakes. Both Collier and Myrna—such amateurs." He shook his head. "They panicked. They worried. They were scared." He rolled his eyes. "They had to go."

"So the paintings actually exist? They weren't ruined?"

Tom laughed out loud, genuinely pleased. "You really are a pathetic excuse for a private eye, aren't you? I don't know why I was so worried when Bill wanted to hire you." He paused, and in the silence we all became aware that the siren was actually getting quieter—it was going in the other direction. My heart sank. "Of course the paintings exist. Rachel Anschler brought them out of Amsterdam in 1940 to sell them, to get the money to get her family to America. Bill's father loaned her money against them…but it was too late. The Germans swooped in, and as hard as she tried, Rachel wasn't able to do anything to save her family, so she gave the money back and took the paintings and came to New Orleans. She refused to sell them because they were all she had left of her family. She went mad with grief, you know, poor thing. It's really a shame. Even when she was going broke and eating cat food, she refused to part with the paintings." He moved the gun from me to Abby and back again. "The paintings are masterpieces. Bill never saw them, but his father had photographs of them. Bill wanted them, was willing to do anything to get them. He tried any number of times to get Rachel to sell them, but she refused. He was even willing to let her keep them while she lived and take possession only when she died. But she refused. No matter what he offered, she always refused. She was clearly crazy by the time she died."

"So what happened? How did the paintings not wind up in the museum?"

"Myrna's father." He laughed. "Oh, yes, this goes back that far, Chanse. Surprised? You'd only begun to scratch the surface. And that was how Myrna knew. Myrna's father was even more unscrupulous than Bill when it came to art. He knew Bill wanted the paintings, so he was paying the nurse who took care of Rachel to keep him abreast of everything. He found some copies of the paintings—done by one of Anschler's students—and deliberately ruined them. Myrna's father, you see, was a long-term planner. He paid the nurse remarkably well to swap out the real paintings for the ruined ones. Since the paintings the museum found when they inventoried Rachel's home were ruined, they couldn't really authenticate them... they just assumed they were the paintings in question. And Myrna's father had them now."

"So why didn't he sell them to Bill in the first place?"

"He was killed before he could. The police figured it was a random break-in, robbery, some junkie, and because of course the paintings weren't supposed to be there, their theft wasn't reported." He smiled.

"You killed Myrna's father."

"He was one of my clients." Tom smirked at me. "Yes,

Myrna's father liked his closet, but he liked to be tied up, you know, and he liked to brag about things. He told me about the paintings—he liked to pretend like he was educating me about art, but he was really just bragging about how much smarter he was than the great Bill Marren, about how he'd managed to get the paintings Bill wanted when the great business mind hadn't been able to. He even introduced me to Bill, who also hired me." His eyes widened. "Poor Bill. It was incredibly easy to seduce him, you know, and once I had the paintings...well, they were my insurance. I knew when Bill tired of me, decided he wanted a younger protégé again, I would sell the paintings and I'd be set for life."

"Myrna knew, though, didn't she?"

His lips compressed. "She didn't know I killed her father but she knew I had the paintings. And she was desperate for money." He rolled his eyes. "They both were. They were such idiots. It's a wonder they didn't wind up in jail themselves. Myrna actually tried to blackmail me, if you can believe such a thing."

"So that's why you let her take the paintings and sell them to Bill."

"I didn't want her telling Bill—"

"She knew about your past, didn't she?" It was all starting to make sense to me now.

"His past?" Abby asked.

"His real name is Rand Barragry."

Tom's eyes narrowed. "So, you found out. How?"

"The wrestling." Abby looked at me with a startled expression on her face. "I called one of Paul's friends from the wrestling world. He told me your name wasn't Tom Ziebell."

He nodded. "The stupid wrestling videos. I knew those would come bite me in the ass someday." He smiled. "Maybe you're not as stupid as I thought. Nice work, Detective."

"That wasn't how Myrna found out?"

"Myrna went to see the real Tom's family. She got his mother to show her a picture of him from high school—that's when she knew I wasn't really Tom. She didn't know who I really was, of course, but she knew enough to force me to go along with her paintings scam."

Never blackmail a murderer—they've already killed and they will again.

"It must have been infuriating to have to go along with them on such a small scale."

"They were idiots. They deserved to die, both of them, for being so fucking stupid if for nothing else." He rolled his eyes again. "I told them withholding the provenance wouldn't do them any good. But they wanted to 'steal' the paintings, keep the escrow money, and then sell the paintings back to Bill. He would have gone along with it, too. And then they would fake the provenance—showing that Rachel Anschler had sold the paintings before she died, and then they would split the money with me."

"But why didn't they just do that to begin with? Why go through the whole charade with the robbery?"

"Because they wanted to have something on me." He shook his heads. "Bill was going to leave me everything—I'd already seen the will—and his heart was bad. They wanted leverage, you see, to hold over me for the rest of my life so I would have to keep paying them." He shook his head. "You'd think they would have learned their lesson. So when Collier cashed out the escrow account, I knew they both had to go." His eyes glinted. "They'll never find Myrna."

"And Bill?"

"He began to suspect, of course. That was *my* big mistake. I thought I could control Bill. But I heard him talking to his lawyer—he was going to change the will. So he had to go." He smiled. "I've always been able to think on my feet. I invited you to dinner, knowing I could drug your wine and drive out here, kill him, and drive back."

"How are you going to explain away me and Abby?"

"By the time they find you two, I'll be long gone." He smiled. "I've already got the paintings secured somewhere. And I have the escrow money." He shrugged. "Bill's fortune would have been nice, but don't worry about me. I've always managed to find a way."

"*We have the house surrounded. Come out with your hands up!*"

"What the hell?"

And in that moment of distraction I jumped at him. We crashed to the ground together—he was incredibly strong, and fiery pain raced through my body from my lower back.

We struggled for the gun, rolling over and over again, and I could hear Abby screaming.

The gun fired.

Beneath me, Tom's body went limp.

His eyes went glassy.

And my back was screaming in agony.

EPILOGUE

The New Orleans Museum of Art had a special reception to unveil the Anschler paintings about a month after Rand Barragry died at Belle Riviere.

Rory and I went together. The cortisone shot was amazing. The procedure was like nothing, and I was pain free for the first time since the accident. My doctor told me that it could last for weeks, or it could last for months. All I knew was it was amazing to be able to make it through the day without having to take a pill, and be able to sleep through the night without having to worry about waking up in agony.

After everything that happened out at Belle Riviere, I called Rory to let him know I was okay—it was going to be in the news and I couldn't guarantee they'd keep my name out of it—and he brought dinner over that night. We had a long talk—we both realized we had to get over our worries and fears about commitment. So we committed to each other. It wasn't perfect, but if you wait for perfection you could spend the rest of your life alone. And Rory was, whether I wanted to admit it or not, the best thing to happen to me since Paul died. He wasn't Paul, but no one was.

We stood in front of the three Anschler paintings, with their glowing, vibrant colors, Rory and I and Paige and Ryan.

"They're so beautiful," Paige said.

I squeezed Rory's hand. "It's going to take me a while to forget their bloody history," I said, "the Holocaust and all the murders of the last ten years or so. But I can see why Bill Marren was so driven to own them. They're extraordinary."

"How's the house hunting going?" Ryan asked, with a bit of a wink.

"Well, if I could convince Chanse that we don't need to live uptown it would be going a lot faster," Rory replied, giving me an exasperated look. "The uptown market is out of control. A double shotgun in the lower Garden District is going for a ridiculous price."

"You know," Barbara Castlemaine said as she joined us and put her arm around my waist, "I've been thinking about letting my rental properties go here in the city. It's really not worth the aggravation." She winked at me and Rory both. "You two make me an offer on the Camp Street house. It was originally a one-family dwelling, no reason why it can't be converted back."

"Are you serious?" Rory gawked at her, and then at me.

"I'm always serious, darling," she said, brushing her lips against his cheek. "Oh, there's Margery Lautenschlager—I need to speak to her, if you'll excuse me?" And just like that, she was gone.

"So, Chanse, what do you think?" Rory said, his voice shaking in excitement. "Do you want to buy the house?"

I looked down into his beautiful blue eyes and smiled at him. "I can't think of anything I'd rather do."

About the Author

Greg Herren is a New Orleans–based author and editor. He is a co-founder of the Saints and Sinners Literary Festival, which takes place in New Orleans every May. He is the author of over twenty novels, including the Lambda Literary Award–winning *Murder in the Rue Chartres*, called by the *New Orleans Times-Picayune* "the most honest depiction of life in post-Katrina New Orleans published thus far." He co-edited *Love, Bourbon Street: Reflections on New Orleans*, which also won the Lambda Literary Award. His young adult novel *Sleeping Angel* won the Moonbeam Gold Medal for Excellence in Young Adult Mystery/Horror. He has published over fifty short stories in markets as varied as *Ellery Queen's Mystery Magazine* to the critically acclaimed anthology *New Orleans Noir* to various websites, literary magazines, and anthologies. His erotica anthology *FRATSEX* is the all-time best-selling title for Insightoutbooks. He has worked as an editor for Bella Books, Harrington Park Press, and now Bold Strokes Books.

A longtime resident of New Orleans, Greg was a fitness columnist and book reviewer for Window Media for over four years, publishing in the LGBT newspapers *IMPACT News*, *Southern Voice*, and *Houston Voice*. He served a term on the Board of Directors for the National Stonewall Democrats and served on the founding committee of the Louisiana Stonewall Democrats. He is currently employed as a public health researcher for the NO/AIDS Task Force and is serving a term on the board of the Mystery Writers of America.

Books Available From Bold Strokes Books

Murder in the Arts District by Greg Herren. An investigation into a new and possibly shady art gallery in New Orleans' fabled Arts District soon leads Chanse into a dangerous world of forgery, theft… and murder. A Chanse MacLeod mystery. (978-1-62639-206-9)

Rise of the Thing Down Below by Daniel W. Kelly. Nothing kills sex on the beach like a fishman out of water…Third in the Comfort Cove Series. (978-1-62639-207-6)

Calvin's Head by David Swatling. Jason Dekker and his dog, Calvin, are homeless in Amsterdam when they stumble on the victim of a grisly murder—and become targets for the calculating killer, Gadget. (978-1-62639-193-2)

The Return of Jake Slater by Zavo. Jake Slater mistakenly believes his lover, Ben Masters, is dead. Now a wanted man in Abilene, Jake rides to Mexico to begin a new life and heal his broken heart. (978-1-62639-194-9)

Backstrokes by Dylan Madrid. When pianist Crawford Paul meets lifeguard Armando Leon, he accepts Armando's offer to help him overcome his fear of water by way of private lessons. As friendship turns into a summer affair, their lust for one another turns to love. (978-1-62639-069-0)

The Raptures of Time by David Holly. Mack Frost and his friends journey across an alien realm, through homoerotic adventures, suffering humiliation and rapture, making friends and enemies, always seeking a gateway back home to Oregon. (978-1-62639-068-3)

The Thief Taker by William Holden. Unreliable lovers, twisted family secrets, and too many dead bodies wait for Thomas Newton in London—where he soon enough discovers that all the plotting is aimed directly at him. (978-1-62639-054-6)

Waiting for the Violins by Justine Saracen. After surviving Dunkirk, a scarred and embittered British nurse returns to Nazi-occupied Brussels to join the Resistance, and finds that nothing is fair in love and war. (978-1-62639-046-1)

Turnbull House by Jess Faraday. London 1891: Reformed criminal Ira Adler has a new, respectable life—but will an old flame and the promise of riches tempt him back to London's dark side…and his own? (978-1-60282-987-9)

Stronger Than This by David-Matthew Barnes. A gay man and a lesbian form a beautiful friendship out of grief when their soul mates are tragically killed. (978-1-60282-988-6)

Death Came Calling by Donald Webb. When private investigator Katsuro Tanaka is hired to look into the death of a high profile lawyer, he becomes embroiled in a case of murder and mayhem. (978-1-60282-979-4)

Love in the Shadows by Dylan Madrid. While teaming up to bring a killer to justice, a lustful spark is ignited between an American man living in London and an Italian spy named Luca. (978-1-60282-981-7)

In Between by Jane Hoppen. At the age of fourteen, Sophie Schmidt discovers that she was born an intersexual baby and sets off on a journey to find her place in a world that denies her true existence. (978-1-60282-968-8)

The Odd Fellows by Guillermo Luna. Joaquin Moreno and Mark Crowden open a bed-and-breakfast in Mexico but soon must confront an evil force with only friendship, love, and truth as their weapons. (978-1-60282-969-5)

Cutie Pie Must Die by R.W. Clinger. Sexy detectives, a muscled quarterback, and the queerest murders…when murder is most cute. (978-1-60282-961-9)